Reading Order for Green Mountain/Butler, Vermont Series

The Green Mountain Series

Book 1: All You Need Is Love *(Will & Cameron)*
Book 2: I Want to Hold Your Hand *(Nolan & Hannah)*
Book 3: I Saw Her Standing There *(Colton & Lucy)*
Book 4: And I Love Her *(Hunter & Megan)*
Novella: You'll Be Mine *(Will & Cam's Wedding)*
Book 5: It's Only Love *(Gavin & Ella)*
Book 6: Ain't She Sweet *(Tyler & Charlotte)*

The Butler Vermont Series

Book 1: Every Little Thing *(Grayson & Emma)*
Book 2: Can't Buy Me Love *(Mary & Patrick)*
Book 3: Here Comes the Sun *(Wade & Mia)*

CHAPTER 1

"I love those who yearn for the impossible."
—Johann Wolfgang von Goethe

Even with snow swirling around him, Wade Abbott knew the way home. He could find it blindfolded, which he was basically doing since the whiteout snow made it so he had to rely on everything but his vision. He'd been out with his brothers for hours looking for two young boys who'd gone sledding in the foothills of Butler Mountain and disappeared in the blizzard.

They'd found them alive but hypothermic forty-five minutes ago and dispersed to head home to warm up. His younger brothers, Lucas and Landon, both paramedics, had transported the boys to the hospital, where they'd be reunited with their grateful parents.

The snowmobile's headlight illuminated the Nelsons' mailbox, a green monstrosity that indicated Wade was about five hundred feet from his own driveway. He noticed a pattern in the snow that looked an awful lot like footprints. Who would be foolish enough to be out in a full-on blizzard if they didn't have to be?

Was he hallucinating, or were the footprints leading to his place? A trickle of unease traveled down his back, which was odd because he never felt unsafe in Butler, Vermont. Hell, he never even locked his door. He didn't have to. His place wasn't easy to find unless you knew where it was.

He hung a right into his driveway and followed the deep footsteps for a quarter mile of twists and bends until his cabin came into view, nestled into a copse of evergreens, his own piece of paradise.

Biting one of the fingers of his glove, he pulled it off and reached for the flashlight strapped to his hip to further illuminate the yard. The flashlight's beam cut through the snow to identify a huddled lump on his porch.

"What the hell?" Wade cut the engine and jumped off the snowmobile. Fighting the foot-high snow, he crossed the yard and went up the stairs. "Hello?"

Nothing.

He nudged the lump with his foot.

It moaned.

He scooped up the bundle and carried it inside, where heat from the woodstove he'd stoked earlier swept over him. Dropping to his knees in front of the fire, he deposited his visitor.

She moaned again.

Dear God, it's a woman—a half-frozen woman. Moving quickly, he threw two more logs on the fire and began unwrapping the ice-crusted scarf that covered her face so the heat could penetrate. Bruises. Her face was black, blue and swollen, so much so he didn't immediately recognize her.

And then he knew.

His heart skipped a beat and shock reverberated through him as he began to frantically remove her wet coat and gloves.

"Mia." He could hear the panic in his own voice. *"Mia!"*

She moaned again. Her lips and fingers were blue.

Wade rubbed her hands between his. "Mia, talk to me." What was she doing here, and who had beat the hell out of her? Rage simmered in his gut. He'd suspected from when he first met her almost two years ago at a yoga retreat that the man in her life— Wade assumed it was her husband—was hurting her, but they'd never reached the point where he felt comfortable asking her about it. Throughout their friendship, he'd seen the signs: skittish, jumpy, secretive, scared, but she hadn't shared anything overly personal with him.

She'd broken off contact with him a year ago, and he'd suffered ever since, wondering why she'd stopped calling him and worrying whether she was safe.

"Mia, honey... Wake up. Please wake up." He would've called for help if anyone could've gotten to them in the storm. Since outside help wasn't an option tonight, it was up to him to get her warm. Unzipping his parka, he pulled it off, removed his boots, kicked them aside and then took off the survival suit that allowed him to be out in a storm for hours without suffering hypothermia. He stripped down to underwear so he could use his body heat to warm her.

Then he went to work on her clothing, moving carefully in case she had other injuries. Working from her boots up, he took off soaking-wet clothes that had him wondering just how long she'd been out in the storm.

Other than the violent tremors that rattled her body, she never stirred as he stripped her down to panties and a tank top, both of which were damp. He laid her wet clothes on top of the woodstove to dry and then stopped short at the sight of arms and legs mottled with bruises of various colors.

Wade choked back the rage that burned through him. He blew out a deep breath, grabbed a down comforter from the sofa and pulled it over them as he molded his body to hers, hoping his body heat would help to raise her core temperature. It would be better, he knew from his lifesaving training, if they were both bare, but he didn't think he could handle that.

Hopefully, he could get her warm without having to strip down completely.

He was enveloped in the sweet, fresh scent of her hair, while his heart beat erratically, his palms felt sweaty despite the cold and his mind raced. What had brought her here? Who had hurt her? What did she want from him? Could he bear to see her again and then watch her go back to wherever she'd been the last year? He tightened his hold on her. He wouldn't let her go back to the man who'd been hurting her, that much he knew for certain.

"Mia, honey, you're safe. It's Wade. I'm so glad you're here. We're going to get you warm." He ran his hand gently up and down her arm, wishing she would wake up and talk to him. He'd missed her so much. Talking to her had once been his favorite thing. After they first met at the yoga retreat, they'd connected a few times at coffee shops between his home in Butler and hers in Rutland. He'd driven more than an hour each way for the chance to spend thirty minutes in her presence.

The last time he'd heard from her, she'd told him she couldn't talk to him anymore. He'd begged her to reconsider and promised to keep his distance so as not to cause her any further difficulty. But he hadn't heard from her again, until he found her on his doorstep, nearly frozen and obviously injured.

Her poor face was so terribly swollen that it made his heart hurt to look at her.

God… He'd gladly kill the man who'd done this to her, and he had no doubt it'd been a man.

He pressed his lips to her forehead. "Sweetheart, wake up and talk to me. It's Wade. It's okay now. No one will ever hurt you again."

The only reply he got was a tortured-sounding moan.

"Mia."

Her lids fluttered open, revealing the gorgeous navy-blue eyes that had once looked at him with such affection. She stared at him, almost as if she couldn't believe her eyes. "Wade," she whispered.

"It's me, honey. You're safe with me."

She began to cry.

Her tears broke him. "Shhh, it's okay. Everything is okay now."

She shook her head as her teeth chattered. "N-no, it isn't."

"It is for right now. The only thing you need to worry about is getting warm. Hold on to me and let me warm you up."

Mia burrowed deeper into his embrace, her arm sliding around his waist and her leg slipping between his.

Wade swallowed hard. Here in his arms was the woman he'd dreamed about since the day he met her. He was supposed to be helping her get warm, but her nearness was making him hot in more ways than one. He took a deep breath and scooted his hips back a crucial inch so she wouldn't be able to feel what her nearness had done to him.

What did it mean that she'd come to him? He'd once written down his home address and phone number as well as the address and phone number for the office and told her to use the info if she ever needed him for anything at any time. With cell phone service nonexistent in Butler, he didn't own a mobile phone, so he'd given her all the other ways to reach him. After so much time, he figured she'd thrown away the scrap of paper and forgotten about him.

He had never forgotten her. Thoughts of her and what she might be going through had tormented him through months of sleepless nights and long days at work in which he'd moved through his life in a perpetual state of despair. He'd known Mia a year when he first shared his complex feelings for her with his sister Hannah. His sister Ella knew about her, too, and he'd told his grandfather a little about her, but he hadn't told anyone else, preferring to keep his feelings—and his despair—to himself.

As one of ten kids, most of whom worked together running the family's Green Mountain Country Store, it wasn't easy to keep secrets in his family. But he'd been aided by the fact that he was considered the "quiet" one of the bunch. No one thought much of it when Wade sat back and took in the madness of their family rather than actively participating. So he'd been able to keep his situation relatively private, which, in his family, was saying something.

He had so many questions for her—especially why now and what now—but he didn't ask any of them. Rather, he stayed focused on warming her and containing the desire zipping through his body, a reminder of how much he'd wanted her from the first time he laid eyes on her.

For a long time after Wade settled them in front of the fire, Mia shivered so hard, her teeth ached. She'd never been so cold in her life. Her car had gotten stuck in a snowdrift on the outskirts of Butler. Fortunately, she'd spent hours studying road maps into and out of Butler. In the back of her mind every second of the last miserable year had been Wade's address, the phone numbers she'd memorized, along with the map of Butler that had represented her path to freedom.

Her biggest concern as she'd plotted her escape was that Wade might not be willing to help her. She'd had to hope and pray that he would still want her the way he once had, even if he'd never said the words. A woman knew these things, and her life now depended upon him still feeling the same way.

He was so warm and solid as he caressed her back in small, soothing circles that made her want to purr with pleasure. She had no idea how long they lay cuddled up to each other under the heavenly blanket, but after a while, her teeth stopped chattering and sensation returned to her extremities in painful pricks. The warmth flooded her mind and body, filling her with a sense of security that was even more blissful than the heat coming from the woodstove—and his muscular body.

For so long, she'd had to wonder what it might be like to be touched by Wade Abbott, and now she knew what heaven must be like. She took deep breaths of the woodsy, natural scent of him and noted that he'd cut his hair since she'd last seen him. Once upon a time, she'd sat across from him in coffee shops and wished she could run her fingers over the sharp planes of his face and touch the longish hair that wasn't brown or blond or red, but rather, an interesting golden mix of all three colors.

During those visits, she'd memorized every detail, right down to the flecks of gold in his eyes that glittered with pleasure whenever he looked at her while they talked until their coffee grew cold and the sun dipped toward the horizon.

Every time she'd left him, she'd done so under a veil of panic, certain this would be the time her secret friendship with Wade would be discovered by a man who would kill her before he'd let anyone else have her. But somehow, they'd gotten away with it. Other things had transpired that'd convinced her to stay away from Wade, for his safety as much as hers, but she'd never stopped thinking about him, wondering about him or wishing that things were different.

Had he thought about her, too? Or had he moved on with someone else? Was there a woman sleeping in his bedroom at this very moment? Would he hold her this way if he had someone else? If it meant saving her life, she knew for sure he would. But once her body was warm, would he leave her to join the woman he loved?

That was like a knife to her heart. Thoughts of him had kept her alive long before tonight, and all her hopes were pinned on him being willing to help her now. She wiggled even closer to him and encountered evidence that he wanted her as much as he always had.

He gasped as she rubbed against him. "Mia…"

The proof of his desire freed her to ask for what she wanted more than anything. "Will you kiss me, Wade?"

He stared at her, seeming incredulous. "Are you really here asking me to kiss you? Will I wake up tomorrow to find out I dreamed this?"

She placed her hand on his face because she'd wanted to for so long and now she could. "It's not a dream. I'm really here, and I've been dying for your kiss for as long as I've known you."

Closing his eyes, he took a deep breath and released it before opening them again. "What about your husband?"

"I don't have a husband."

A strangled sound escaped his tightly clenched jaw in the second before his lips found hers with the light of the fire and years of yearning to guide them. "I don't want to hurt you."

"I'm okay, and I really want you to kiss me."

He kissed her like a man possessed. His fingers dug into her hair and shaped her skull, making it impossible for her to escape, not that she had any wish to be anywhere but right there with him. She'd waited what felt like forever for him to kiss her, and the reality was a thousand times better than the fantasies had ever been.

To call this a kiss didn't do justice to the feelings that exploded inside her as his tongue found hers in an erotic, sensual dance that made her dizzy and weak with longing.

"Mia…" He withdrew slowly, gently kissing the uninjured side of her face, jaw and neck. "You have no idea how long I've wanted to kiss you."

"Don't stop." She sounded desperate and wanton but couldn't be bothered to care. Combing her fingers through his hair, she brought him back for more.

They kissed like they were afraid this was all they'd ever have. Perhaps it was. Perhaps he wouldn't be able to help her, and if that were the case, she'd have no choice but to leave him. For his sake, as well as hers, it would have to be all or nothing.

One kiss became two and then three, and when they came up for air, he was pressed up against her, and she wasn't cold anymore. Not even kind of.

He gazed at her, the firelight turning his hair and skin to pure gold. "Who hurt you, Mia?"

"The man I used to love."

"Why would he do this to you?" He ran his fingertips gently over the bruise on her left cheek.

"That's a very long story."

"You can't go back to him," he said fiercely. "I *knew* he was hurting you, but I couldn't prove it, and you'd never talk to me about him."

"Because I couldn't."

"How did you get here?"

"I drove as far as I could, but my car got stuck in a drift on the way into town. I walked the rest of the way."

"That's *miles* from here!"

"I don't know how far it was, but it took a long time, and then when I got here and you weren't home… The last thing I remember is reaching for the door hoping you wouldn't mind."

"I wouldn't have. Of course you could've come in."

"I must've passed out before I made up my mind."

"My place isn't easy to find. You'd have to know where it is to find it, especially in this weather."

"After you gave me your address, I looked it up on a map, and I memorized the route."

"*Why*, Mia? Why did you memorize the way to my home?"

"Because I knew I'd come to you as soon as I could. I only hoped that I'd still be welcome after all this time."

"You're always welcome with me. You know that." He looked at her with love and joy and hope. So much hope that her heart contracted. "You still haven't told me what happened or why you came tonight, in the middle of a blizzard."

"Because..." She swallowed hard, summoning the fortitude she needed to say the words. "I need you to do something for me."

"I'd do anything for you."

His fierce words made her want to weep from the relief of knowing she hadn't misjudged him or his feelings for her.

"Tell me what you need, Mia. There's nothing you could ask of me that would be too much."

Looking up to meet his intense brown-eyed gaze, she said, "I need you to marry me."

CHAPTER 2

*"Only I discern infinite passion, and the
pain of finite hearts that yearn."*
—Robert Browning

Wade stared at her, certain this couldn't actually be happening. The woman he'd longed for was lying in his arms asking him to *marry* her? Where did he sign?

"Wade?" She waved her hand in front of his face, which was when he realized he was staring at her.

"All this time, I thought you were already married and that he was hurting you. I've been tortured wondering what became of you."

She shook her head. "I'm so sorry I put you through such an ordeal. I never intended for that to happen."

He absorbed the information with a soaring feeling of hope he'd never experienced quite so acutely before.

"Are you okay?" she asked.

Taking a deep breath, he said, "Um, yeah, I'm good. Better than good. I'm excellent, in fact."

She smiled. "I know this is totally shocking and completely out of the blue, but—"

He kissed her. Because he could. Because he was crazy about her. Because she was here and asking for his help, and because there was absolutely nothing he wouldn't do for her. "Yes," he said, his lips still pressed to hers. "I'll marry you."

She pulled back from him. "Don't you want to hear why?"

"I care very much about how you got hurt and what's being done to punish the person who hurt you. But I don't care why you want me to marry you. I'm in."

"Wade—"

He kissed her again, losing himself in her, wanting her more than he'd ever wanted anything in his life, and now she was asking him to commit to her for a lifetime? *Yes, hell yes.*

Mia pulled back from the kiss but kept her hands on his face. "You need to know why."

"No, I don't." What he needed was to keep kissing her for the rest of his life. If he could do that, he wouldn't need anything else. Ever.

She turned away to break the kiss. "Wade. You *do* need to know why. When you know, you might change your mind."

"I believe I've already given you my answer, but if there's more you want to tell me, I'm listening. And PS, I'm not going to change my mind."

"I need to sit up for this, and I need you to not touch me and scuttle my brain cells so badly I forget what I need to say."

He flashed a smug smile as he helped her sit up, wrapping the blanket around her shoulders. "Do I scuttle your brain cells?"

She took a long, hungry look at his bare chest that only added fuel to the fire simmering in his groin. Did she have any idea how beautiful she was to him? And when she looked at him like that, it took all his willpower to keep his hands to himself. "You've scuttled my brain cells from the minute we first met, and you know it."

"No, I didn't know that until right now. For a long time, I wondered if it was just me."

"It wasn't just you."

Her face lost all expression as she seemed to withdraw into herself.

Because he couldn't be this close to her and *not* touch her now that he was allowed to, Wade took her hand and kissed the back of it. "Whatever it is, we'll deal with it together. Now that you're here, I'll never let you go."

"You need to know what you'd be getting into before you decide anything." The dull, flat tone of her voice made him wary.

"Tell me what you think I need to know, and we'll go from there. But I've already decided."

She looked up at him, and the sadness in her gaze made him hurt for her. "Did you hear about the big drug bust in Caledonia County a few months ago?"

"I remember reading something about that." And he recalled his grandfather, Elmer, asking him if he knew anything about it a month or so ago. He sat up straighter, wondering what the connection could possibly be. "What about it?"

"The ringleader was a guy named Brody Dennison. He... He's the one I was involved with for the last three years, and the one I've been trying to get free of for almost that long, but he..."

Suddenly, Elmer's fishing expedition made sense. He'd known this and wanted to know if Wade knew, too. How in the hell had he known? "What, honey?" Wade tried to contain the rage he felt growing with every word she said. "What did he do?"

"He told me if I ever left him, he'd find me and he'd kill me."

Wade released a pained sigh.

"I... I was afraid he'd kill you if he ever found out about our... our friendship. That's why I stopped returning your calls. I was afraid for you."

"I can take care of myself. I don't want you to ever worry about me."

"I *was* worried. You have no idea what he's capable of. I've only recently learned the full extent of what he was doing when he was bullshitting me about his 'successful contracting business' that was actually a front for a huge heroin operation. So many people were hurt by him, lives destroyed... It makes me sick."

Wade reached out to stroke her bruised cheek. "Did he do this to you?"

She nodded. "It turns out I know just enough to be a threat to him in the criminal case. He's out on bail and has been pressuring me to marry him so I won't have to testify against him. When I refused to marry him, he…" She took a deep breath and released it. "He beat me, and he said there'd be more where that came from unless I changed my tune—quickly." Lowering the blanket, she raised the hem of her tank to display a badly bruised abdomen and ribs.

Wade gasped. "Mia, oh my God. You need to be in the hospital! What if you have internal injuries?"

"It happened a couple of days ago. I think I'm okay."

"I know you said you didn't want me touching you while we're talking, but I really need to. Can I, please?"

Her chin quivered. "I wish you would."

He scooped her up off the floor, blanket and all, and moved them to the sofa, arranging them so they were facing each other with the blanket pulled over their shoulders so she wouldn't get cold again. "How did you get away?"

"He had a mandatory court appearance today, and I left while he was gone. He said when he got back, he was bringing someone to marry us so I'd have no choice but to keep my fat mouth shut. I'd been preparing to run for weeks, but after he beat me, I knew he wouldn't give up until I was shackled to him for life. I figured the only way I can get him to stop pressuring me is if I'm legally not able to marry him, because I'm married to someone else. And the only person I'd ever want to be married to is this gorgeous, sweet guy I met at a yoga retreat a couple of years ago who's been giving me a reason to live just by being out there somewhere."

Wade brushed away a tear that rolled down her cheek. He couldn't bear to see her cry. "He's been hurting you for a while now, hasn't he?"

"Not like this, but in other ways. Grabbing my arms or handfuls of my hair… Things that wouldn't show to the outside world but would keep me terrorized enough to toe the line. I kept asking myself how the nice guy I'd fallen for had turned into such a monster. It took me a while to realize he's always been a monster. He'd just hidden it well when we were first together, back when I thought I'd finally found a good guy. It wasn't until I met you, a truly good guy, that I could see just how far off I'd been with him."

"I'm wondering how you were able to go to the yoga retreat in the first place."

"He went on a weekend fishing trip to Maine with his brothers. I left after he did and was back before him. He never even knew I was gone. I worked as a waitress, and he never asked where my money went, probably because he was so flush with drug money, he didn't need my pitiful contribution. I squirreled away as much as I could, so I'd be ready when I got the chance to run. I'm not without resources, if you're wondering about that."

"I'm not wondering about that. In fact, that's the last thing on my mind. Not only will I marry you so you can't marry him or anyone else, but I'll protect you from him and anyone who'd try to harm you. You'll have me and my entire, formidable family behind you. We'll have your back, sweetheart, and I'll get my cousin Grayson to represent you in any legal matters. Everything will be okay. I promise."

"He won't go quietly," she said. "I have no way to predict how he'll react to finding out that I married someone else."

"He won't get near you. Not as long as I'm alive."

"I almost didn't come here. I thought about heading west and disappearing."

"I'm so glad you didn't do that. I would've missed you for the rest of my life."

"Wade…" Her eyes filled again. "What I'm asking of you could endanger you. I have to be sure you understand that."

"I get it."

"You need to think about this, to be sure—"

He kissed her. "I'm sure. My aunt is the town clerk. My grandfather is a justice of the peace. We'll get a license and get married as soon as the blizzard ends."

"What will your family say?"

"I don't care what they say."

"Yes, you do. I know you well enough to know you care very much what they think."

"Not about this." He stared into her eyes. "There is nothing—and I do mean *nothing*—anyone could say or do that would keep me from offering you this protection. By helping you, I get everything I want, too. The way I see it, it's a win-win."

"You say that now... I'm going to be tied up for months, if not years, in the case against Brody."

"We'll take it one day at a time until it's in the past and we never have to think about that again."

"I'll understand if you want me to sign something that protects you and your assets for after."

"For after what?"

"After our marriage ends, of course."

"Sweetheart, let's get one thing perfectly clear. I'm going to do everything in my power to make sure you never want to be anywhere but with me for the rest of your life. So let's not talk about how it's going to end. Let's talk about how we're going to make it work."

"We've never even been on a date."

"Every time we sat across from each other in a coffee shop was better than any date I've ever been on with anyone else. But if you want an official date, you got it. As many as you want—after we get a ring on your finger so no one can try to take you away from me."

Her eyes flooded with new tears. She closed them to contain the flood.

"What?" he asked, alarmed.

"I was so afraid you would've forgotten about me," she said in a whisper.

"I could never, ever, *ever* forget about you. I never want you to be afraid again. You've got me now, and we're going to face whatever comes head on, until the bad stuff is so far in the past, you can't even remember it. We'll make so many happy new memories that you won't have the space in your brain to accommodate the bad stuff anymore."

"You make me believe that's actually possible."

"It's more than possible." He snuggled her in close to him. "Close your eyes and get some rest. You're safe now. I've got you, and I'm never letting you go."

CHAPTER 3

"The secret of a happy marriage is finding the right person. You know they're right if you love to be with them all the time."
—Julia Child

If anyone had told Wade Abbott earlier that he would end this day with Mia Simpson sleeping in his arms, he would've laughed. As if that would ever happen. And now... Now they were *getting married*. Stranger things had happened, for sure, but never to him.

There were details to be seen to, but not until the storm passed, probably tomorrow sometime. As soon as he could dig them out, he'd take her to town first and get the ball rolling. First and foremost, they had to go to the big red barn his family called home so he could introduce her to his parents.

Thinking about that gave him his first twinge of anxiety since Mia had asked him to marry her. His parents wouldn't understand, and he had to find a way to make them see how badly he wanted this—how badly he wanted *her*. She was right about one thing—their approval would matter to him.

Not that anyone could talk him out of marrying Mia, but he expected them to push back against his plans—and they'd push back hard, because he'd never talked to his parents about her. They didn't even know she existed.

At the very least, they'd try to talk some sense into him. However, he didn't need sense or anything else talked into him. His mind was made up. He would marry her as soon as he could make it happen. And then he'd do everything he could to make theirs a successful union.

Were they starting under the best of conditions? Absolutely not. But marriages had begun under worse situations. At least there were genuine feelings between them, and Wade had to believe those feelings would grow and flourish once they were together every day.

Together every day. With Mia, my wife.

The thought of it made him deliriously happy. There were still so many things he didn't know about her, like where she was from originally, if she had siblings, where her parents lived or who her friends were. He couldn't wait to talk to her until they ran out of words, hopefully fifty or sixty years from now.

Having her in his arms was like having every dream he'd ever had come true all at once. Before this, he'd never even gotten to hug her, even though many a time he'd desperately wanted to wrap his arms around her and beg her to come home with him. But she'd been so skittish and afraid—and he'd thought then that she was married, so he'd stuck to the platonic side of the road when he'd been drawn to her on a cellular level. To hear she wasn't married to the man he'd known was hurting her… That was the best news he'd ever gotten.

He breathed her in, memorizing the scent of her hair and the satiny feel of her soft skin. His mind wandered back to the first time he saw her, in a room full of people at the yoga retreat. He'd thought then that she looked like an angel with her halo of golden curls, pale white skin and big navy-blue eyes. That was the first time in his life he'd experienced instantaneous attraction to another human being, and he hadn't yet spoken a word to her.

The words had come later, when she sat at his table for dinner and they'd struck up a conversation that had lasted well into the night. He couldn't recall what they'd talked about, but he remembered thinking he never wanted to stop talking to her. In the long months since the last time he talked to her, he'd missed the sound of her voice almost as much as he'd missed the sight of her gorgeous face.

And now… God, it was almost too much to wrap his mind around.

He released a shaky-sounding deep breath.

"What's wrong?" she asked.

"Nothing at all. Everything is perfect."

"If you've changed your mind, I'll understand."

He rested a finger over her lips. "I'm not going to change my mind, about any of it, so don't worry about that."

She closed her eyes, tears once again leaking from the corners.

As he brushed them away, he kissed her forehead. "Why the tears?"

"I'm so *relieved*. I didn't know what I'd do if you couldn't or wouldn't help me. I'd have to go somewhere and disappear. Change my name… I'd always be looking over my shoulder, waiting for him to find me."

"None of that is going to happen. We'll get through this together, and he'll never get the chance to hurt you again."

"I feel kind of guilty, too."

"Why?"

"Because this has nothing to do with you, and the minute I marry you, I'm putting you squarely in the middle of it."

"I told you I don't care about that. The only thing I care about is that you are safe and happy and free of worries."

She took a deep breath, her body trembling as she exhaled. "Thank you. I don't know if I've said that enough or—"

He kissed her. "You don't need to thank me. Having you here with me feels like a dream come true. You're giving me as much as I'm giving you."

"That's hardly true," she said with a laugh.

"It's entirely true. You have no idea how concerned I've been about you, how sad I was that I couldn't talk to you anymore or see you… And now I get to *marry* you, so you can stop feeling guilty, because nothing has ever made me happier—or more worried—than coming home to find you half frozen on my porch."

She laughed at the way he said that. "I hope you still feel that way after we're married."

"I have a sneaking suspicion I'll always feel that way."

For the first time in weeks, Mia could finally relax a little. Wade was everything she'd hoped he would be—and then some. All the things she'd worried about—that he'd be involved with someone else by now or would have forgotten about her—hadn't materialized. He was free and clear, and his feelings for her seemed as strong as they'd always been.

"Are you hungry?" he asked.

"No, thank you. I'm good." Her stomach had been in knots for so long that eating had become a chore.

"Let's go sleep in my bed. It'll be more comfortable than the sofa."

She'd been more comfortable on the sofa with him than she'd been anywhere else in months, but she willingly took the hand he offered and followed him to the bedroom.

"The bathroom is in there if you need it, and there's an extra toothbrush in the cabinet."

"I have one in my bag." She gasped. "My bag. Please tell me it was with me when you found me."

"Let me go look." He went into the other room and returned with the nylon bag she'd worn wrapped around her waist as she trudged through the snow in what had seemed like an endless trek.

"Oh, thank goodness. I'd be lost without that." She took it from him and ducked into the bathroom.

When she came out a few minutes later, he had a pair of flannel pajama pants and a long-sleeved T-shirt laid out on the bed for her. She happily donned the clothing, since her teeth had begun to chatter again when she left the heated cocoon next to the fire.

"I'll throw some more logs on the woodstove," Wade said. He'd changed into flannel pajama pants, but his splendid chest was on full display.

Mia found herself wanting to stare at him, like a person who'd been starving and stumbled upon a banquet. The rush of emotion that came from being with him, from being safe and under his protection, made her legs go weak. She sat on the edge of the bed and focused on breathing. There'd been a time, not that long ago, when she'd been fully independent and in need of no one's protection. But that was before she met Brody and got lost in the web of an abusive relationship the likes of which she'd only heard about before it happened to her.

Once upon a time, she'd had friends and a decent job as a waitress in an upscale restaurant and an apartment and a life she had built for herself. Once upon a time, she'd been a woman who'd never believe she could be so completely controlled by a man. She shuddered thinking about him punching her until she blacked out. How had she gotten from her former life to being beaten by the man who'd professed to love her?

Wade returned to the bedroom with a glass of water that he handed to her. "You need to stay hydrated after being so cold."

"Thank you." When she took a sip of the water, she realized how thirsty she was.

"I also have this stuff we sell in the store that works wonders on bruises." He produced a green container that he held up for her to see. "You want to try it?"

"Sure."

Wade sat next to her. "You want to apply it, or do you want me to?"

"Would you mind?"

"Not at all," he said with a wolfish smile. He opened the jar and dabbed his fingers into the white cream. "Close your eyes and tell me if anything hurts."

His touch was light and gentle as he spread the cream over the bruised side of her face.

Right away, she experienced cool, soothing relief. "What's in that?"

"Eucalyptus, among other things."

"Feels really good."

"It helps with the pain and the healing."

"Could we put it on my ribs, too?"

"Sure. Lie back."

Mia stretched out on the bed and raised the T-shirt and tank to expose her abdomen.

His face tightened with tension as he studied the bruises. "How could he do this to you?" He leaned over her and kissed the darkest, meanest-looking bruise.

Mia sucked in a sharp deep breath.

"I'm sorry. I didn't mean to hurt you."

She combed her fingers into his hair. "You didn't. That wasn't a pain sound."

He looked up at her with eyes gone hot with desire. "No?"

She shook her head.

Wade kissed every one of the bruises before applying the soothing cream to them. "That ought to make them feel a lot better by tomorrow."

"They already do."

He eased her tank back down and adjusted the T-shirt. "Are you warm enough?"

"Yes, much better. Thank you." She glanced at the bedside table that had a stack of books and a framed photo of his family that she picked up for a closer look. Everyone wore denim shirts and khakis along with big smiles. They looked so happy.

"That right there is the Abbott family circus."

"Introduce me."

"Get under the covers so you don't get cold." He took the photo, went around to the other side of the bed and got in next to her. When she was snuggled up to him, he pointed to the three people at the center of the gathering. "That's my mom, Molly, Dad, Lincoln, and grandfather, Elmer, along with my parents' dogs George and Ringo."

"Ringo?"

"My dad is a crazy Beatles fan. My mom refused to allow him to name a kid Ringo, so the dogs are named after them. Incidentally, George and Ringo are both girls."

Mia laughed. "That's awesome. I *love* the Beatles."

"My dad will love you. That's all it takes. When we go to the store, I'll show you his Beatles memorabilia collection. People come from all over to see it."

"I'd love to see it."

"This is my oldest brother, Hunter, the CFO of our company, and his wife, Megan, who runs the family restaurant in town. That's Colton and his fiancée, Lucy, Max and his former girlfriend Chloe. Max is the youngest of us and was the first to produce a grandchild. A month after the baby was born, Chloe took off and left him to raise their son, Caden."

"Oh wow. How old is Max?"

"Almost twenty-three."

"That's a lot of responsibility for someone so young."

"It is, but he's got a lot of help, and he seems to be adjusting. He works with Colton at the family sugaring facility on the mountain. It gets pretty crazy up there for about three weeks in the spring."

"Does Colton's fiancée help out, too?"

"Everyone helps during sugaring, but Lucy is a partner in a website company, and she works from home on the mountain, one of the few places around here that has a reliable internet connection and cell signal."

"I wondered why my phone didn't work. I tried to call you when I first got stuck in the snow."

"Your phone is basically useless in this town."

"That'll take some getting used to..."

"So I'm told. I've never had one, so I wouldn't know."

"I'm trying to remember the last time I met someone who didn't have a cell phone."

"You already busted my balls about that when we met. Remember?"

"I remember everything."

"I do, too. Anyway, this is my brother Will and his wife, Cameron. She's known in town as the girl who hit Fred, the town moose, on her way into Butler. He was fine. Her car wasn't. Will rescued her from Fred and Vermont mud season, and they've been together ever since. She's expecting their first child later this year. He oversees our Vermont Made line at the store. That's my sister Hannah, she's Hunter's twin, and her husband, Nolan. Her first husband, Caleb, was killed eight years ago in Iraq."

"Oh, that's so sad."

"It was awful. Truly terrible for all of us, but we're thrilled to see her happy again with Nolan. He owns the garage in town and was a close friend of Caleb's. I'll send him after your car as soon as the storm lets up. They just had a baby daughter who they named Caleb, but they're going to call her Callie."

"I love that they named her Caleb."

"It's an amazing tribute to someone we all loved." He pointed to a dark-haired man. "That's Caleb's brother, Gavin, who's engaged to my sister Ella. She was crazy about him forever, but he was a mess after he lost his brother. They're so happy now that they're engaged and living together. I'm really close with Ella."

"She's lovely."

"Inside and out. That's Charley. We joke that she's a pain in our asses, which she is, but of course we love her to pieces and so does her boyfriend, Tyler. He saved her life when she fell off the mountain on a run back in December."

"Whoa. She fell *off* the mountain?"

"Yep. Stepped right off the side in a snowstorm and fell about thirty feet, tearing her ACL. He ran back to get help for her and then insisted on nursing her back to health. The rest, as they say, is history. She moved in with him at the beginning of the year, and she's less of a pain in our asses now that she's a pain in his."

Mia laughed. "I bet she's a doll."

"Right… I'll let you decide for yourself when you meet her. These two lunatics are Lucas and Landon. In case you can't tell, they're identical twins and full of the devil. When they aren't causing grief for the rest of us, Lucas is a woodworking genius who lives at the family Christmastree Farm that Landon runs—with Lucas's help, not that Landon would ever admit that. They're also paramedics and volunteer firefighters."

"They're adorable."

He glared at her.

"Almost as adorable as you are."

"Haha, very funny. They'll flirt shamelessly with you, but I'll pound them into the ground if they cross the line."

"That's good to know. Where do you fall in the family order?"

"I'm number six, after Charley and before Colton." Pointing to each person as he named them, he said, "It goes Hunter, Hannah, Will, Ella, Charley, me, Colton, Lucas, Landon and Max."

"It'll take me a year to remember all their names."

"Nah, they leave an immediate impression. You'll catch on quickly."

"Do you think…"

"What?"

"Will they like me, or will they hate me for dragging you into my nightmare?"

"They'll love you because I ask them to."

"Is it really that simple?"

"In my family, we stick together and we have each other's backs. So yeah, it is that simple."

"You're really lucky to have that."

"I know. Sometimes they drive me nuts, but I always feel lucky to have them and my cousins. Did I mention my mom's sister has eight kids who grew up with us?"

"So, really, there're actually *eighteen* of you?"

"Yep, the Abbotts and the Colemans were a force to be reckoned with back in the day. My cousin Isabella took this photo."

"Your cousin is *Isabella Coleman*, the photographer?"

"Uh-huh. You know her?"

"Not personally, but I'm certainly familiar with her work. I've always wanted to meet her."

"Now you'll get the chance. Her older brother, Grayson, is the one I mentioned who can represent you in any legal issues you may have with what's-his-name."

"Is that what we're calling him?" she asked with a small smile.

"Works for me."

"Me, too."

"Anyone who would hurt you the way he did has no place in our home."

His support made her stronger and more determined than she'd been in years. Her body ached from her injuries, but he made her believe she could face whatever came next and survive it.

"Get some rest," he said, caressing her hair.

"I'm afraid I'm going to wake up and still be out in the cold, that you're not really here, that I wished so hard for you, I made myself believe..."

"You can believe. I'm right here, and I'll still be here when you wake up. I promise."

She had so many things she wanted to talk to him about, but she couldn't keep her eyes open any longer. They had tomorrow to spend together, and she couldn't wait.

CHAPTER 4

*"Happy is the man who finds a true friend, and far
happier is he who finds that true friend in his wife."*
—Franz Schubert

Wade woke to sunlight peeking in around the closed blinds in his bedroom.
As silky hair brushed against his chest, the events of the day before came
rushing back to him. Mia, half frozen on his porch, her marriage proposal,
kissing her, holding her, sleeping with her. All his dreams had come true
in one unbelievable day, and today would be about keeping his promises
to her.

The office was closed on Saturdays, and usually he slept late and then
spent most of the day in one outdoor pursuit or another. This time of
year, skiing or snowboarding took precedence over the rock-climbing he
did the rest of the year.

Moving carefully so he wouldn't disturb Mia, he got out of bed. He
needed to dig them out so they could get on with their plans. They needed
a marriage license, but he couldn't tell his aunt Hannah before his parents
knew. Without a doubt, their first stop needed to be the barn.

Eager to get going, he took a quick shower, brewed a pot of coffee
and donned thermals and ski pants. He was putting on his boots in the
mudroom when Mia appeared, wrapped up in the down blanket, her hair
like spun gold around her bruised face. Those bruises, which had faded

somewhat overnight, gutted him. The thought of someone *punching* her...
Wade honestly believed he could kill the guy if he had the chance.

"Morning," he said, forcing a cheerful tone. She'd had enough anger
and violence in her life. She didn't need more from him. "Sleep good?"

"Better than I have in years."

"Glad to hear it. I'm going to dig us out, and then we can see to
our plans."

"Oh. Today?"

"Are you doing something else?" he asked with a teasing grin. He
hoped she hadn't changed her mind about wanting to marry him.

"No, but... I just..."

He stood and went to her, placing his hands carefully on her shoulders,
hoping she wouldn't flinch from his touch.

She flinched and then schooled her features, almost as if hoping he
wouldn't notice.

"What's wrong?"

"I... Would it be okay if we maybe waited a while, until the bruises
heal? I don't want to meet your family looking this way."

His heart ached at the shame he saw in her eyes and heard in her
voice. "I understand what you're saying and why you're saying it, but
you have *nothing* to be ashamed of. This was done *to* you, and when we
tell my parents that, they'll want to help you as much as I do." He ran
a gentle finger over her unbruised cheek. "Besides, I'm not going to rest
until we've made it impossible for you to be married to anyone but me."

She swallowed hard and looked up at him. "Your parents are going
to freak out when you tell them you're marrying a bruised and battered
woman they've never even met."

Yes, they would, but that wouldn't stop him. "Let me worry about
them." He stepped back from her to pour coffee into a travel mug. "Coffee?"
He remembered that she liked it with soy milk, which he drank, too.

She nodded. "Thanks."

"Let me go plow us out, and then I'll make some breakfast. I'll also
call my brother-in-law about seeing to your car."

"I could make breakfast while you plow. If you don't mind, that is..."

"I don't mind." He handed her a mug of steaming coffee with the soy milk stirred in. "Anything I have is yours. Make yourself completely at home here."

"Thank you so much for making me feel so welcome."

Wade put his arms around her and kissed her gently. "You are so very, *very* welcome here." He punctuated his words with a grin that had her smiling back at him. "I'll be back as soon as I get the driveway clear."

"Okay."

He pulled on a parka, hat and gloves and went out to the frigid tundra. From the looks of things, about two feet of snow had fallen overnight. While his truck warmed up, he sipped his coffee and thought about how best to approach his parents with the news of his impending marriage. They were a significant hurdle standing between him and his desire to marry Mia as soon as possible.

At thirty-one, he certainly didn't need their permission, but he'd like to have their approval. He had to convince them that this was something he wanted. *She* was what he wanted. He wavered between talking to them privately and bringing her with him, but he didn't want to leave her alone for any reason until they were married.

He would call them, he decided as he used the plow attached to his truck to push aside the snow on the driveway. Before they left for town, he'd call his parents and give them a heads-up that he was bringing someone to meet them and they had news. He'd warn them about the bruises and ask his parents not to ask about them.

It was a lot to ask. He knew that, but he'd ask it just the same.

An hour later, he had a path carved out of the snow that would get them to the main road into town, which had been plowed. He returned to the house, eager to see her, talk to her, *be* with her. Clomping off the snow in the mudroom, he removed his boots and gloves and hung up his coat.

In the kitchen, Mia stood at the stove, wearing jeans and a flannel shirt of his she'd knotted at her waist. Her hair was contained in a ponytail and her feet encased in his slippers. The sight of her did crazy things to his insides. Since the TV was on in the living room, he cleared his throat, hoping he wouldn't frighten her.

She spun around, and fear was the first thing he saw on her face. Fear morphed into relief when she saw him there.

"Something smells good," he said, choosing to ignore the fear. There was no need to question it when he certainly understood the reason for it.

"I made tofu with veggies and toast."

"Sounds good to me." He refilled his coffee mug and leaned against the counter to watch her finish cooking.

"You're staring," she said, her face flushing with embarrassment.

"You're beautiful. Before, I had to resist the urge to stare when I wasn't allowed to, but now that I am, there's probably going to be a lot of staring."

Her lips quivered with amusement that made her eyes light up with joy.

Wade liked that look on her. He liked it a *lot* and wanted to see as much of it as possible. Tearing his gaze off her, he got out plates and silverware. They sat together at his small kitchen table, and a feeling of profound *rightness* came over him as he sat across from her. His parents had always told him to trust his gut, and his gut and every other part of him was screaming out in favor of starting every day like this. Just like this.

"My shirt looks good on you."

"I hope you don't mind. Mine was still damp…"

"I don't mind. In fact, I'd love to see you in *only* my shirt. Someday." As soon as he said the words, he hoped he hadn't gone too far.

The sweet flush of heat in her cheeks made him want to drag her into his arms so he could devour her. But he couldn't do that. Not yet anyway. Despite the hot kisses they'd shared last night, despite sleeping together in his bed, he understood that he would have to proceed with caution. The last thing he wanted was to scare her or ask for more than she was ready to give. They had all the time in the world to get comfortable with each other.

After they ate, they cleaned up the kitchen together. Wade called his brother-in-law, Nolan, and asked him to see about retrieving Mia's car from the snowbank on the outskirts of town. With her help, he described the make and model of the car and roughly where it was. Nolan promised to go after it as soon as the roads were clear.

"You can just bring it to my place if you would."

"Sure," Nolan said. "Will do."

"Thanks again." Wade ended the call and turned to Mia. "You ready to go to town?"

She nodded. "Could I borrow your shower first?"

"Of course. There're towels in the closet, and you can use anything you need in there."

"Thank you. I'll be quick."

"Take your time. We're not in any rush." He was in a huge rush, but she didn't need to know that. Underneath the euphoria of being with her and sharing his home with her was the fear of her violent ex showing up. The odds of that were slim, since Brody didn't know that Wade existed, at least as far as they knew. But he wasn't taking any chances when it came to her safety.

While she was in the bathroom, he used the phone in the kitchen to call his parents. His mom, Molly, answered.

"Hey, Mom."

"Morning, honey. Can you believe this snow? Dad said we got two feet!"

"I know. I just spent an hour plowing." He eyed the closed door to the bathroom. "So Mom... I've got some news I wanted to share with you and Dad."

"What kind of news?" she asked warily, as only the mother of ten grown children could. She'd seen and heard it all—well, almost everything...

"It seems I'm getting married."

"*What? Married?* To who?"

"I'm going to bring Mia by to meet you, and we're going to be married right away."

"Wade Michael Abbott, what the hell are you talking about?"

"Mom, listen to me." He kept his voice down. "I'm asking for your support, not your permission. And I need you to please proceed carefully when you meet Mia. This is what I want. *She* is what I want. I've wanted her for a long time, and... I just need you to be supportive."

"You're asking a lot of me—and your father—when you tell me you're planning to marry a woman we've never met or even heard you speak of."

"Hannah and Ella know about her. Gramps does, too."

"I don't know what to say to this, Wade. When you get here, we'll talk more."

"Mom, please, when you meet her... Please don't say or do anything that can't be undone."

"Give me a little credit, will you? I'm not going to run her off, but you have to understand that we have questions."

"It's a somewhat delicate situation. She's injured and... Well, that's all I can say for now. I'll explain the rest when I can, but don't say anything about her bruises."

"Wade... What's really going on?"

The bathroom door opened. "I've got to go," he said. "I'll see you soon."

"Wade—"

He set the phone down on the cradle. "Ready?" he asked Mia.

She nodded. "Were you talking to someone?"

"My mom."

"Oh. Did you tell her?"

"Yep."

"And?"

"It was fine. Nothing to worry about." He only hoped that would be the case.

Molly Abbott heard the phone go dead and, in a state of total shock, turned to her husband, Lincoln, who'd been perusing the morning paper until the phone rang.

"What's up?" he asked.

"Wade said..." Molly shook her head. In nearly forty years of raising children, she'd seen and heard just about everything. But this...

"What did Wade say?"

"Apparently, he's getting married."

Linc stared at her. "He's getting *what?*"

"*Married.*"

"Wade Abbott is getting married."

"That's what I said."

"To *who?*"

"He said her name is Mia."

"*Ohhhhhh,*" Linc said, his eyes going wide. "Oh my God."

"What do you know?" Molly asked, hands on her hips.

"Something your dad mentioned a while back…"

"How does he know about this and I don't? And you…" Her eyes narrowed. "Have you been keeping this from me?"

Linc held his hands up in self-defense. "No, no, nothing like that. Your dad rode with Wade to Burlington for Thanksgiving."

"That was three months ago! And you're just telling me this now?"

"Molly, honey, listen to me. Wade mentioned to your dad that he had met a woman named Mia who was apparently involved with someone else. Wade became friendly with her at a yoga retreat, but he told Elmer he hadn't seen her in a while. I've never heard a word about him seeing her since then."

Crossing her arms, she took a deep breath and eyed her husband. After forty years of marriage, she knew when he was keeping something from her. "What else?"

"That's it. That's all I know."

"You've never lied to me before, Lincoln Abbott. Don't you dare start now."

He sighed and seemed to slump in his chair. "Elmer did some digging, and he figured out that the woman Wade was interested in was associated with that Brody Dennison, who was—"

"*The heroin kingpin?*"

"Yeah."

"And you knew our Wade was involved with her and never said anything to me?"

"I knew Wade met her. As far as I knew, his 'involvement' with her was all about yearning, and that's it. I've never heard otherwise until now."

"He can't marry her."

"Yes, he actually can."

"You can't honestly tell me you support this."

Lincoln stood and went around the table to where she stood. "He's thirty-one years old, Mol. The days of us telling any of them what to do are long past. And this is *Wade* we're talking about, the most reasonable, deliberate one of the bunch. There's no way he'd be planning to marry her if he didn't honestly want to."

"Who's getting married?" Max asked as he appeared in the kitchen carrying his son, Caden.

Molly reached for the baby, welcoming the distraction. "Wade called to say he's getting married."

Max's eyes bugged. "To *who*?"

Everyone had the same question.

"A woman named Mia, who he's bringing here to meet us. He mentioned she has bruises, and we're not to say anything about them."

"He's marrying someone none of us have ever met?" Max asked.

"That's what he said."

"Wow. And I thought my life was screwed up."

"Your life is hardly screwed up." Molly gazed at the grandson who'd brought them so much joy. At three months old, he was the picture of Max as a baby.

"Listen," Lincoln said, "before they get here… We need to proceed with caution if he's dead set on marrying this woman. Anything we say and do in the next hour will set the tone for our entire relationship with her—and possibly him, too."

Molly knew he was right. She had preached a similar approach to other issues that had confronted them and their children over the years. But if this woman was going to put her son in danger, Molly wouldn't stand silently by and let that happen.

"Molly?"

"I know." Snuggling Caden was far better than worrying about Wade and what he was getting himself into. She passed an hour entertaining the baby while Max and Linc dug them out. George and Ringo were out there, too, chasing each other around in the snow. She took Caden to the mudroom to look out at the yard. "There's Daddy." When she said the word *Daddy*, Caden got excited. "He'll be in soon."

With every minute that passed while Molly waited for Wade to arrive, her anxiety seemed to multiply. She had a bad feeling about this news of his. A very bad feeling, and as the mother to ten kids, she'd learned to trust her instincts.

CHAPTER 5

"If my son is happy, then I am happy."
—Chris Paul

Molly was still in the window with the baby when Wade's truck made the turn into the driveway. George and Ringo barked and circled the truck, excited to greet him. Wade always paid a lot of attention to them and usually brought treats, so the dogs recognized his truck. He got out and pet the dogs before going around to help a woman from the passenger side.

Mia.

She was so bundled up that Molly couldn't see much beyond the blonde hair that peeked out from under her hat. "Let's go heat up some milk," she said to Caden. "They're going to want hot chocolate."

Having something to do helped to pass the ten minutes it took for the others to come into the house, bringing a rush of cold air with them.

The first thing she noticed when Wade brought Mia into the kitchen were the bruises on her face. Remembering Wade's warning about not mentioning them, Molly bit back a gasp. Someone had beaten the hell out of her. Had it been the drug dealer? Her stomach turned at the thought of her son being caught up in such a thing.

"Mom and Caden, this is Mia," Wade said. "Mia, my mom, Molly, and my nephew, Caden."

With Caden on her left hip, Molly extended her right hand. "Pleased to meet you."

"Likewise. Wade speaks so fondly of you all."

"That's nice to hear. Could I interest you in some hot chocolate or coffee?"

"Hot chocolate sounds great. Thank you."

"Got any soy milk?" Wade asked. "That's what Mia likes, too."

"Always." She handed him the baby and got busy filling mugs and stirring in the soy milk she kept on hand for her son the vegan. He looked… happy. She couldn't deny that. And Mia… God, the bruises were awful, and the thought of someone doing that to her or anyone made Molly sick.

"He's such a cutie," Mia said of the baby, who offered a gummy smile to the newcomer.

"This guy has never met a stranger," Wade said, gazing proudly at his nephew. "He takes to everyone he meets."

When Mia offered her finger, Caden wrapped his chubby fist around it. Her eyes softened with emotion. "He's so sweet."

Molly was thankful to the baby for providing an icebreaker. As she placed mugs of hot chocolate on the table in front of Mia and Wade and went back for a plate of cookies, she heard Linc and Max come into the mudroom, stomping the snow off their boots. "Help yourselves to hot chocolate," she said to them.

They brought their mugs to the table. Max immediately reached for his son, who let out a happy squeal at the sight of his father.

"Gotta say I'm getting sick of snow," Linc declared, helping himself to one of the cookies and then offering the plate to Mia.

She took one and placed it on a napkin. "Thank you."

"I know you're all wondering what's going on," Wade said.

Mia put her hand on top of his. "Would it be okay if I explain it?" she asked him.

"If you want to."

"I'd like to try."

He gestured for her to go ahead.

"Wade and I met at a yoga retreat almost two years ago. We struck up an immediate friendship that we continued over the next few months by meeting for coffee and talking on the phone. We were friends. Just friends. But I liked him. A lot. I don't have to tell you what a great guy he is, and he was a good friend to me at a time when I really needed one."

Wade squeezed her hand, and she offered a tremulous smile.

The connection between them was obvious and seemed sincere. At least Molly hoped it was sincere.

"For the last couple of years, I've been trying to extricate myself from a very difficult domestic situation. The first time Brody beat me was the first time I tried to leave him. I calmly told him our relationship was over and I was planning to move in with a friend. He just as calmly told me that if I moved so much as a pair of underwear out of our house, he would kill me—and my friend. Just to make sure I knew he meant it, he beat the crap out of me and made it so I couldn't leave the house for two weeks. I lost my job because I was out for so long, which only made me more dependent on him." She wiped a tear and winced when her hand brushed against the bruises on her face.

Molly glanced at her husband, who had a ferocious expression on his face as he waited for Mia to continue. They despised bullies and men who beat on women because they could.

"I tried to leave again a few months later. I'd gotten another job in a store, and one of my coworkers volunteered at a shelter for women who were escaping abusive relationships. I found out later that she'd suspected someone was hurting me and asked me to help at one of their events. Afterward, she asked me to stick around to speak to the director, who offered to help me if I needed it. I had decided to take their help when my coworker landed in the hospital after an 'accident' and the home of the shelter director burned to the ground. Suddenly, neither of them would take my phone calls, so I'm sure there were other threats made against them."

With every word she said, Molly became more appalled for what Mia had endured and more frightened for her son. What would this man who would beat up women and burn someone's house do when he found out Wade was married to Mia? The list of possibilities terrified her.

Wade moved his chair closer to Mia's and put his arm around her. "We don't have to do this now if it's too much."

"No, we do have to. It's not fair to expect your family to understand if they don't know why." She took the tissue Molly offered her and wiped her eyes and nose. "The best day of my life was when Brody got arrested. I thought maybe then I could finally get free of him. But before I could make a plan, he was released on bail and was back home plotting his way out of the charges. I've seen and heard things that could be incriminating to him. I've seen him with other people who've been arrested. I've been to the building they used as their headquarters, although I've never been inside. I know where it is. He came up with the big idea to marry me so I couldn't be forced to testify against him and began pressuring me relentlessly go to along with the plan."

"Jesus," Linc muttered.

Gesturing to the bruises on her pretty face, she said, "This is what happened when I said no. That was the first time he left me unconscious. When I came to, he had left for a mandatory court appearance, so I ran. I got in the car with the clothes on my back and came to Butler, to the only friend I had left. I… I thought if I was married to someone else, Brody would have no choice but to let me go."

"I want to be clear," Wade said. "I'm doing this for one reason and one reason only—because I *want* to. Not because of the legal case or to get her free of him, but because, from the moment I met Mia, I've wanted to be with her, and now…" He gazed at her. "I'm going to marry her as soon as possible. Today, if we can make it happen."

"And then what?" Linc asked.

"What do you mean?" Wade replied.

"What happens after you say 'I do' and he finds out she's married someone else?"

"I'm going to get Gray involved with the legal end of things," Wade said. "He can file for a restraining order and advise us on other things we can do to keep Mia safe until after the trial, when we hope he'll be sent away for a long time."

"If you report the fact that he beat you," Linc said, "they're apt to revoke his bail."

"You wouldn't have to get married if they put him in jail," Molly added.

"What if they don't?" Mia asked. "Brody... He... He isolated me. My mother, the only real family I have, lives in New Mexico with her third husband, and I've lost touch with the friends I had before I met him. His efforts to control me started slowly. Over time, my friends stopped calling, and the only new friend I made in years is Wade. I stopped contacting him after a while because I was afraid Brody would find out and think it was something it wasn't. I... I didn't want him to cause trouble for Wade."

"So what'll happen when he finds out you're married to Wade?" Max asked. "Won't he cause trouble for Wade then?"

Molly wanted to thank him for asking what she most wanted to know.

"I don't suppose there's anything he can do after we're married," Mia said, glancing at Wade.

"He could have my brother killed to get him out of the way," Max said bluntly. "If he would beat a woman the way he did you, burn down someone's home and threaten people, I'd be concerned about what he'd do to the man who took the woman he considers his from him."

Molly felt like she was going to be sick.

Mia's face had gone pale. "I... I don't think..."

"That's not going to happen," Wade said emphatically. "I'm more than capable of taking care of myself and Mia."

Lincoln cleared his throat, and all eyes turned to him. "I want to say something, and I want you to listen to me, son. I totally and completely understand why you want to do this. You care for Mia, and she's obviously in a bad spot. After hearing what she's been through, *I* want to help her. I want to get Gray over here and find out what we can do from a legal standpoint to protect her from this guy. There've got to be things we can do, short of you two getting married."

"I'm sure there are things we can do, and we will do all of them—after we're married." Wade stood and offered a hand to Mia. "Let's get going. We've got things to do."

Molly stood. "Wade—"

"I heard you," Wade said. "I heard everything you all said, and I appreciate your concern. I'm going to marry Mia—today. I really hope we can count on your support."

"We'll always support you both," Lincoln said, "but you have to understand why we feel the way we do."

"I understand," Mia said. "And I'm so sorry to have dragged Wade and the rest of you into my nightmare. If I'd had anywhere else to go..."

Wade put his arm around her. "You did the right thing coming to me, and we're going to get you free of him. Let's go see my aunt Hannah about a marriage license." To his mother, he said, "Later, we'll have a real wedding and have everyone there. Today is about legalities."

As she watched them go, a jolt of panic made Molly want to chase after them and try to talk some sense into her son. Her husband's tense expression told her he felt the same way.

"This is totally F'd up," Max said softly. "He can't *marry* her. He barely knows her."

"You heard what he said," Linc said. "Not only can he marry her, he fully intends to."

"What can we do?" Max asked, expressing the same desperation Molly felt.

"There's nothing we can do," Linc said. "Your brother is thirty-one years old and has the right to do whatever he wants, even if we don't agree."

"Linc..." Molly stared at him imploringly.

"We can't stop him, honey," he said gently. "All we can do is support them and hope for the best."

Molly had never felt so anxious or afraid.

His ears ringing from the things his parents and brother had said, Wade helped Mia into his truck. It wasn't like him to disregard his parents' advice or do something that obviously upset them. He tended to toe the line and do what was expected of him, so he understood that his plans had shocked and dismayed them, especially after they heard the circumstances under which Mia had sought him out.

He got where they were coming from, and if the roles had been reversed, he'd probably say the same things. But they had no way to know how he'd felt about Mia from the day they met, and how he'd suffered over not knowing if she was safe after she'd stopped contacting him.

Now that she had sought him out and asked for his help, there was nothing that would stop him from helping her, not even his parents' obvious disapproval.

"I'm really sorry," she said as he backed the truck out of his parents' driveway.

"You have no reason to be sorry."

"Your parents are very upset, and rightfully so. They don't know me from Adam, and here I am showing up, asking their son to marry me so I won't be forced to marry a violent drug dealer."

Wade reached over to take her hand. "They have no way to know about the bond we've shared from the beginning, because I never told them about you. If I had, this wouldn't come as such a shock to them. My sisters Hannah and Ella won't be surprised. They know how I feel about you and how upset I've been since you stopped calling me."

"I've caused you so much heartache. Maybe it would be better if you took me to the airport and I disappeared."

"It wouldn't be better. If you think there's been heartache before, that's nothing compared to what would happen after having you here with me and us talking about getting married. I'd never get over it if you ran away, so please don't do that to me."

They drove in silence the short distance to his aunt's house, but his mind raced with thoughts and details and an almost desperate need to permanently bind himself to her. He'd certainly never had such a thought about any other woman, which was why he felt so certain he was doing the right thing by marrying her.

He pulled into his aunt Hannah's driveway and cut the engine. "She's apt to say some of the same things my parents said. It won't matter, so please don't worry that I'm going to change my mind, okay?"

"Okay," she said with a sigh.

Wade got out of the truck and went around to help her out, guiding her over the snow-packed sidewalk that led to his aunt's mudroom. He and his siblings had been walking into the Colemans' house all their lives, so he pushed open the door and stepped into the cinnamon-scented house where his aunt had raised his eight cousins. They kicked off their boots and hung their coats on hooks.

He was surprised to see Ray Mulvaney sitting at the kitchen table, having a cup of coffee with his aunt.

"Hey, Wade," Hannah said. "Come on in. This is a nice surprise."

He kissed his aunt's cheek. "Hi, Auntie. This is Mia. Mia, my aunt Hannah and Ray Mulvaney. His daughter Lucy is engaged to my brother Colton, and his daughter Emma is engaged to my cousin Grayson."

"Pleased to meet you both," Mia said, shaking their outstretched hands.

Hannah gasped when she caught sight of the bruises on Mia's face. "Honey... Good God. What happened to your face?"

"That's part of why we're here," Wade said. "I need a favor."

"Sure thing," Hannah said. "Whatever I can do for you."

"I need a marriage license."

CHAPTER 6

"May this marriage be full of laughter, our every day a day in paradise."
—Rumi

Mia watched the shock register on his aunt's face as well as Ray's. Like Wade's parents, they had to be wondering who the hell this woman was who'd suddenly appeared and wanted to marry their son and nephew. And how could she blame them? If her son came home with a bruised and battered woman and wanted to marry her to save her from the man who'd hurt her, she'd feel the same way they did.

"You're getting *married*?" Hannah asked, visibly stunned.

"That's the plan. Can you help me out? I know it's a Saturday, but our situation is somewhat urgent."

"Are you... I mean, it's none of my business, but is there..."

"She's not pregnant." Wade smiled at her. "Not yet anyway." He went on to explain why they were getting married and why they wanted to do it right away.

Listening to him, Mia felt overheated and lightheaded at the same time. The thought of being pregnant with his child filled her with a powerful sense of yearning. In the twelve hours since he'd come home to find her on his doorstep, he'd been more devoted to her than anyone had ever been, and it wouldn't take long for her to become addicted to the way he made her feel—safe, protected and adored.

After what she'd been through with Brody, she ought to be fearful of becoming involved with another man, but she already knew Wade was Brody's polar opposite, and she wasn't strong enough to walk away from the help he offered, even if she knew that would be best for him. She'd once been a strong person, but Brody had systematically chipped away at her self-esteem until she questioned her every instinct except for the one that had led her back to Wade.

Mia could only hope she hadn't made another huge mistake by involving him. If anything happened to him because of her... She shuddered.

"Are you cold?" he asked.

"A little." That was better than telling him she was so afraid for him that she felt sick.

Wade got up and put another log on his aunt's woodstove. "Can you issue us a license, Aunt Hannah?"

"I, um... What did your mother have to say about this?"

"She's not thrilled, but she and my dad understand that I'm old enough to make my own decisions, and my choice is to marry Mia right away."

The statement was met with a long silence.

Wade never blinked as he met his aunt's gaze.

Then she sighed, stood and said to Ray, "Excuse me for a minute. I'll be right back."

"Take your time," Ray said.

"If you'll both come with me." Hannah led them through the mudroom, where she unlocked a door Mia had missed on the way in. From there, they were taken into her office, which had another door on the far side that Mia assumed was how the public accessed the town clerk's office.

Hannah sat at her desk, fired up her computer and requested Mia's date of birth, her parents' names, place of birth and Mia's address.

"I don't know my father's name or place of birth. I know nothing about him."

"Okay," Hannah said, making a note.

"Use my address for her," Wade said.

His aunt glanced at him but continued to type. "Have either of you ever been married?"

"I haven't," Wade said, grinning at his aunt.

"I was. Once."

Wade glanced at Mia, surprise registering in his expression.

"It was a brief moment of madness a long time ago, and we've been divorced for eight years."

"Normally I'd require proof of the divorce."

"I don't have it, but I could request a copy of the divorce decree."

"How long would that take?" Wade asked Hannah.

"A week or more at best."

"I don't want to wait that long. She said she's divorced. Isn't that enough?"

"I'm going to take your word for it because I trust you, Wade."

He released an audible sigh of relief. "Thank you."

Hannah printed the form and asked them both to sign it. "After you're married, the officiant will sign here," she said, pointing, "and then return it to me within ten days of the wedding. You can be married anywhere in Vermont by a judge, justice of the peace or licensed clergy member."

"I'm going to get Gramps to do it today," Wade said.

Hannah folded the form and put it in an envelope before handing it to Wade.

"Thanks again for this. I really appreciate it."

"No problem. I just hope you both know what you're doing."

"We do," he said, kissing her cheek. "Come on, Mia. Let's go see my grandfather."

"Thank you, Mrs. Coleman," Mia said before Wade could lead her from the office.

"Call me Hannah, and you're welcome."

They donned their coats and boots in the mudroom.

"See you, Ray," Wade called.

"Bye, Wade. Congratulations to both of you."

"Thank you," Wade said, smiling broadly at Mia.

He was so damned handsome when he smiled like that.

"He's the first one to congratulate us," Wade whispered. He held the door for her and followed her to the truck.

She hoped that Ray wouldn't be the only one to congratulate them, but she had a feeling the good wishes might be few and far between.

"What the hell just happened here?" Hannah asked when she rejoined Ray in the kitchen.

"Seems to me that you just issued a marriage license for your nephew and the woman he's crazy about."

"You mean the woman we've never laid eyes on before today?"

"It's a little odd. I'll give you that, but he sure seems happy."

"Yeah, he does." Hannah stewed over it for a minute. "I need to call my sister. Do you mind?"

"Go right ahead. This is the most excitement I've had since we saw that action flick last week."

"I prefer my Saturday mornings a little less exciting," she said.

"Good to know."

Hannah had butterflies in her belly—and not for the first time since Ray Mulvaney moved to Butler with his daughter Emma and granddaughter, Simone. He immediately began seeking out her company—and giving her butterflies with the way he looked at her. It had been a very long time since any man had looked at her the way Ray did.

She dialed Molly's number and waited for her sister to answer.

"I thought I might hear from you," Molly said. "I assume Wade has been there?"

"Come and gone."

"Did you give him a license?"

"I did, and I hope it was the right thing to do."

"As Linc said, there's not much else we can do but support him, as he's very determined to go through with this."

"It's not like him to be impetuous."

"I just talked to my Hannah, and she told me that Wade told her about Mia back when she was first starting to date Nolan. Hannah wasn't at all surprised to hear he'd jumped at the chance to marry her."

"That gives me some comfort."

"Me, too, but the fact that she's running from an obviously dangerous man is what worries me most. How will he react to hearing she married someone else? Max came right out and asked what's to stop this guy from murdering his brother when he finds out Wade married Mia."

"Oh, my Lord."

"I know. It's very frightening, but he seems so…"

"Happy?"

"Yes! He's usually so serious and quiet, and today I saw a side of him I've never seen before."

"I saw it, too. I suppose we'll have to hope for the best."

"While preparing for the worst."

"One thing all our kids know how to do is take care of themselves. Wade is no exception."

"I sure hope you're right."

"When have you known me not to be?"

Molly responded with a huff of laughter. "I walked right into that."

"Let me know if you need anything. I'm here."

"Thanks, Han. Talk to you later."

"How're they holding up over there?" Ray asked.

"She's worried but resigned. They do reach an age where we can't tell them what to do anymore."

"Very true."

"So, in case you hadn't heard, it seems that my nephew Wade is getting married."

"How about I take you out to dinner to celebrate?"

Hannah felt her face get very warm, which happened often when he was around. "That would be lovely."

Wade drove to his grandfather's house and wasn't surprised to see Elmer's driveway already plowed. Even the sign outside the house had been cleared of snow.

"Justice of the peace, notary public, free advice," Mia said, reading the sign. "He's a jack of all trades."

"He really is," Wade said. "Especially the free advice."

When she laughed, he glanced over at her.

"What?" she asked.

"I don't think I've ever heard you laugh like that."

"I haven't had much reason to laugh in the last few years." She looked down at her hands, which were encased in gloves she'd borrowed from him. "You must wonder why I stayed…"

He put the truck in park and turned to face her. "I don't wonder. Obviously, you stayed because you were afraid to leave. I don't think less of you for that. You did what you had to in order to survive, and I'm extremely thankful that you survived and were able to get out and that you came to me. Why do you think I told you how to find me?"

"You have no idea how hard I clung to that information. I had it memorized a year ago. I kept waiting for an opportunity. Then when he got arrested, everything got worse, if that's possible. The DEA had infiltrated his organization, which took him totally by surprise. He was so infuriated. They froze his assets and had him on an ankle monitor after he was arraigned. He wanted me with him all the time, I think because he knew I could bury him with the things I've seen and heard. A week ago, after a meeting with his lawyers, he started talking about how we were going to get married so I couldn't be forced to testify. That's when I knew I had to get out of there before…"

"What? Before what?"

"Before he either killed me or forced me to marry him."

"Neither of those things will happen now, so you can stop worrying."

"I wouldn't put it past him to kill me to keep me from testifying."

"We'll get a restraining order and hire bodyguards if it comes to that, but he won't get near you. Not while I have a breath left in me. You hear me?"

She offered a wan smile. "You're too good to be true."

"I'm not. I'm a regular guy who met an amazing woman two years ago and has thought of her every day since then. You have no idea what a relief it is to have you right here with me rather than having to wonder if you're okay."

"I'm sorry you were worried. I didn't mean to do that to you."

"No more apologies. The past is the past, and now we need to see to the future. You still want to marry me?" he asked with a cajoling grin.

Her lips curved into a smile. "Yes, please."

"Let's go see a man about a wedding."

As they made their way up the path to Elmer's porch, the front door swung open. "What're you doing out so early, boy?"

"I've got important business," Wade replied, charmed as always by his grandfather. Inside, they took off their boots and handed over their coats. "This is Mia."

Elmer stopped in his tracks. "*Ohhhhh*. Oh. Well…" He put the coats over a chair. "This is a very nice surprise." He kissed her unbruised cheek. "It's a pleasure to finally meet you."

Mia smiled at him. "You, too. Wade thinks the world of you."

"The feeling is entirely mutual. What can I get you? Coffee? Hot chocolate? Tea?"

"What we really need, Gramps, is a JP."

Elmer blinked, glancing from him to her and then back to him. "Excuse me?"

Wade produced the marriage license from his pocket and handed it to his grandfather. "We need you to marry us. If you wouldn't mind, that is."

"You… you want to… Married?"

Wade laughed. "You heard me right. Mia and I would like to get married. Today. Right now, if possible."

"Oh. So, now, then?"

"Please."

Elmer glanced at Mia. "And this is what you want, too, honey?"

"Yes, sir."

"Call me Elmer. Everyone does."

"Thank you, Elmer."

To Wade, he said, "Does your mother know about this?"

"She does."

"And she approves?"

"I'm not sure I'd say that, but I wasn't asking for approval when I told her and Dad."

Elmer studied him for a long moment before he cleared his throat. "You need witnesses."

Wade groaned. Another delay. He ran through a quick list of family members who would be readily available and settled on Ella and Gavin. "May I use your phone?"

"Of course. Help yourself."

Wade picked up the portable phone next to his grandfather's recliner and placed the call to his sister.

Her fiancé, Gavin Guthrie, answered. "Hey, Elmer. What's up?"

"It's Wade. I'm at Elmer's, and I was wondering if you and Ella might be able to come over to do me a favor."

"Sure, what do you need?"

"Would you mind if I explained when you get here?"

"Okay… Ella is in the shower. We'll be there in thirty."

"Thanks very much." Another half hour, and then Mia would be his wife. He could stand to wait that long. Just barely… "They'll be here in half an hour."

"That gives us time to get to know each other." Elmer ushered Mia into his cozy kitchen, where he held a chair for her.

She glanced at Wade as she sat.

He took the seat next to her and reached for her hand, hoping to provide reassurance. His family could be overwhelming on an average day, and there was nothing average about *this* day.

Elmer put mugs of hot chocolate in front of each of them. "Wade told me about you a few months back. I've been hoping ever since that I'd get to meet you someday."

"I was hoping I'd get the chance to meet the big family Wade told me so much about."

"Someone hurt you, honey."

She nodded.

"I'm very sorry that happened to you."

"Thank you."

"Is that the reason you two kids are in such an all-fired rush to make it official?"

"The man who hurt her was recently arrested for running a heroin organization."

"I suspected that might be the case."

"That's what you were talking about that day you asked me about Mia."

"Yes, but I wasn't entirely sure it was the same Mia, so I didn't want to say any more. I was afraid you'd go off on a rogue mission to rescue her and get yourself killed."

"I probably would have. He's been pressuring Mia to marry him so she can't testify against him. If she's married to someone else, that makes it impossible for her to ever be forced into marrying him. And we believe that if he were to get the chance, he'd threaten her life to get her to do what he wants." Though he understood the necessity to explain it to his family, he was looking forward to putting the explanations in the past and getting on with the being-married part of the program.

"Have you filed a report on the assault?" Elmer asked.

"N-no," Mia said. "I was focused on getting away from him."

"You need to report it. They may revoke his bail."

Mia glanced at Wade, seeming to seek his opinion.

"I agree with Gramps, and we'll do that next if you're comfortable with reporting it." His body vibrated with tension as he waited impatiently for Ella and Gavin to arrive.

"I have the phone number of the prosecutor from the state's attorney's office," Mia said. "I could call him."

"You should do that while the bruises are still visible," Elmer said gently.

Wade had no doubt that seeing her bruised and battered had affected his grandfather almost as deeply as it had affected him. Elmer had no patience for violent men who beat up on women—or anyone else for that matter.

The three of them chatted until they heard car doors closing outside. Wade jumped up to greet Ella and Gavin as they came in.

"What's going on?" Ella asked. "Gavin said you were acting mysterious, and I said that's not like you." She stopped short when she saw Mia standing with Elmer.

"El, Gav, this is Mia. Mia, my sister Ella and her fiancé, Gavin."

"Oh my God!" Ella went right over to Mia and hugged her. "I'm so glad to finally meet you!" Pulling back, she added, "And you're hurt…"

"I'm okay," Mia said, looking at Wade. "Now."

Ella turned to Wade. "You told Gavin you needed a favor. What can we do?"

"We need witnesses to our wedding."

Ella's mouth fell open as Gavin gasped. "You're getting *married*?" Ella asked.

"Yes, right now, if the two of you are willing to be our witnesses."

"Holy shit," Gavin muttered. "Didn't see that coming."

"Will you do it?" Wade asked, feeling more anxious by the second to make it official.

"Yes, of course we will," Ella said. "Right, Gav?"

"Yeah, sure. Happy to help."

"Great, thanks. Gramps? Can we get this show on the road?"

His grandfather hesitated, but only for a second. "Give me a minute to get myself together."

After already waiting for years for her, Wade could stand to wait one more minute. But not a second more.

CHAPTER 7

"A happy marriage is a long conversation
which always seems too short."
—André Maurois

Wade's beautiful sister and her handsome fiancé were shocked by their news. His grandfather had been, too. Everyone was. And naturally, they were worried about what Wade was getting himself into. The only one who didn't seem worried about that was Wade himself. He had been steadfast since she'd first presented the idea to him, and he'd never wavered.

Her belly fluttered with butterflies when Elmer arranged them in front of the woodstove with Ella to her right and Gavin positioned next to Wade and instructed Wade to hold her hands.

"Dearly beloved," Elmer said with a warm smile. "We are here today to celebrate the marriage of my wonderful grandson Wade Michael Abbott and Mia Elizabeth Simpson. Wade and Mia, have you both come here willingly, of your own free will, to join your lives in wedded matrimony?"

"I have," Wade said, looking at her as he said the words.

At that moment, everything but him faded into the background. "I have," Mia said.

"Wade, if you'll repeat after me: I, Wade, take you, Mia, to be my wife. To have and to hold from this day forward, barring all others, to love, honor and protect all the days of my life."

Wade repeated the vows, his gaze never wavering as he bound himself to her.

"Now, Mia, if you'll repeat after me: I, Mia, take you, Wade, to be my husband." Mia repeated the words Elmer gave her, holding tight to Wade's hands and the belief that they were doing the right thing. Whether they'd make a go of the marriage remained to be seen, but he was saving her from being forced into marrying Brody, and for that, she would always be thankful.

"Do you have rings?" Elmer asked.

Wade looked stricken. "Crap. I never even thought of it."

"Hold tight." Elmer disappeared into his bedroom and returned a minute later with two plain gold bands in the palm of his hand. "These were mine and your grandmother's. I had to take mine off when my arthritis made my knuckles swell." To Mia, he added, "My Sarah died quite some time ago, but I think she'd approve of you having her ring."

"Gramps," Wade whispered. "We can't. They're yours."

"If I didn't want you to have them, I wouldn't have offered. Take them. Please. It will make me happy to know they've found a good home."

Wade took the rings from his grandfather and then hugged him. "Thank you."

"I hope you two are as happy as Sarah and I were."

When he pulled back from his grandfather, Mia saw tears in Wade's eyes that touched her deeply. He took her right hand and curled his grandfather's ring into her palm. Then he slid his grandmother's ring on her left hand.

"Look at that," Elmer said. "Fits like it was meant for her."

"So it does," Wade said, visibly moved.

Ella sniffed and dabbed at her eyes.

"Wade, if you would, repeat after me: With this ring, I thee wed."

He squeezed her hand and said the words. Then she put his grandfather's ring on his finger and repeated the words.

"By the power vested in me by the state of Vermont, it's my honor to declare you husband and wife. Wade, if you'd like to kiss your bride…"

He wrapped his arms around her, and after gazing at her for a long moment, he kissed her softly and then hugged her tightly. "Everything's going to be okay now," he whispered in her ear. "I promise."

Mia hoped he was right, but was afraid of what would happen when Brody found out she'd married someone else.

With the formalities completed, Wade could breathe easier. Mia was his *wife*. His wife. Despite the circumstances that'd led to this moment, he had never been happier about anything than he was about marrying her. It was the most foolish and impulsive thing he'd ever done, but so be it. He had what he wanted, and he would spend the rest of his life making sure she had everything she wanted or needed.

"Thank you, Gramps." Wade hugged his grandfather. "For marrying us, for the rings, for a lifetime of everything."

"Love you, son. I hope this marriage makes you very happy."

"It already has."

Elmer released him and hugged Mia. "Welcome to our family, honey. Now that you're one of us, you have a formidable crew standing by you in good times and in bad."

"That's very nice to know. I hope the good times far outweigh the bad. Thank you again, Elmer."

"My pleasure."

They accepted congratulations and hugs from Ella and Gavin.

"I sure didn't think you'd beat me to the altar, little brother," Ella said when she hugged Wade.

"Neither did I, but we both got the one we wanted."

"That we did. I wish you nothing but the best."

"Thanks, El. And thanks for coming when I needed you."

"Always."

Gavin shook Wade's hand. "Congratulations, man."

"Thank you for being a witness."

"Happy to do it. Didn't expect to go to a wedding today."

"That's the Abbott family for you. You never know what's going to happen next."

"True that."

"I need signatures from Ella and Gavin before you get away," Elmer said.

"And we need a picture of the bride and groom," Gavin said, pulling out the phone he carried for work.

"I don't know," Mia said, her hand covering the bruises on her face.

"If we turn you this way," Ella said, arranging them so Wade stood behind Mia. The camera would capture the unbruised side of her face. "How's that?" Ella asked.

"That'll work," Mia said. "Thank you."

Gavin took a picture of the two of them together and one with Elmer. Then Elmer took one of Wade, Mia, Ella and Gavin.

As Ella and Gavin signed the marriage license, Wade took Mia's hand and brought it to his lips. "How're you doing, Mrs. Abbott?"

"Mrs. Abbott. Wow. I'm doing great. Better than I've been in a very long time."

He stepped closer and kissed her. "Me, too, sweetheart." Leaning his forehead against hers, he closed his eyes, swamped with relief after wishing for so long to have what he did now—Mia in his life and in his arms. "Me, too."

Before he left his grandfather's house, Wade called his cousin Grayson to see if he was home.

"Yep," Gray said. "We're hanging out and watching movies."

"Would you mind if I stopped by to discuss some business?"

"Legal business?"

"Yeah. I know it's the weekend and everything, but—"

"Sure, Wade, come over. It's no problem."

"Thanks a lot. I'll see you in a few."

He held Mia's coat for her and then donned his own. Ella and Gavin had left to do some errands. Wade hugged his grandfather. "Thanks again for this—and for the rings. I'll get them back to you when we have a chance to buy some."

"Keep them. I like that you have them, and I think it's a sign of your grandmother's approval that they both fit so perfectly."

"We will treasure them always, Gramps." Wade kissed his grandfather's cheek and hugged him again. When he released the older man, he saw tears shimmering in Elmer's eyes.

Elmer turned to Mia. "If there's ever anything I can do for you, I'm here."

Mia hugged and kissed him. "Thank you so much."

In the time they'd spent at his grandfather's, the sky had gotten dark and thick with clouds.

"I can't believe it's going to snow again," he said, holding the door to his truck for her. "We'll go see my cousin, and then we'll go home and get comfortable before it starts to snow again."

"That sounds good to me."

It sounded like heaven to him. Mia was his wife. Maybe if he thought it a few more million times, it would finally register. Wade wished he had the time to fully wallow in his new reality, and he would, as soon as he'd taken the necessary steps to ensure her safety. Nothing was more important to him than that. For so long, he'd wished there was something he could do for her, and now there was nothing he wouldn't do, as he'd just proven by legally binding himself to her. Nothing had ever pleased him more than looking into her gorgeous navy-blue eyes and saying, "All the days of my life," to her, to *them*.

Grayson and his fiancée, Emma Mulvaney, lived with her daughter, Simone, in a converted church about a mile from Elmer's place. That mile was slow going on roads caked with slushy snow that would freeze during the night. They needed to make this quick and get home before the driving became more treacherous.

"This is where your cousin lives?" Mia asked of the white church with the steeple.

"Isn't it cool? Wait till you see the inside. Ray lives in the cottage in the back."

"It's nice that he lives close to her."

"They just moved up here recently."

"From where?"

"New York City. Grayson met Emma when she and her daughter, Simone, came up with Ray for my brother Hunter's wedding and Christmas."

"And they're already living together. That was fast."

"When you know, you know," he said with a meaningful look for her. She smiled and nodded in agreement.

Hand in hand, Wade and Mia ran through the frigid cold to the side door that led to the mudroom. Wade rang the doorbell and stepped inside, since his cousin was expecting him, and it was freaking freezing.

They were kicking off their boots when Gray appeared in the doorway, wearing flannel pajama pants and a Boston Red Sox sweatshirt. "I understand congratulations are in order for you two."

"Welcome to the Abbott and Coleman families," Wade said to Mia, "where news travels faster than the speed of light, even though none of us has cell phones."

"How do you guys *live* without cell phones?" she asked.

"It's surprisingly nice to be untethered," Grayson said. "You do get used to it after a while." He led them into the kitchen. "Can I get you anything?"

"I'm good," Wade said. "We've had enough hot chocolate this morning to float a battalion."

"Me, too," Mia said. "Thanks."

Simone came into the kitchen, skidding to a stop when she saw Wade and Mia.

"Hey, Simone," Wade said. "Come meet my wife, Mia." *My wife…* His heart could barely handle the surge of emotion that came with those words.

"You got *married*?"

"I did. Mia, this is Simone."

"It's nice to meet you."

Simone shook Mia's hand. "You, too. What happened to your face?"

"Simone," Grayson said. "Don't ask that."

"Why not?"

"Because it might be private."

"Oh. Sorry."

"It's all right," Mia said, smiling at Simone. "I had an accident, but I'm okay."

Emma came into the kitchen, also wearing pajama pants and a sweatshirt. "There you are," she said to her daughter. "I told you Gray had business to do."

"I just wanted to say hi to Wade. He got *married*!"

"So I heard," Emma said, smiling at Wade. "Congratulations."

"Thank you. This is Mia."

"Nice to meet you." Emma shook Mia's hand. Unlike her daughter, she didn't ask about the bruises on Mia's face, but she certainly noticed them. With her hands on Simone's shoulders, she said, "Let's go watch *Frozen* for the nine millionth time."

"*So* sorry to miss that," Grayson said.

"He's being sarcastic," Simone said as her mom steered her out of the kitchen.

"She's adorable," Mia said.

"She's too cute for her own good—and ours," Grayson said. "Now what can I do for you newlyweds?" With a good-natured grin, he added, "And way to get everyone talking about you by popping a surprise wedding on us, Wade."

Wade grimaced. "Because you know how much I *love* being the center of attention in this family." He reached for Mia's hand. "We need some legal help."

"Whatever I can do."

Wade told the abridged version of Mia's story, hoping to spare her from having to tell it again. "We're wondering what our options are to keep Brody far away from her."

"First thing, you need to report the assault. Right away."

"Mia has the number for the U.S. attorney overseeing the drug case," Wade said.

"I'll start there. I'll also ask about a restraining order to keep him away from you, Mia."

"He's going to be very angry when he finds out I got married," Mia said softly. "Would it be possible to include Wade and his family in the restraining order?"

"I'll see what I can do. Before we go any further, I need you to tell me everything. Start at the beginning and don't leave anything out. Every detail matters. Tell me what you know about his operation, what they'll ask you to testify about and anything that might help to build a secondary case against him."

"A secondary case?" she asked.

"For domestic assault," Grayson said gently.

By the time they left Grayson's two hours later, Wade was completely drained from hearing the full extent of what Mia had endured. Brody had abused her physically and emotionally while isolating her from anyone who might be able to help.

Grayson had arranged for an officer from the state police and the prosecutor himself to come to Wade's house in the morning so she could report the assault.

They drove home in snowy darkness that required all of Wade's attention and focus.

After hearing more about what she'd been through, Wade wanted to find that bastard Brody and beat the shit out of him. But more than that, he wanted to put his arms around her and do everything in his power to make her feel safe and loved.

Yes, he loved her. How else could he explain why he'd thought of her every day since he met her, why he'd yearned for her during the long months with no word from her, or why he'd jumped at the chance to marry her, to bind her to him legally and every other way? If that wasn't love, he didn't know what else it could be.

"I'm sorry you had to hear all that," she said in a tone he now recognized as shame.

It infuriated him that she felt ashamed of anything. She was a victim, and she had nothing to be ashamed of.

"You have no need to apologize, especially not to me." He would keep telling her that until she stopped feeling the need to apologize for what had been done *to* her.

They arrived at his house after a long, tedious drive to find a box sitting right inside the mudroom door. They went through the now-familiar routine of removing boots and coats and gloves and hats, and then Wade took the box into the kitchen to see what it was. He found a note written in his mother's familiar handwriting.

Wade and Mia, I thought you might appreciate not having to cook dinner on your wedding day. Dad and I love you very much. Mom

Touched by the gesture, and his stomach growling at the smell of his mother's famous stew, Wade shared the note with Mia. "She always makes the all-vegetable version for me."

"That's very nice of her, especially since our news upset her."

"That's my mom for you. She may not agree with everything we do, but she's always supportive of us."

"That must be nice," Mia said wistfully.

"Your mom isn't like that?" Wade asked as he put the stew in a pot on the stove to heat.

"My mom had me at eighteen, and my childhood was somewhat of a slow-moving train wreck. She had no idea what she was doing and made it up as she went along. Sometimes I felt more like the adult than the child."

"The older I get, the luckier I feel to have been born into my family."

"You didn't always feel that way?"

"God, no. They used to drive me crazy when we all lived at home. I was always a little different from the rest of them. I like my space and crave solitude, which is hard to come by in a house with eleven other people underfoot."

Mia winced. "And now I've invaded your space and your solitude."

Wade turned to her and put his arms around her. "I wanted space and solitude from the lunatics I grew up with. That's the last thing I want from you."

"Oh. Really?" She looked up at him, seeming uncertain.

"Really," he said, kissing her.

"You might not say that after I've been here awhile and—"

"I will *always* say that. Having you here with me is ten million times better than wishing you were here, or wondering if you're okay, or hoping I might hear something from you." He kissed her again, lingering for a full minute this time with just his lips pressed to hers.

"Wade…" Her gaze zeroed in on his lips.

"What, honey?"

"I like when you kiss me."

A low rumble of laughter shook him. "I fucking *love* kissing you."

"Maybe you could, you know, do some more of it."

"Is that what you want?"

She nodded and licked her lips with a delicate swipe of her tongue that made him instantly hard.

He set the stove to low, took her hand and led her around the island to the sofa. When she was settled, he tossed a few more logs on the woodstove and then sat next to her, drinking in the sight of her lovely face.

"You're staring," she said, flushing.

"I'm memorizing every little detail," he said, kissing the mole above her top lip. "I had to rely on memories for so long. Now that I have the real you here, I'm probably going to be doing a lot of staring."

"As long as I'm allowed to stare, too."

"You're allowed to do any damn thing you want."

"That's going to take some getting used to. It's been awhile since I could."

"Take all the time you need. I'm not going anywhere, and I'm never going to turn into someone who wants to control you. I promise." With his arm around her, he drew her closer to him, moving slowly so he wouldn't overwhelm her with the powerful desire he felt for her.

After hearing what she'd endured with Brody, Wade wanted her to have all the tenderness she'd been denied. He wanted to worship her, treat her like the precious angel she was and make her feel safe—always.

Being with her, being *married* to her, kissing her... It felt like a dream come true. The best dream he'd ever had was right here in his arms, eagerly returning his kisses while running her fingers through his hair.

Her touch had him trembling from the effort it took to go slow, to be gentle and careful with her.

"Wade..."

"What, honey?"

"Don't hold back. I want you to kiss me like you did before you heard all the ugly details."

It made him ache to realize his hesitancy had hurt her. "I'm sorry. I don't want to do anything that'll scare you."

"I know I'm safe with you. You can't scare me."

He laughed when he wanted to groan. If she had any idea how badly he wanted her, she might indeed be frightened.

Her hands on his face brought him back for another kiss, her tongue tracing his bottom lip.

This time, he did groan from the sheer pleasure that made every nerve ending in his body stand up to take notice of what was happening. Whatever it was, it had never happened before. Not to him anyway. He'd never felt so consumed by desire or experienced anything like the intense, sharp need she'd aroused in him from the start.

Now that she was here and in his arms, that need grew and multiplied with every kiss, every touch, every smile or sweet look or shared moment.

Her tongue touched his, and he moaned, the helpless sound seeming to encourage her to do it again and again and again, until he snapped out of the daze to discover he was on top of her, her legs entangled with his and her arms tight around him. She'd completely and thoroughly trapped him, and there was nowhere he'd rather be than right here with her.

"Honey, your ribs… Don't want to hurt you."

"Nothing hurts. I promise."

The kiss became more desperate with every passing minute, until Wade had to come up for a deep breath or pass out. Leaning his forehead on hers, he kissed her nose and both cheeks and the lids of her closed eyes. Her lips were pink and swollen and damp… He'd never seen anything more beautiful in his life than the sight of her flushed with desire for him.

She raised her hips ever so slightly, pressing her heat against the hard ridge of his erection.

He gasped, so hard he ached with wanting her. "Mia…"

"I know… We probably need more time, and we shouldn't do this, but I want to." She opened her eyes and looked up at him, her every emotion shining through. "For so long, I've wondered what it would be like to be with you this way. And it's so much better than anything I could've imagined."

"For me, too," he said, his voice gruff with emotion. "Sometimes I worried it was possible to die from wanting someone so badly and having her so far out of reach."

"I'm not out of reach anymore."

"Believe me," he said with a huff of laughter. "I know." After a long pause to get himself together, Wade sat up and withdrew from her out of self-preservation. If he continued to kiss her, they were going to end up naked, and he wasn't sure she was ready for that. "How about something to eat?"

"Sure," she said.

Was that disappointment he saw in her expression? "Mia…"

"Yes?"

"There's no need to be disappointed."

"I'm not disappointed."

"I'm hungry, and I need to eat so I'll have the energy I need for our wedding night."

Her eyes widened. "Oh…"

"You might want to fuel up, too." He kissed her quickly and got up to see to their dinner, pleased to have erased all signs of disappointment in her.

CHAPTER 8

"Don't marry the person you think you can live with. Marry only the individual you think you can't live without."
—James Dobson

Mia ate the delicious stew his mother had left for them and drank the glass of wine he poured for her, but she might as well have been eating or drinking cardboard for all she knew. His reference to their wedding night had scrambled her brain, making it hard to focus on anything but going through the motions of eating so they could get to the next part of their evening.

But before they could take that step together, there were things she needed to tell him. She took a sip of her wine and forced it down over the lump in her throat.

"I... I want you to know," she said hesitantly. "Since I met you, I never once did anything... with him... willingly." She paused to take a breath. "Even before I met you, it had stopped being consensual. But that doesn't mean I don't want to... with you."

Wade put down his spoon and wiped his mouth before rolling the paper napkin into a wad that disappeared into his fist. "He forced you."

She nodded. "I didn't want to be with him. I wanted to be with you, and he knew I was looking for a way out, which made everything worse."

"Why didn't you come to me sooner?"

After a long pause, she said, "Before I met Brody, I had a good life. I had a job and an apartment and friends, and I took care of myself. Other than the very brief time I was married, I'd been on my own since my mom got married and moved away when I was eighteen. The worst part of what happened in the last few years is that he stole my independence. Before I met you, all I thought about was escaping from him and trying to get back what I'd lost. But then I met you, and all I thought about was you and how much I wished I had met you under different circumstances."

She met his gaze. "I want you to know that it goes against everything I used to be to come here, to ask you to marry me, to ask for your protection. But as he became more desperate about his legal situation, he became fixated on making it so I couldn't testify against him. I was afraid if I continued to refuse to marry him, he would kill me to get me out of the way. I'm beaten down enough to know I can't fight this battle on my own."

"You don't have to. You're an Abbott now. You'll never be alone—unless you want to be."

"That means the world to me."

"And just because we're married, that doesn't mean you can't be as independent as you want to be. Do what you want. I'll never object to you following your dreams or seeing your friends or anything you want to do. As long as what you want doesn't involve other guys..."

She smiled. "So you plan to be a jealous husband?"

"Extremely."

"I can live with that."

He took her hand. "I know it's going to take a while to get past what happened with him and to regain your confidence, but I'll be right here to support you every step of the way. If you want something, all you have to do is say so, and I'll do anything I can to help you get it."

She blinked back tears. "That's very sweet of you. Thank you. And you're right, it'll take some time to unravel myself from the hold he had over me."

"Would you consider maybe getting some counseling to help you deal with everything that happened?"

"That might be a good idea."

"I'll get you added to the company health plan tomorrow, and we'll go from there."

"Wow, all this and health insurance, too. I've never had it before."

"Never?"

"My mom couldn't afford it, so we did the pay-as-you-go thing and hoped for the best." After a pause, she said, "She did the best she could with what she had."

"What about your father?"

"He was never in the picture. She refused to talk about him."

"Well, she raised a beautiful, sweet daughter. I look forward to meeting her."

"She'll like you."

"You think so?"

"I know so. She *hated* Brody. She met him once and said once was enough."

"Does she know what's been going on?"

"Only that he was arrested and charged and out on bail, but not the rest. The last time I talked to her, I told her I was making plans to get away."

"Do you want to call her and let her know you're safe?"

"I will tomorrow."

The phone rang, startling them both. Wade got up to answer the call from his sister Hannah.

"Wade! I just heard the news. *Oh my God!* She came looking for you—and you married her! I'm so excited I can't even *breathe!*"

Wade held the phone away from his ear so her high-pitched shrieks wouldn't deafen him. "Hello to you, too, Hannah." He smiled at Mia, who could hear every word his sister was saying.

"I'm so, so happy for you, even if the circumstances aren't entirely ideal."

"Thank you."

"When can I meet her?"

"Soon."

"How soon?"

"I'll let you know. I don't want her hit with all the Abbotts at once, or she might change her mind about me."

Mia shook her head.

"I've got to go, Hannah. My *wife* is waiting for me."

"Wade... I just..."

"I know, Han. Love you, too. I'll call you tomorrow."

"You'd better."

Wade put down the phone and started clearing the table.

"Is she always like that?" Mia asked.

"She's one of the few people who knew about you, so I expected some excitement from her."

"I'm looking forward to meeting her and the others."

"Maybe we can go to Sunday dinner, if you can deal with meeting the Abbotts all at once. I'm not sure that would be the best idea."

"It's fine with me. I know your family is huge, and I've already met a few of them." She brought the last of the dishes over to the sink and helped him load the dishwasher before wiping down the counter and table. They worked like they'd been living together for months rather than hours. Everything was so easy with him, and it'd been like that from the beginning. They'd struck up a conversation at the retreat that had flowed with the kind of ease she'd rarely experienced with a man. Right away, she'd had the inappropriate wish that she'd met Wade before Brody. How different things might've been for her.

When Wade slid his arms around her from behind, Mia startled.

"It's okay," he whispered. "Just me."

"I'm sorry. That might happen for a while until my subconscious catches up."

"If it happens another thousand times, it'll still be okay."

She relaxed into his embrace, loving the feel of his arms around her and the rich, woodsy scent of him.

"What I said before about the wedding night... I don't want you to think I expect anything. I'd be perfectly content to hold you in my arms all night long." His whiskers brushed against her jaw, sending goose bumps down her back. "I don't want you to feel pressured or rushed or anything other than safe and comfortable."

Moved by his sweet words, she said, "I do feel safe—safer than I've been in a long time."

"But not comfortable?"

"Not entirely."

"What do you need?"

"I seem to have this ache..."

"Is it your ribs? We can put some more balm on them."

Holding back a laugh, Mia turned so she could see his face. "It's not my ribs. This ache is a little bit lower."

His eyes widened with understanding. "*Oh.*"

Mia's cheeks flamed with heat. She'd never been one to be forward with a man, but everything about *this* man was different. He'd made it so easy for her to be entirely herself with him, even before they were able to be anything to each other but friends.

He ran a finger over her cheek. "Does it embarrass you to tell me that?"

"A little."

"Don't be embarrassed. I've been nursing a very similar ache for quite some time now."

"I'm sure you've had plenty of willing candidates to help you with that." Mia was surprised by how furious it made her to think of him with other women, even if she had no right to feel that way.

"A few here and there, but since I met this gorgeous woman at a yoga retreat a couple of years ago, I haven't been able to work up enthusiasm for any of them."

It took a minute for his words to register, and when they did, she looked up at him, shocked. "Does that mean... in all this time..."

Cupping her face gently, he kissed her. "There hasn't been anyone else."

"Wade! Oh my God. You've got to be kidding me. It's been *two years* since we met."

"I'm *painfully* aware of how long it's been," he said with a playful grimace.

"What were you going to do... if I hadn't come here?"

"I don't know. I suppose eventually I would've had to get back in the game, but as long as I knew you were out there somewhere, I didn't want anyone else."

Mia rested her forehead against his chest, overwhelmed by his devotion to her even when he'd had no good reason to be devoted. "Wade... I'm so sorry I put you through such a difficult ordeal."

He drew her in closer to him and buried his face in her hair, breathing her in. "Now that I know where it was leading, every second of that ordeal was worth it, because it brought you to me."

"I want to be with you, Wade. I feel like we've already waited so long..."

"We've waited forever, or so it seems."

Wade kept his arms around her and steered her toward his bedroom. "Give me a minute to throw some wood on the stove and lock up." He kissed her and had to tear himself away from the sweet taste of her lips to see to practicalities. They would freeze in the night if he didn't stoke the fire, and now that she was here and possibly in danger, he would start locking his doors.

He made quick work of tending to the fire, and then locked the front door, for the first time employing the dead bolt the previous owner had installed. Then he did the same on the back door and checked every window to make sure they were locked. He'd never once, in all the years he'd lived in Butler, felt the need for that kind of security, until he had something more precious than his own life to protect.

When he returned to the bedroom, she was already in bed with the covers pulled up to her neck. "Are you cold?"

"No. I'm okay."

Standing beside the bed, he unbuttoned his flannel shirt and pushed it off his shoulders, draping it over a chair in the corner. Now that he was sharing his living space, he couldn't drop it on the floor the way he would've when he lived alone. He pulled off his long-sleeved thermal and unbuttoned his jeans.

Mia watched his every move, her gaze flickering from his face to his chest to his groin and back up again. When she licked her lips, he went hard as stone, like he used to when they'd sit across from each other in coffee shops and the movement of her tongue over her lips had tortured him.

He kicked off his jeans and ducked into the bathroom to brush his teeth and get a condom. Realizing once wouldn't be enough, he grabbed a strip of them. Maybe that was wishful thinking, but now that he could touch her and kiss her and make love to her, he wanted to gorge on her. Splashing water onto his face, he tried to calm himself. He wanted her so badly, but after what she'd been through, he needed to be careful with her. The last thing he wanted was to scare her by letting her see the full extent of his desire for her.

He'd had his share of women, but never one who mattered to him like she did. For a time, he'd wondered if there was something wrong with him, because he never got emotionally involved with women. Until he met her and was instantly captivated in every possible way. So while he certainly had had plenty of sex, he'd never before made love.

He took a couple of deep breaths, changed into pajama pants and left a nightlight on so she could find the bathroom if she needed it during the night. Emerging from the bathroom, he half expected to find her asleep, but her eyes were open and fixed on him as he put the condoms on the bedside table and got into bed.

"Are you okay?" she asked.

"Never better. You?"

"The same."

"You're too far away over there." He held out an arm to invite her to come closer to him and gasped when she pressed her naked body against him. "*Jesus*," he said on a long hiss. "A little warning would be nice."

Laughing, she said, "And miss that reaction?"

He turned on his side and pulled her in tighter to him, until her breasts were flattened against his chest and her leg was tucked between his. "This must be what heaven feels like."

"Mmm," she said, her lips vibrating against his neck. "Definitely."

"I still can't believe you're here with me, married to me, naked in bed with me."

"Well, I hate to be technical, but one of us isn't entirely naked…"

He released his hold on her. "Feel free to rectify that oversight."

"Don't mind if I do."

Wade thought he would go mad when she sat up on her knees and gave him his first view of her bare breasts. Tight pink nipples peeked out from behind her hair, and a vine tattoo he'd missed the night before curved from her hip to the unbruised side of her ribs. She was the sexiest thing he'd ever seen, and he wanted her fiercely. But he forced himself to stay still while she worked the pajama bottoms over his straining erection and down his legs, reminding himself he needed to go easy with her. She was injured, and the last thing he'd ever want to do was cause her more pain.

"You're very, very sexy, Wade Abbott. I watched you that first day in yoga class. I couldn't take my eyes off you."

"I didn't know you watched me in class. You never told me that."

"I felt like a weirdo because I couldn't stop staring at this incredibly hot guy who could do every move, even the ones no one else could do. And PS," she said, resting her hands on his thighs as his cock throbbed. "*All* the women in the class were watching you."

"You're the only one I remember from that retreat." He reached for her and brought her down on top of him. The feel of her lush body pressed against his had him sucking in a sharp deep breath. "I dreamed about this."

"About me?"

"Every night since I last saw you, I would think about what it would be like to be with you this way."

"And?"

"My wildest dreams couldn't have done it justice."

For the longest time, he simply held her, breathing her in and wallowing in the sensations that had every nerve ending in his body alive with desire and love and relief. He couldn't recall ever being more overcome by emotion. They came at him so fast and so furious, he could barely process one before another hit him.

"When we were in yoga class," she said after a long period of quiet, "I used to think about all the things I'd do if I got you naked in a bed."

Wade nearly swallowed his tongue. "Like what?" he asked gruffly.

"Like this," she said, kissing his chest and using her tongue to drive him mad. "And this..." She moved down to fully explore his abdomen. "I wanted to kiss every well-defined muscle you have."

Her hair brushed against his cock, and he held his breath. *"Mia..."*

"Hmm?"

"It's not going to take much to..."

As she took him into her mouth, she looked up at him with those big navy-blue eyes, and he wanted to freeze that image so he would never forget it. He buried his hands in her hair and tried to control the looming explosion. *Goddamn...* "Mia, honey..."

"Let me, Wade. I've wanted to for so long."

Dear God... He relaxed into the mattress and let her have her way with him. Pleasure zinged through him as she licked and sucked and stroked him with unbridled enthusiasm. "Mia..." He tried to warn her, but the words were trapped in a brain that wasn't firing on all cylinders. The climax, when it hit, was a full-body event that engaged every muscle.

She never let up on him until he was completely drained—in every possible way.

Son. Of. A. *Bitch.* Wade could only breathe as his heartbeat roared in his ears. He couldn't have moved if he tried.

Kissing a trail from his belly to his chest, she returned to her perch on top of him.

He forced his eyes open.

She looked rather pleased with herself, her lips plump and swollen, her cheeks flushed with a rosy glow. Then she smiled, and his heart skipped a beat. "How's it going down there?"

"Umm, can I let you know when my brain starts working again?"

Her low, husky laugh sent a charge of lust boiling through him. He would've thought he was done for the time being. He would've been wrong.

"That was a quick recovery," she said, releasing that sexy laugh that made him crazy for her. Then she squirmed on top of him and took him from half hard to desperate once again.

Cognizant of her bruises, he turned them so he was on top and waited a second to make sure she was with him, that there was nothing about the position that frightened or pained her. When he recalled what she'd said about Brody forcing her...

"What is it?" she asked, her brows knitted with concern as her hands cupped his face.

"I don't want to do anything to scare you."

"You couldn't. Everything is different with you. It always has been."

Moved by her words and the knowledge that all this time, she had felt the same way he did, he studied her intently. "Will you promise to tell me if I do something that makes you uncomfortable?"

"I promise, but you should know..." She raised her hips, pressing her heat against his cock. "I'm already quite uncomfortable."

"I'm not going to survive you," he said, gritting his teeth against the already insistent need to come again.

That laugh... Dear God, that laugh. He wanted to hear it every day for the rest of his life.

He kissed her with deep thrusts of his tongue.

Her arms encircled his neck while her legs curled around his hips. One slight move by either of them would seal the deal. Condom. He needed a condom. Now. Before this got any more out of hand. He wanted to kiss her everywhere—and he would. But he needed to be inside her more than he'd ever needed anything. "Hold that thought," he said against her lips.

Reaching for the bedside table, he grasped a condom and had it on in record time. He was about to make love to his wife. His wife, *Mia*. Best. Day. *Ever.*

She welcomed him back into her arms, her tongue meeting his as he settled on top of her, mindful not to put too much weight on her injured ribs.

This was love. This was what drove sensible people to do crazy things such as marry a woman they hadn't seen in more than a year. The only thing that mattered to him now was that she was here, in his bed and in his arms and in his life to stay, if he had anything to say about it.

He entered her slowly, giving her time to accommodate him.

She gasped. "*Wade…*" Her hands slid over his back to grasp his ass, dragging him deeper into her.

Fuck. Even though she'd taken the edge off, this would be over fast unless he managed to find some control—and quickly. Then she began to move under him, and he decided control was overrated.

Her fingers dug into his ass, and he gave in to the burning need she aroused in him. All thoughts of being gentle with her were forgotten in a sea of desire so intense, it drowned out everything but the pleasure.

She never stopped kissing him or touching him or responding to him.

Nothing had ever felt this good. *Ever.* Reaching between them, he pressed his fingers to her clit. "Come for me, sweetheart. Let me hear you." He drew her nipple into his mouth and sucked hard as he coaxed her.

Her sharp cry of completion had her muscles clamping down hard on his cock.

He pushed into her and gave in to his own release.

"Holy crap," she whispered.

Wade laughed and gathered her into his arms as he rolled onto his side, taking her with him. Still joined with her, his body hummed with satisfaction and bone-deep pleasure. "Wow."

"I knew it would be good with you, but… *Damn.*"

"We might need to do it again really soon, just to be sure that wasn't a one-off."

"That would be the responsible thing to do."

She was everything—sweet and sexy and funny and easy to talk to. She liked yoga, was vegan like him and enjoyed the same things he did, even rock-climbing. His dream woman was now his wife, and he'd never been happier in his life.

CHAPTER 9

"Sensual pleasures have the fleeting brilliance of a comet;
a happy marriage has the tranquility of a lovely sunset."
—Ann Landers

Wade dragged himself out of a sound sleep when his alarm went off at seven, the usual time he got up every day. He and Mia hadn't gone to sleep until well after four, and his body ached from the decadent workout. The lack of sleep and the aches were well worth it to finally make love to the woman he'd fallen for so long ago. It had been everything he'd hoped it would be and more than he ever could've imagined.

She was facedown asleep next to him, her golden hair spread out on the pillow.

For a long moment, he simply stared at her, drinking in every detail as a pang of fear struck his solar plexus when he recalled that she had to testify against Brody and that the police were coming this morning to take her statement about the beating she had withstood at his hands.

Their "honeymoon," such as it was, would be short-lived, with real-life concerns intruding to remind him of what had brought her to him in the first place.

No doubt Brody had friends who would be more than willing to fight his battles for him if he got locked up again, which meant neither of them would be safe when word got out that they were married.

The thought of her in any kind of danger made Wade crazy, because the reality was that he couldn't be with her every minute of every day. He had to work and could take a day or two off, but not much more than that with the big rollout of the store's intimate line coming soon. Not to mention the catalog shoot that was also on the docket for later in the month. His dad had roped him, his siblings and cousins into "modeling" the store's clothing.

Wade cringed at the thought of that shit show, but his dad had argued that they couldn't have hired a better-looking group of men and women to represent the family business. Even Caden and Callie had been recruited to model the baby clothes. It would be a true family affair, Abbott-Coleman style.

He could bring Mia to work with him, he thought, brightening at the possibility. There was always plenty to be done at the store, especially now with the catalog in production, the warehouse being built in nearby St. Johnsbury and more business than ever flooding into the store since the website had gone live.

They could find a job for her. Hell, they'd created a whole new *department* for Will's wife, Cameron, when she'd joined their staff as webmaster. Surely, they could find something for his wife to do. *His wife.* A day later, the words were still surreal. The most beautiful words he'd ever uttered.

Wade got out of bed and brewed a pot of coffee. Then he called his brother Hunter, the company's chief financial officer.

"Mmm, what?"

Wade glanced at the clock and winced. "Sorry. Call me back when you're awake."

"I'm awake. What's up?"

"I need some time off this week."

"What's the occasion?"

"You didn't hear what happened yesterday?"

"Um, no. Megan and I... We took a snow day off the grid."

In other words, Hunter and his new wife had spent the day in bed.

"So, what happened?" Hunter asked.

"I got married."

"You did *what?*"

"You heard me right the first time. I'm going to be out tomorrow and possibly Tuesday, too, but I'll let you know for sure. And if you could, find a job for my wife, Mia. There's got to be something she can do. She's got office experience and some retail. I think."

"Wade… What the hell? You got *married?* Who is she?"

"Someone I've known a long time. You can ask Hannah. She knows about her."

"You married someone the rest of us have never even met?"

"It's a long story that I don't have time to tell right now."

"Wade—"

"Find her a job, Hunter."

"Have her come in and fill out an application so we know where to put her. And PS, you can't be off this week with Amanda coming for training on the new product line from hell."

Wade groaned. How had he forgotten about that? "I'll come in for that, but I won't be around much otherwise."

"You have to be there for that. We can't do it twice. Once will be bad enough."

"I'll see you then, if not before." Wade ended the call before his older brother could reply. If he knew Hunter—and he knew him well—he'd be on the phone with his twin, Hannah, within thirty seconds. If it took that long.

Long after it went dead, Hunter stared at the phone, still trying to wrap his head around what Wade had told him.

Megan turned over, awakened by the phone. They'd decided to close the diner after getting another foot of snow overnight. "Who called?"

"Wade. Apparently, he got married yesterday."

Megan blinked. "Seriously?"

"Ah, yeah, sounds that way."

"Who'd he marry?"

"Her name is Mia, and apparently, he's known her a long time."

"Whoa. That's unexpected."

"No kidding, but then again, if any of us were going to show up out of the blue with a wife, it'd be Wade. He keeps to himself. We never know what's going on with him. But he said Hannah knew about it, so I'm going to call her and get the scoop."

He'd put through the call before he questioned the wisdom of calling his sister so early. Hopefully, they were up.

"What?" Hannah mumbled.

Okay, not up. "Sorry. Call me back when you're awake."

"I'm awake now."

"I thought Callie would have you up."

"She was up at five thirty, and I got her to go back to sleep."

"Call me later. I wanted to know the deal with Wade."

"Mia came, and he *married* her," Hannah said, sounding wide awake. "It's the best thing *ever*!"

"Who the hell is Mia, and how do you know about her when no one else did?"

"I think Ella did, too."

"Hannah! Who is she?"

"Quit your bellowing, will ya? He met her at a yoga retreat almost two years ago."

"Why haven't we ever heard about her?"

"Because he wasn't *with* her, until now."

"Wait a minute..."

"She's been in a bad relationship that got worse when the guy got arrested in that big drug bust in Caledonia County. From what Mom told me, he was pressuring her to marry him so she couldn't testify against him. He beat her up, she bolted the first chance she got and came to find Wade."

In total shock, Hunter tried to wrap his head around what she was saying. "Are you kidding me right now?" He wouldn't put it past her to make up a crazy story and then tell him it was a joke.

"Not kidding."

Hunter felt sick at the thought of his brother in any kind of danger, and this sounded dangerous, at the very least. "How could you know this and not tell me?"

"I heard about it last night and tried to call you, but your machine picked up."

"Oh. Sorry. I was... busy."

She snorted out a laugh. "I remember what that was like. Then I had a baby..."

"Who's the most beautiful little girl in the entire world."

"She is rather perfect."

"Let me know if you hear anything else, will you? I don't like the sound of this. I can only imagine what Mom and Dad had to say about it."

"Mom was freaked, but Dad reminded her that Wade is thirty-one and doesn't require their permission—or ours, for that matter—to get married."

"It's weird, Hannah. People don't just get married out of the blue. It doesn't work that way."

"All I know is that he's wanted her from the time he first met her, and he's been worried sick about her for a long time. When she showed up asking him to marry her, he got exactly what he wanted."

"I... I don't even know what to say."

"When you see him, you say, 'Congratulations, Wade. I couldn't be happier for you.'"

"Even if I have huge reservations about this?"

"Even if. Like Dad said, he's a grown man who has the right to make his own decisions, just like you did when no one was certain Megan was good enough for you. We had to let you decide for yourself."

"Touché. Is she good enough for him, Han?"

"I don't know, but he thinks so, and that has to be good enough for us. For now anyway."

"He wants me to find her a job at the store."

"So find her a job at the store."

"Just like that?"

"Hunter, he's *married* to her. That makes her family. You're running a *family* business. Find her a job."

"All right already, I will."

"Remember what it was like when you first got together with Megan and show him some support."

"Anything else, bossy one?"

"Yes, let me know when you and Megan want to babysit your godchild. She's been asking for you both, and her parents desperately need a date night."

Hunter laughed. "Sure thing. Next weekend."

"Don't commit until you're sure. I couldn't handle the disappointment."

Hunter glanced at Megan. "Can we babysit the adorable Callie Roberts one night next weekend?"

"Yes, please."

"Did you hear my wife? We'd love to. It's on. Pick your night."

"Saturday, seven o'clock. I'll have her fed, bathed and ready for night-night."

"We'll be there."

"I'm hanging up before you can change your mind." The line went dead.

"She hung up before I could change my mind," Hunter said to Megan.

Megan cracked up. "Needs a break, does she?"

"Sounds that way."

"What'd she say about Wade?"

"That we need to be supportive and I need to find a job for his *wife*, who I've never met."

Megan patted his chest. "You'll meet her soon enough."

"You don't think it's at all weird that he married someone none of us have ever met?"

"It's definitely weird, but so is he—and I say that with true affection. He's a very cool person, but he's nothing like the rest of you. If he didn't look like Will and Max, I'd think he was adopted."

Pondering what she'd said, Hunter put his arm around her to bring her closer to him. "He's always been 'unto himself,' as my mom used to say when we were younger. The rest of us would be doing one thing, and Wade would be off on his own doing something else. It wasn't that he didn't get along with us, because he did. He just marched to his own beat."

"Then it should hardly surprise you that he's married someone none of you know."

"Sorry, but that does surprise me. Even for Wade, that's bizarre."

"But you won't say that to him, right?"

"No, I won't, and don't worry, Hannah has already said the same thing. I'm to be 'supportive,' the way everyone tried to be with me when you and I first got together and they weren't sure how they felt about it."

"Because they thought I was too caught up in my former crush on Will to ever be what you need."

"Something like that." Smiling at her, he said, "But we know you turned out to be *just* what I needed, don't we?"

"Uh-huh. I believe we did a very good job of proving that yesterday."

Other than the few hours he'd given to the search for the missing boys, they hadn't left the house since Friday night.

"Do you think it worked? Did I succeed in knocking you up?"

"We'll find out soon enough."

"How soon?"

"Soon."

Hunter groaned. "I can't wait that long."

Laughing, she patted his arm. "I'll keep you very well occupied so you don't have time to think about it."

"It's all I'll think about until we know."

CHAPTER 10

*"We make no greater voluntary choice in this life
than the selection of a marriage partner."*
—James E. Faust

While waiting for Mia to wake up, Wade went through his morning yoga and meditation routine, needing to find his center to face the day ahead. While she gave her statement to the police, he would stay by her side every second. Never again would she be alone with the terrible burden she had lived with for so long on her own. She had him now, and he was determined to get her through whatever had to happen to gain her freedom from Brody and the horror of their relationship.

No matter what she needed, he would find a way to get it for her. Whatever it took to make her whole again. In the meantime, he would surround her with love and a big supportive family, and he would have her back, come what may.

Wearing only his flannel shirt from yesterday, buttoned once over her breasts, Mia came out of the bedroom as he was finishing Savasana, also known as the "corpse pose" in yoga, the most relaxing of all the many poses.

"Did you start without me?" she asked, smiling.

Wade could only stare at the face that had haunted his dreams for so many lonely nights, and now she was here, vividly real and married to him.

She waved her hand. "Earth to Wade. Are you there?"

"Yeah, I'm here, but I'm still having trouble believing *you're* here, too, and that last night really happened."

Kneeling on the foot of his mat, she rested her hands on his knees. "I'm here, this is real and last night most definitely happened."

Wade sat up, framed her face with his hands and kissed her. "Morning."

"Morning. I was sad to wake up without you."

"I was awake and didn't want to bother you."

"Next time, bother me. I would've worked out with you. If you wanted me to."

"I want you to." He who had craved space and solitude his entire life now wanted to spend every waking moment in the presence of another human being for the first time ever. "Definitely."

"Then you'll wake me up tomorrow?"

"I will." He kissed her again. "And now I need a shower."

"So do I. Someone got me dirty last night." Her lips curved into a coy smile that stopped his heart. "You want some company?"

Picturing her naked and wet made him immediately hard. "Ah, yeah, but only if it's you."

She raised a brow as she stood and offered him a hand to pull him up. "Were you expecting someone else?"

Wade was thrilled to discover that under her serious exterior lay a playful side she'd had to keep hidden until now. "I wasn't expecting you, and look at us now."

"Mmm," she said, laying her hands on his bare chest. "Look at us now." She curled her hand around his neck and brought him down for a deep, sexy, toe-curling kiss. "Now that I'm allowed to do that anytime I want to, you might get tired of me wanting to."

"No. Never." She made him pant with desire. "Kiss me anytime you want, anywhere you want."

"Anywhere?"

"Anywhere." Wade felt like a dog in heat as he followed her into the bathroom. The lower hem of his shirt just missed covering the bottom of her gorgeous ass. He wanted to sink to his knees and kiss the sweet, tantalizing curves that taunted him.

"Wade?"

Tearing his gaze off her ass, he realized she'd been speaking to him. "Sorry. The stupendous view inspired some rather detailed fantasies."

"Is that so? Like what?"

He turned her away from him, dropped to his knees and ran his hands up the backs of her legs to cup the cheeks that had held him captive. "Such as this." He kissed and nibbled and licked each inch of delicious flesh until her legs trembled so hard, she had no choice but to lean on the sink or fall over.

"Grab the shirt," he said gruffly.

She lifted it up and out of his way.

Using his thumbs, he opened her to his tongue and made her come hard in a matter of minutes.

He whipped off the shorts he'd worn to do yoga and buried himself in her, riding the waves of her orgasm.

Her fingers gripped the edge of the sink as he sank into her over and over again until she came again. In a single moment of clarity, he realized he'd forgotten a condom and pulled out before it was too late, coming on her back.

Good God… He'd never been so completely overtaken by desire. Not like that anyway, and not so much that he didn't give a thought to protection until it was nearly too late. When his head stopped spinning, he helped her up and out of his shirt and into the shower, where he washed off her back and held her under the steamy spray. "I was rough with you. I'm sorry."

"Don't be sorry. In case you couldn't tell, I loved it."

"You made me so crazy, I forgot the condom. That's never happened before."

She smiled up at him. "I've always been careful about protection. The last thing I wanted was a baby with Brody. I'm on the pill."

"Still… We should, you know, get tested before we give up the condoms."

"I was tested recently. I'm clean if you are."

"I am. So this means…"

"No need for condoms."

"*Thank you, Jesus.*"

They took turns washing each other, and he was fully aroused again in no time. "I'm not sure what kind of spell you've cast on me, but whatever it is, it sure feels good."

She turned to face him, her breasts pressed to his chest and her arms curled around his neck. "You've put the same spell on me."

Wade kissed her, slowly, deeply, tenderly, never stopping until the water began to run cool. He helped her out of the shower, dried her off and led her right back to bed to finish what they'd started in the shower. It had taken less than forty-eight hours to become completely and utterly addicted to her.

They dragged themselves out of bed to clean up and get dressed with minutes to spare before the officers arrived to take her statement about the assault.

She put on another of his shirts over the same pair of jeans she'd been wearing when she arrived. "I need to go home to get my clothes and stuff at some point."

"Point of order," Wade said. "*This* is your home now."

"My apologies. I meant the place I used to live."

"Let's see what the cops say about getting you in there." He fixed her coffee and made toast for her, offering peanut butter or jam for her to choose from.

She picked the raspberry preserves they sold in the store and had just finished eating when a knock on the door brought them back to reality.

Wade went to answer the door to two uniformed officers and another man. He stepped aside to invite them in.

The men in uniform introduced themselves as officers Brinkman and St. Germain from the Vermont State Police.

"I'm Larry Herschler," the third man said. "US attorney for Vermont."

As he shook the man's hand, Wade experienced a sinking feeling. The US attorney *himself* had come? "I'm Wade Abbott."

"Pleased to meet you," Larry said.

"Hi, Larry." Mia greeted him with a handshake. "Thanks for coming."

"I heard from your attorney, Mr. Coleman, yesterday, and I understand congratulations are in order," he said, glancing from her to Wade.

"Yes, thank you."

"I wish you'd called me rather than taking off."

Mia raised her chin defiantly. "I came to the one person I knew I could trust to look out for me."

Hearing that, Wade felt his heart swell with love for her. That she had so much faith in him amazed and humbled him.

"Fair enough." Larry took a long, intense look at the bruises on Mia's face. "I can't believe he did this on top of everything else."

"I believe it," she said, her voice returning to the dull, flat tone Wade recognized from when she'd first arrived. She sounded nothing at all like the happy woman she'd been only a few minutes ago when it had just been the two of them. "Nothing makes Brody unhappier than not getting his own way. It's not the first time he did this to me."

Wade put his arm around her. "But it will be the last."

"Yes, it will." Larry turned to the officers. "Go ahead and give the order."

One of the cops nodded and stepped outside.

Wade sat with Mia on one sofa while Larry sat across from them. The other cop stood by the door.

"What order is he giving?" Wade asked.

"They're going to arrest Brody for domestic assault," Larry said. "His bail will be revoked until he goes to trial."

Mia released a deep sigh of relief. Over the next hour, she gave a detailed account of the assault to Officer Brinkman, who took notes and asked what seemed like a hundred questions.

Wade hoped she wouldn't have to tell that story again anytime soon. Each telling seemed to diminish her more than the one before.

Then Brinkman took pictures of the bruises on her face and ribs.

Mia held up her shirt, her gaze fixed on the ceiling, humiliation radiating from her.

Wade hated that she had to go through this, but whatever it took to nail the bastard who had hurt her. "What happens now?" he asked when Brinkman said he had what he needed to file the report and would get it into the system before the end of the day.

"We need to talk about keeping you safe until the trial," Larry said.

A pang of fear hit Wade in the chest. "When will that be?"

"Six to nine months, possibly longer."

That seemed like a lifetime to have this hanging over her head, and judging by the rigid set to Mia's shoulders, she felt the same way.

"I know it sounds like forever," she said softly.

Clearly, she'd already been told how long it would take.

"It's a very complicated case, as you know," Larry said. "We want to ensure we've built an airtight case before we go to trial. The last thing we want is for him to walk."

"That's the last thing I want, too," she said.

"If Brody will be in jail until the trial, why are you worried about Mia's safety?" Wade asked.

"He has friends," Larry said bluntly. "A lot of friends, many of them caught up in the case against him."

Wade felt sick at the thought of her being stalked by criminals intent on keeping her from testifying against that scumbag Brody.

"Our case hinges on your testimony, Mia," Larry said.

"Wait a minute," Wade said. "Your case *hinges* on her?" He looked at Mia. "What does he mean?"

"I was the one who figured out what Brody was really doing," she said in a small voice. "I reported him."

As if a trapdoor had been opened under him, Wade experienced a dropping sensation. She hadn't thought that was an important detail to convey to him before he married her? Not that he would've done anything differently, but it left him wondering what else he didn't know about the woman he'd married.

"Your wife missed her calling as a detective," Larry said with a warm smile for Mia. "By the time we were brought in, she'd built one hell of a case against him. She made our jobs a thousand times easier than they would've been without her."

"And quadrupled the danger for herself," Wade said, looking at her. "Was that the real reason he beat you up?"

"No, he doesn't know that I reported him or that I gathered evidence that will be used against him. But he does know that I could bury him with what I've seen and heard. He beat me up because I refused to marry him, just like I said."

Wade, who'd been holding Mia's hand, released it and stood, needing to move, to do something to help him process this new information.

Mia got up and came to him, resting her hand on his chest. "What're you thinking?"

"What's going to happen when he finds out that you did this to him, Mia?"

"He did this to himself," she said. "And you heard what Larry said. He's going to be in jail until the trial."

"What about his friends and the other people who were implicated? Are they all in jail, too?"

"That's one of the things I wanted to talk to you about today," Larry said. "We'd like to put you, both of you, under police protection until after the trial."

Wade had an immediate, visceral, *negative* reaction to being watched by cops for as much as a year—maybe even longer. It hadn't even happened, and he already chafed against it. The thought of being watched by strangers made him crazy.

Mia looked to him. "Is that okay with you, Wade?"

No, he wanted to say. *None of this is okay with me, except for the part about wanting to keep you safe.* "I don't think it's necessary. Correct me if I'm wrong, but he would have no way to know you're here in Butler."

"He knows nothing about Wade," Mia said to Larry. "I was very, very careful to never give anything away about my friendship with him."

"Can he track your phone?" Larry asked.

"We have no cell service in Butler," Wade said. "So even if he could, it won't get him anywhere."

"I'd be more comfortable with police protection," Larry said.

Mia looked to Wade.

"Could we reserve the right to request it should it become necessary?" Wade didn't even want to think about the scenarios that could make it necessary.

"Of course."

Wade took hold of Mia's hand. "Then we decline for now."

"I don't like it, but I'll respect your wishes, but we will keep an officer in the area for the time being. That's nonnegotiable."

They spent another hour with Larry, discussing the next steps in the criminal cases against Brody.

"Mia needs to get into the house in Rutland to get her clothes and other belongings," Wade said.

"That won't be possible," Larry said, shaking his head. "I don't want you anywhere near Rutland. I'll ask a court-appointed officer to go in and pack up your things. If you make a list of what you want, we'll have it delivered to you here as soon as tomorrow."

When Larry stood to leave, the day was already half over, and Wade's nerves were shot. He now had a much better idea of the true nature of the case they were building against Brody and how essential Mia was to the prosecution, which filled him with fear. Larry shook both their hands and said he would be in touch with Mia. Since her cell phone was useless in Butler, they gave him Wade's home and office numbers.

"If you need anything at all," he said, handing them each a business card, "don't hesitate to call me. My cell number is on there. Don't be afraid to use it."

Wade prayed they'd never need it.

"Brody has been telling everyone you'd never testify against him—and that you're going to marry him so you won't have to," Larry said. "It may be unprofessional for me to say this out loud, but I'm looking forward to letting his attorney know that you won't be marrying Brody because you're already married—and you *will* testify against him."

"Tell him I can't *wait* to testify," Mia said defiantly.

"Is that a good idea?" Wade asked. "If we tell him Mia is off the market and planning to testify, won't that put her in greater danger?"

"I want him to know," Mia said fiercely. "I want him to know that he might've beat me with his fists, but he didn't defeat me. I want *him* to be scared of *me* for once."

Wade gazed at her, filled with pride—and fear for her safety. But he had to take his lead from her, and he was so damned proud of her show of strength. "Okay."

"I'll pass it along," Larry said. "And we'll keep eyes on you around the clock. They won't get near you."

Long after the door closed behind Larry, a sense of uneasiness hung over Wade. He had no idea what to say to her, which was a first. He'd never been at a loss for words with her. That had been one of the first indications he'd had that she would be special to him—he *loved* talking to her more than he'd ever loved talking to anyone else. And for the first time since he'd known her, he couldn't think of a single thing to say now that they were alone again.

Mia came over to him, seeming hesitant. "I'm sorry, Wade. I know you're angry, and with good reason. I should've told you that I was the one who reported him and that I helped the police and prosecutors."

"Yes, you really should've told me that."

"I'll understand if you..." She took a breath and looked up at him. "If you want me to leave, I will."

"I don't want you to leave, but I don't like feeling as if I've been played."

Her face fell, and he immediately regretted the words he'd used, even if they were accurate.

"I haven't played you, Wade," she said softly. "I... I meant what I said about coming to the one person I had left who I could totally trust."

"I know you did. I want to feel that I can trust you as much as you trusted me by coming here the other night."

"You can trust me."

He wanted to. God, how he wanted to, but a seed of doubt had been planted. As much as he wanted to ignore it and go back to the way things had been only a few hours ago, the doubt took root, refusing to be ignored.

CHAPTER 11

"A good marriage is one which allows for change and growth in the individuals and in the way they express their love."
—Pearl S. Buck

She'd screwed up badly by not telling Wade that she'd been the one to report Brody to the police, and now she had to find a way to repair the damage.

"I hurt you," she said, "and that's the last thing I ever want to do."

"Why didn't you tell me?"

"It wasn't because I don't trust you."

"Okay... So why, then?"

"I thought you might find it strange that I stayed after I figured out what he was really doing." She took a step closer to where he stood with his arms crossed and his body rigid. "I thought you might be disappointed that I didn't leave him as soon as I could." She took another step closer. "I thought you might be angry that I endangered myself to gather evidence against him." Looking up at him, she said, "I screwed up by not telling you everything, and I apologize for that. I'm sorry I hurt you."

A ticking muscle in his cheek was the only reaction he seemed to have to her apology. Maybe she ought to give him some space. He was used to having his home to himself.

Mia took a step back, intending to find somewhere else to be for the time being.

"Don't go," he said, reaching for her.

When he put his arms around her, Mia released a sigh of relief. "I'm so sorry, Wade."

"I know, but I have a request."

"Anything."

"Is there anything else I should know—about you, your life, Brody, the case? I'm out on a limb with you, Mia. My family thinks I'm crazy for marrying you the way I did, and I'm willing to defend our decision for the rest of my life, if that's what it takes, but I don't want to be blindsided again."

She looked up at him. "There's nothing else. I swear."

"What about the first husband you mentioned yesterday?"

"A boy I went to high school with. I freaked out when my mom got married and moved so far away. I married him when I never should've. It lasted six months and has been over for almost ten years."

"Okay, then." He hugged her, seeming as relieved as she was to put the awkward episode behind them. "Will you tell me how you figured out what Brody was doing?"

Mia nodded. She wished she never had to talk about Brody again, but she owed Wade the truth after everything he'd done for her.

Wade put some logs in the woodstove and sat next to her on the sofa, pulling a blanket over them.

Mia gathered her thoughts and let her mind wander back in time. "The first sign of trouble was the money. He was suddenly flush with it."

"How long ago was this?"

"About a year. Shortly after the last time I saw you. We'd always been comfortable, but he started coming home with extravagant gifts for me that he said were the result of bonuses he got from his customers who were happy with his work. The sad thing is he's a master carpenter and woodworker. He can build anything and makes gorgeous furniture that people came from all over to buy.

"At first, I believed him when he said his customers were happy, but then he came home with a brand-new, fully tricked-out pickup truck. I looked it up online and saw that the model started at seventy thousand dollars. He made furniture and built bookshelves. Where would he get the money for something like that? I started paying closer attention to everything he said and did. I wrote things down—his comings and goings, who he was with, what I heard them say. One night, I followed him."

"Jesus, Mia."

"I had to know. It took about a month for me to realize he was selling heroin."

"Why didn't you go right to the cops?"

"Because I couldn't prove it. Not yet anyway, and I didn't want him to get away with it."

"Earlier, you said you were afraid to go to the cops in Rutland after he beat you up because Brody grew up there and was tight with many of them."

"Yes, that's right."

"So how did you get around that when you reported him the first time?"

"I went right to the state police with what I had. I saw a thing on the news about their drug task force, and when I was ready, I called them."

"But you didn't feel that you could call them when he beat you?"

"I had a two-hour window when he would be out of the house. It was more important to me to get out of there than it was to call the police on him. I knew if I didn't leave then, I might not get another chance, because they had him on house arrest. He was home all the time and ranting about getting railroaded and how I'd better have his back. Then he said he was coming home with a JP and I'd better be ready to say 'I do.' I said I'd never agree to marry him, and that's when he beat me up. He left me unconscious on the floor when he left for court, and I think he expected me to still be there when he returned."

"Going back to when you first became suspicious of him... I'm trying to understand why you would endanger yourself to do a job the cops could've done."

"Because," she said fiercely. "He took *everything* from me—my friends, my life, my independence, my self-confidence. He tried to break me, Wade. This was my chance for justice. And…" Her voice broke, and she looked down, trying to regain her composure.

"What, honey?"

"I had a friend from high school… A sweet girl who'd had a rough life that got worse when she got hooked on heroin. She overdosed four years ago. I was thinking about her when I set out to stop him from selling that poison to people who can't control their addictions." Mia wiped away tears that fell every time she thought of Angie and what'd happened to her. "I know it's hard for you to understand, but I couldn't leave until I knew he would pay for what he's done."

Wade ran a finger over the bruises on her face.

"What I went through with him was a small price to pay," she said with defiance.

"It wasn't a small price."

"I'd do it again if it meant seeing him behind bars."

Wade put his arms around her. "It's a good thing I didn't know before now what kind of chances you were taking with your safety."

"What would you have done if you knew?"

"I might've had to kidnap you and hide you away in my mountain lair, so you wouldn't be able to do anything that could get you killed."

She laughed at the way he said that, with such fierce conviction. Looking up at him, she said, "Knowing you were out there somewhere… You gave me hope, Wade. The whole time, I just kept thinking if I could get rid of him, maybe I'd have a chance with you."

With his index finger on her chin, he held her in place for his kiss. "I want you to promise me something."

"What's that?"

"You'll never again intentionally put yourself in danger. You have a husband now, and he needs you to be safe. Will you promise me?"

"I promise. I'm out of the private-detective business."

"Good."

The phone rang, and Wade reached for the extension to take the call from his brother Will. "Hey, what's up?"

"I should be asking you that."

"Which means you already know what's up with me, so what do you want?"

Will laughed. "Glad to see that marriage hasn't changed you. I'm calling because the lake is frozen and everyone is going skating. We wanted to see if you and your *wife* might want to join us."

"Let me ask her." Holding the phone aside, Wade said, "You want to go ice skating with my family?"

"I don't have skates."

"We can scare some up for you. What size?"

"I love to skate, and I'm a seven."

Wade added that info to the other things he'd learned about her in the last few days. "We're in," Wade said to Will. "Mia is a seven if someone can bring skates for her. What time?"

"About an hour?" Will said. "And I'll put out the word about extra skates."

"See you then."

"Hey, Wade?"

"Yeah."

"Congrats, man. I'm happy for you."

"Thank you."

Mia rolled her bottom lip between her teeth as she wondered how long it would take the cops to get her stuff to her.

"What's this?" Wade asked, tapping on her lip.

"I'm just thinking that I need clothes, and I hope they can get them to me soon."

"Let's go to the store."

"Now?"

"Why not? You need clothes. I co-own a store."

"Sure, I suppose that would be okay. As long as I can pay for whatever I get."

"Sweetheart, you're an Abbott now. That means what's mine is yours. You don't have to pay in our store. Besides, I'd love to show it to you."

"If you're sure…"

He kissed her again. "I'm very, very sure."

Wade couldn't stop thinking about the things she'd told him, the risks she'd taken and the danger she'd been in for months while he'd been completely oblivious to what she was going through. It truly made him crazy to think about how close she probably came to much worse than a beating.

She'd been so courageous to gather the evidence needed to help the authorities build a compelling case against Brody, but now that she was married to him, Wade intended to hold her to the promise she'd made to never again risk her safety.

They drove into town, and Wade became aware that they were being followed by a state police car. "Check it out," he said, gesturing to the rearview mirror.

Mia spun around to look. "They're following us?"

"I like knowing they have eyes on you."

"It's creepy."

"I don't care, if it means keeping you safe." He parked behind the store and led her inside to the store his grandparents had founded more than fifty years ago, which was bustling with customers and activity. A little snow didn't keep Vermonters at home.

"Oh, Wade!" Mia turned in a circle as she tried to take it all in. "This is incredible!"

They'd stepped into the toy department, which was full of board games, toy soldiers, wooden pull toys, picture books and musical instruments.

Wade nudged her forward, past cases of Vermont's famous cheddar cheese. "My sister Hannah makes that jewelry," he said, pointing to the display. "And my brothers Colton and Max oversee our family's maple syrup operation." Row upon row of maple syrup in every shade of amber lined another set of shelves. They walked past barrels of peanuts, coolers full of old-fashioned bottles of Coca-Cola and stopped at his dad's prized Beatles memorabilia collection.

Mia leaned in for a closer look. "Are those original lyrics?"

"They are. My mom got them for my dad at an auction for their anniversary one year. That's one of his most-prized possessions."

"I want to look at everything."

"You can come back anytime you want. But right now, we need clothes." With his hands on her shoulders, he steered her to the women's clothing department. "Get whatever you want. We just have to record what we take in the inventory system, or my sister Charley will have us killed."

Mia laughed.

"No, really, she *will* kill us, and she'll make it hurt, if we mess with her inventory."

"I see how it is."

"We're all a little territorial about our parts of the business."

"Where's your part?"

"Pick out what you need, and then I'll show you."

She perused the racks and settled on a pair of jeans, an inexpensive cotton sweater, a couple of pairs of underwear, long johns and socks. "That should cover me until my stuff arrives."

"That's not enough," he said. "Get more."

"I don't need more."

"Either you pick it, or I will," he said with a teasing glare.

"What would you pick for me?"

"Go look around while I shop."

"Don't go crazy."

"I won't." He kissed her and sent her on her way to further explore the store.

Wade gave careful consideration to the available items, choosing a silky top that would cling to her curves, several silk nightgowns that were more for him than for her, two of the gorgeous hand-knitted sweaters from their Vermont Made line, more of the jeans she'd chosen for herself, five pairs of warm socks, sexy panties in every color they had, a matching hat-scarf-gloves set and the warmest parka they sold.

When he found her in the home goods department, her eyes bugged at the sight of his arms bulging with clothes. "Wade! That's way too much! I don't need all that."

"It's nothing much."

She gave him the withering look perfected by wives the world over, and Wade felt something inside him settle. He had a *wife*.

"What?" she asked. "Why're you looking at me like that?"

"Because I'm so damned glad you're here with me."

"You're very sweet, but I still don't need all that."

"Maybe I need to give it to you." He put the clothes on one of the checkout counters. "Hi, Evelyn."

"Hi, Wade. I understand congratulations are in order."

"Thank you. This is my wife, Mia." He *loved* introducing her as his wife. "Mia, this is Evelyn. She's worked here for forty years."

Mia shook her hand. "That's amazing! So nice to meet you."

"You, too."

"Would you mind charging this to my account?"

"Sure thing, Wade. No problem."

"Come see my department," he said to Mia.

"We're not getting all that," she said one more time, in case he hadn't heard her the first two times.

Wade pretended not to hear her and led her around a corner devoted to books about Vermont and into the apothecary he'd poured his heart and soul into as the director of health and wellness. Dark wood shelves held unique products targeting every imaginable malady, from toe fungus to dry skin, from joint pain to wrinkles. "We offer tonics and elixirs, from pain relief to grooming, from hair loss to hair removal. You name it, we've got something for it."

Mia perused the shelves, picking up bottles to read labels. She pumped a sample of one of their more popular lotions into her palm and rubbed it into her hands. Watching as her hands moved the lotion over her skin was unbearably erotic to Wade, who hung back to give her a chance to fully experience his hard work.

"We're introducing a new line of sex toys this month," he said, breaking a long silence.

She turned to him, her cheeks flushed with what might be embarrassment. "*Really?*"

"Uh-huh."

"Was that your idea?"

"Hell no. It was my dad's."

"I have no idea what to do with that information."

Laughing, Wade pushed himself off the wall he'd been leaning against and went to join her as she took the lid off a tin to sniff the contents, recoiling slightly at the strong scent of ointment for aching muscles. "That'll cure whatever ails you," he told her.

She wrinkled her pretty little nose. "It smells horrendous."

"But it works like a charm. Want to try it?"

"You won't want to come anywhere near me."

"Trust me, that'll never be the case." He picked up the tin. "It's even stronger than the other stuff I used. It'll take the aches away."

"I guess I'll try it, but don't blame me if you have to move out of your own house."

"If you're there, I'm not going anywhere."

She rolled her lip between her teeth and looked up at him. "Could I ask you something?"

"Anything."

"Why me?"

He framed her face and gazed down at her. "I've had good reason to ask myself that question many, many times over the last couple of years. All I know is that from the first time you said hello to me, I've been unable to think of anyone but you."

Mia curled her hands around his wrists. "I've felt the same way. You have no idea how many times I wanted to ask you to take me home with you."

Hearing that, Wade ached with what might've been for all the time he spent missing her. "I would've. All you had to do was ask."

"And I knew that. I always knew that."

"So why didn't you ask?"

"At first it was because I was too afraid of what Brody might do if I tried to leave him. Later, it was because I'd begun to suspect he was dealing drugs and wanted to finish what I'd started. And mostly it was because I didn't want to put you in the middle of the nightmare that was my life."

"It means a lot to me that you thought of me when you had so many other things to think about."

"I thought of you *constantly*. You were like an oasis in the desert, and if I just kept moving forward, I might one day get to you."

"You're here now, and that's what matters. I know there're a lot of difficult days still to come, with the trial and everything, but let's try to compartmentalize that into a box that we only open when we have to. There's no need to let that color everything for us in the meantime."

"I love that idea."

"I would like to take my new wife on a honeymoon."

"You would? Really?"

"Anywhere she'd like to go."

"She's never really been anywhere, so she'll leave that up to her husband to decide."

Wade nuzzled her neck. "Let me give that some thought and get back to you. I've got to be here the next couple of weeks for the launch of the new product line—and the catalog photo shoots." He grimaced at the thought of "modeling" for the catalog.

"What's with the face?"

"Another of my dad's brilliant ideas is having all of us—our family and our cousins—model the clothes for the catalog." He scoffed. "It's ridiculous."

Mia covered her mouth with her hand as her eyes lit up with laughter.

"You aren't laughing at me, are you?" he asked, glowering playfully at her.

"Would I laugh at you?"

"Yes, I believe you would."

She flattened her hand on his chest, the scent of the lotion wafting between them. "I haven't met all your siblings and cousins, but if they look anything like you, I can see why your father wouldn't bother to look outside the family for models."

Though he was ridiculously pleased by the compliment, he couldn't let her see that. "You're either with me or against me on this topic. You can't have it both ways."

"I do want my new father-in-law to like me..."

"*Seriously?*"

She laughed out loud this time. "I can't wait to see your photos. I bet you'll be the sexiest one of all."

"I can't believe my own wife would turn on me this way."

"I'll try to find some way to make it up to you."

"You're going to have to try *very* hard."

"I can do that."

When she looked at him that way, he'd give her anything she asked for—even copies of his modeling photos. "So, about the ice skating... You still want to go?"

"Only if you do."

He wanted to go home, take her to bed and keep her there until sometime next week. But even more than that, he wanted his family to get to know her and hopefully begin to understand why he felt about her the way he did. "Let's go, then." Luckily, it was still freezing out, so the outing wouldn't last more than an hour or two before the cold would drive everyone inside.

Wade gathered up the clothes he'd chosen for Mia, intending to email the inventory notes to Charley when he got home, and shut off the lights. After he locked up, he followed her to his truck.

"I told you I don't need all that."

"I heard you."

"So why do we still have all that?"

"Because I want you to have it. Consider it a gift from your husband."

"My husband is very generous, but he needs to know that the woman he married doesn't require gifts and excess to be happy."

"Your husband is happy to hear that, but he wants to know if his wife has ever been showered with gifts and excess before."

"No, but—"

"Then how does she know she doesn't like it?"

"She never said she wouldn't like it. She said she doesn't *need* it."

Wade put the clothes in the backseat and then held the passenger door for her. "That's good to know, but she'll need to allow her husband to spoil her a little after waiting so, so long to have the chance."

Her face went soft and her eyes glistened as she looked up at him. "That's very sweet of him."

Wade kissed her because he couldn't resist. "He wants to give her everything."

"He's already given her so much—his name, his protection, his support, his friendship."

"That's just the start of what he wants to give her."

She shivered, and he wasn't sure if it was from the cold or the emotion zinging between them. "Sometimes I worry I'm going to wake up, still trapped in my old life, wishing with all my heart that I could be with you."

"You're wide awake and I'm right here, right where I've wanted to be since the day I met you." He kissed her again, losing himself in her sweetness and the feeling of utter completion that came over him every time he touched her or kissed her.

Her arms wound around his neck, and her tongue tangled with his.

He had to remind himself of where they were, that anyone could see them, not that he cared. But he didn't want to subject her to the Butler gossip machine—any more than he already had. Reluctantly, he drew back from the kiss in slow increments. Her damp, swollen lips made him want to forget all about the skating and take her home.

Instead, he helped her into the truck and kissed her once more before closing her door and going around to the driver's side while aching from wanting her. He turned the key and was met with a clicking sound. "What the…" He tried again, but the engine didn't turn over. "Great."

"Pop the hood," Mia said, jumping out of the passenger side before he could ask her what she was doing.

Wade popped the hood and got out as she propped it open and began to tinker with the engine. "Um, excuse me. What're you doing?"

"Checking your engine? Ahh, this is it. Your distributor cap is frozen." She removed the distributor, knocked some ice off the wires and put it back in place. "Try it now."

Astounded, Wade got in the truck, and it fired right up.

Mia dropped the hood, brushed off her hands and got back in. "What?" she asked when she found him staring at her.

"How'd you do that?"

"I know a thing or two about cars."

"So I see. Where'd you learn?"

"My grandpa had a garage. He let me hang around, and I paid attention. There's almost nothing I can't fix."

"I'm extremely turned on by this information."

Mia laughed. "Is that all it takes?"

"Honestly, if you're breathing, I'm turned on, but this… This is a whole other level."

She flashed a pleased smile. "Good to know."

"Seriously—very impressive."

"I do what I can for the people."

"You sure you still want to go skating?"

"Uh-huh. Why? You don't?"

He took her hand and placed it over the hard ridge of his erection. "Oh…"

"Yeah, all your fault."

"I'd say I'm sorry, but I'm really not."

Wade huffed out a laugh as he drove them out of the parking lot, hoping his *situation* would be under control before he had to face his family.

CHAPTER 12

"Be happy for this moment. This moment is your life."
—Omar Khayyam

This is what happiness feels like, Mia thought. Holding hands with Wade while he drove them through town on the way to go skating with his family. She'd loved seeing the store that he'd always spoken about with such affection, and particularly his department, which she knew he was intensely proud of.

He'd talked about his work during their coffee dates, and she'd recognized his passion long before she'd seen it for herself.

They rounded a curve in the road, and Wade slammed on the brakes, the truck fishtailing for a wild second.

"Holy crap," Mia whispered at the sight of a gigantic moose blocking the road.

"Mia, meet Fred, the town moose."

"Your town has a moose?"

"Yep, and Fred likes to show up when we least expect it. He's the one my sister-in-law Cameron slammed her car into on her first trip to town."

"He's... *huge*."

"Yep." Wade laid on the horn, but other than a perturbed glance in his direction, Fred didn't budge. "We could be here awhile." He put the truck in park and turned to Mia. "Want to make out some more while we wait?"

"He's watching us."

"So?"

"I've never made out while a moose was watching me."

Grinning widely, Wade said, "First time for everything." He released her seat belt and reached for her.

She came willingly into his arms, happy for any chance she got to be close to him, to kiss the lips she used to obsess over after seeing him. Those short hours together had never been enough, and now that they were together and married, they could finally make up for all the time they'd lost.

Every time he kissed her, he managed to erase every thought from her head that didn't involve him and the way she felt whenever he touched her.

A loud, indignant *moo* interrupted the kiss.

Mia pulled back and startled at the sight of the moose's face pressed against the windshield.

Wade cracked up laughing.

"It's not funny! He's coming after us!"

"Nah, Fred's a pussycat. He wouldn't harm a fly."

Unconvinced, she snuggled in closer to Wade.

He laid on the horn again and opened the window. "Move it along, Fred. We've got somewhere to be."

"Close the window!"

"You should see my sister Hannah. She walks right up to him like he's a dog."

"That's insane. He could kill her."

"That's what Nolan says every time she does it." He bumped his nose against hers. "More kissing, please."

"I can't while he's watching."

Wade groaned and hit the horn again. "Be a pal, Fred. Move it or lose it." All at once, Wade's eyes went wide and his mouth fell open. "What the..."

Mia sat up straighter, trying to see what he was looking at. A tiny moose on new legs came bursting from the bushes by the side of the road.

"Holy..."

"Um, Wade? Is Fred a girl?"

"I... I swear I've seen him with antlers."

"Well, he/she doesn't have them now."

"This is going to be the biggest news to hit Butler in a decade."

"Bigger than our impromptu wedding?"

"Well, maybe second to that, but right up there."

Fred uttered another loud moo and began moving forward as the little moose scrambled to keep up.

As soon as they were clear of the road, Wade helped her back into her seat. "Put your seat belt on." He shifted the truck into drive and headed for the lake that was located about a mile down Hells Peak Road from his parents' home. They traversed the one-lane covered bridge that preceded the right-hand turn onto Hells Peak.

"I love that covered bridge," Mia said.

"We used to play cops and robbers on it when we were kids. The boys were always the cops, and the girls were the robbers."

"Something tells me the girls prevailed."

"They played dirty. They still do."

"I can't wait to meet them all."

"It's going to be overwhelming. You know that, don't you?"

"I think so."

"I have *nine* siblings, Mia. *Nine.*"

Laughing, she said, "So I've heard."

"That's a lot."

"Yes, it is. I can't even imagine what that must've been like when you were kids."

"One word: chaos. Utter chaos."

"But you love them, right?"

"Very much so, but I love them a whole lot more now that I don't live with them anymore."

"But working with them is okay?"

"Yeah, most of the time. We all oversee different parts of the business, so that autonomy helps." He tightened his hold on the steering wheel.

"I'm kind of worried about what's going to happen when the catalog hits, though."

"How come?"

"My siblings and I are concerned about the business getting too big for us. We like it the way it is, but my dad, he's always reaching for bigger and better, especially lately. Website, catalog, distribution center, expanded maple syrup operation. It's a lot."

"And here I thought you helped to run a simple country store."

"So did I, but Lincoln Abbott doesn't do simple."

"It's funny that he's the one urging modernization while his children push back."

"You're not the first to mention that. Cameron found it amusing when she was first working with us on the website."

"What's your objection to modernization?"

"It runs contrary to what the store's about."

"True, but the store is a business, right?"

"Of course."

"At the risk of siding against my husband, I think your dad is right."

"Why do you say that?"

"You and I both know that Vermont is unique. It's not like anywhere else. Packaging the magic of our home state and selling it to others outside of Vermont is a brilliant idea."

"I don't deny the idea makes sense. It's the implementation that worries me. The business is manageable as it is. What'll it be like if it explodes into something way bigger than we can handle?"

"Then you grow to accommodate the demand. That's how business works."

"I know," Wade said with a sigh. "It's just that bigger isn't always better, you know?"

"I get what you're saying, but I also think it's exciting to imagine what's possible."

"I'm change-averse. I admit it. Most of my siblings are, too. We're steeped in the tradition of the business our grandparents founded in a much simpler time."

"Which is the reason people are so interested—that simpler time is long gone now, but they can recapture that magic if they come to your country store in Vermont."

"Is that how you felt when you came to my country store in Vermont?"

"I *loved* the store. I can't wait to spend more time there."

"I'm glad you liked it. I told my brother Hunter, who's our CFO and personnel manager, to find you a job in the company. If you want one, that is."

"I'd love to work there."

"And I'd love to have you there with me. Is there any particular part of it that interests you?"

"Maybe the warehouse."

"Really?"

She nodded. "It'll be really interesting to see that come together in concert with the catalog."

"There's certainly plenty to do in that area of the business. I'll let Hunter know that you're leaning in that direction." He glanced at her. "Is it weird to be starting a whole new life in a place you've never been?"

"It would be if I didn't have you to guide me through it, but the change is very welcome. My job in Rutland was just that—a job. It wasn't a challenge or an adventure the way this could be."

"My dad does keep things challenging, that's for sure. You're more than welcome to oversee the introduction of his new intimate line if you want a real challenge."

Mia laughed. "I'll leave that to you."

"Gee, thanks."

"Can I be there when you introduce the line?"

"I wouldn't be able to focus if you're there. Besides, the company is sending a rep to do the worst part."

"What's the worst part?"

"Demonstrating how they work." Wade shuddered. "To the grandmothers who make up our sales force."

Mia's peals of laughter rang through the truck's cab. She laughed so hard, she had tears in her eyes. "Can we please, please, please, *please* declare that Take Your Wife to Work Day? *Please?*"

"No!"

She wiped the tears from her eyes. "Yes! I *need* to see that."

"No."

"Yes."

Wade chuckled and shook his head. "My wife is totally unmanageable."

"That's right, and don't forget it." Being able to say anything to him and not fear retribution was the greatest of the many gifts he'd already given her. At some point, she would have to tell him that. But as they arrived at the lake, where numerous trucks and SUVs were already parked at the shoreline, she began to feel nervous about meeting more of his family. What did they really think of her and their spontaneous marriage? She was about to find out.

"Hey," he said. "You just got really tense. What's wrong?"

"Lotta cars, lotta people." The ice was dotted with colorful parkas and bodies in motion.

"I warned you."

She took a deep breath. "It's okay. I'm ready."

"I'll be right there with you. Nothing to worry about."

"Stay close, okay?"

"The only place I want to be is close to you, so no problem."

Mia released a deep breath. With him by her side, she had no reason to be nervous. She got out of the truck and met him in front where he helped her into the warmer coat he had bought for her as well as the hat and gloves. He had black hockey skates tied together slung over his shoulder. As they made their way to the edge of the lake, a man skated toward them, pointing to something on the ground. She looked down to find a pair of skates waiting for her.

He came to a stop, sending a spray of ice into the air that just missed hitting Wade in the face.

"You missed," Wade said. "This jackass is my brother Hunter, the oldest of us."

"And the smartest and most handsome, too."

"He's a legend in his own mind," Wade said drolly. "Hunter, this is my wife, Mia. Be nice to her, or I'll kill you."

Hunter pulled off his glove to shake her hand. "Good to meet you."

"You, too," Mia said.

"Megan had her sister Nina's skates, so we brought them for you," he said. "No idea if they'll fit or not, but you can try them."

"Thank you."

A woman skated up behind Hunter and wrapped her arms around him, the forward motion nearly making him fall. He recovered at the last second and slung an arm around the woman, who was laughing.

"This is my wife, Megan, who knocks me off my feet on a regular basis. Megan, this is Mia, our new sister-in-law."

Megan came off the ice to hug Mia. "Welcome to the family."

"Thank you," Mia said, touched by Megan's warm welcome.

"As a newbie myself, I can give you some pointers on navigating this mob."

"That would be very welcome."

Sensing fresh meat, the others began making their way over to say hello to her. She met Wade's brother Colton and his fiancée, Lucy.

"You met her sister, Emma, yesterday," Wade said. "She's engaged to Grayson. And their dad is Ray, who we met at Aunt Hannah's."

Mia's head spun as she tried to keep up. "Nice to meet you."

"You, too," Colton said. "Way to keep secrets, bro."

Before Wade could respond, Lucy smacked Colton. "You said you weren't going to do that."

Ignoring Colton, Wade said, "These two morons are Lucas and Landon."

Both young men said hello and kissed the back of her hand as she looked from one to the other and then back to Wade. The only difference between them was the beard one of them sported. Lucas. Or was it Landon?

"Identical twins," he said, "and total fools. Get your hands off my wife."

"That's not nice," the one with the beard said.

"But it's true," Wade said. "Now go away so I can introduce Mia to everyone else."

They took off in a sprint that sent them flying across the ice at breakneck speed.

"Watch out for them," Wade said. "They'll try to steal you away from me."

"Not possible."

Smiling, he gestured for her to have a seat on one of three overturned milk crates and helped her tie the skates Megan had brought for her. "How do they fit?"

"They're a little big, but they'll work."

Wade sat on the milk crate next to hers to put on his own skates. "Good. We're sold out of them in the store this time of year, or I would've gotten you your own."

"I have some. I put them on the list for the officers who are getting my stuff." She looked out on the happy, laughing group on the ice. "Do you think they've told Brody yet that I married you?"

"I hope so."

Imagining his rage had her cringing, even though she was nowhere near him.

"Hey."

Mia looked at Wade, who nodded toward the cop car parked a discreet distance from them. "He can't touch you in any way. Nothing to worry about."

"Old habits die hard."

"I know, but he'll have to get through me and everyone else," he said, gesturing to the people on the ice, "to get to you, and that's not going to happen. The Abbott family makes for a formidable wall when push comes to shove."

"They don't even know me."

"Doesn't matter. They'd do it for me."

"You're so lucky to have them."

"I didn't always think so, but the older I get, the more I realize how lucky I am, especially when I encounter people who are so alone in the world."

"Being somewhat alone in the world never bothered me too much, until Brody started to isolate me from the people who'd become like family to me."

"You should reach out to them now that you're free of him."

"They've probably forgotten me."

"Doubtful. You're unforgettable."

"I stopped taking their calls, and after a while, they stopped calling. They're probably mad."

"Maybe, but if you explain to them that you couldn't take their calls because you were in an abusive relationship, they'll understand."

"Sometimes I wonder what was wrong with me that I let it go on as long as I did."

"There was nothing wrong with you, Mia. He had you terrorized and under his thumb. That's on him, not you."

"Still... I let that happen."

He put his arm around her and kissed her. "We're going to talk more about this when we get home. Right now, we're going to have some fun, okay?"

She nodded, forcing a smile for his benefit. The darkness wouldn't recede overnight. It would take time and patience and determination, but she would get past it. With him by her side, she felt that anything was possible.

CHAPTER 13

"There is only one happiness in life, to love and be loved."
—George Sand

Wade lent Mia a hand and led her onto the ice, tamping down the rage he felt at hearing her blame herself for what that douchebag Brody had done to her. His rage was entirely directed at the man who'd terrorized her, and he forced himself to get it under control because Mia had seen and experienced enough rage to last her a lifetime. Skating backward, he held both her hands as they glided onto ice that had been cleared of snow by the others. Wade had skated here hundreds of times, but never with the woman he loved.

Everything he did with her, even if it was something he'd done many times before, felt new and exciting because she was there to experience it with him.

Will skated over and came to a stop a few feet from them.

"Mia, meet my brother Will."

"Wow, he looks like you," she said, as people often did. "Even more so than Max."

"*He* looks like *me*," Will said. "I'm the older and wiser brother, and it's nice to meet the woman everyone is talking about. In a good way, of course."

"Of course," Wade said drolly.

Will laughed. "It's all good, bro. I swear."

"Where's your much better half today?"

"No skating while pregnant," he said. "She's over at Mom's making food for after and helping with Caden so Max can skate." Will gestured to their youngest brother, who was off by himself on the far side of the lake.

"Didn't see him over there," Wade said. "What's he doing?"

"Not sure. He's been over there awhile. I'll go check on him."

Will took off, and another couple approached them.

"Incoming," Wade muttered, trying to prepare Mia to meet his sister Charley.

"What?"

"You'll see." The couple came to a stop in front of Wade and Mia. "Charlotte."

"Wade."

"This is my wife, Mia. Mia, my sister Charley and her boyfriend, Tyler, who is a saint among men for taking her on."

"Whatever," Charley said. "He's the luckiest man in Butler."

"I wouldn't say that," Wade replied, smiling at Mia.

"It's so nice to meet you, Mia," Charley said, shaking her hand. "And congratulations on your marriage. Everyone thought the story of the year would be me finally getting a man who could handle me, but Wade scooped us all." She leaned in and lowered her voice. "It's the quiet ones you have to look out for."

"Is he quiet?" Mia asked, glancing at Wade. "I haven't noticed that."

Charley's mouth fell open. "You mean he's not closed off and remote with you like he is with the rest of us?"

"Not even kinda," Mia said, grinning.

That smile... God, he was crazy about her. And watching her hold her own against his formidable family made him so damned proud of her.

"Wow," Charley said, giving Mia an admiring look. "You've done what no one else has ever been able to do—crack the Wade code."

"I don't know that I've fully cracked the code, but I'm having fun trying."

Charley laughed. "I like her."

"So do I," Wade said.

"Congratulations, you guys," Tyler said. "On your marriage and on Charley liking you, Mia. That's a hard like to come by. I ought to know."

She elbowed him in the belly. "You be quiet. He had to like me after he pushed me off a mountain."

"That is so *not* what happened," Tyler said in a long-suffering tone.

"That's my story, and I'm sticking to it."

"This I need to hear."

Tyler extended his arm to Mia. "Come with me, and I'll tell you the *real* story."

"Don't mind if I do." She took his arm and skated off with him.

"Wade," Charley said, hugging him. "I couldn't be happier for you."

"Thanks, Charl. I'm pretty damned happy myself, even if the circumstances aren't ideal. Who cares, if it means I get her?"

"Well, we care, and I won't lie to you. We're concerned about what you've gotten yourself into."

"Don't be." Wade fixed his gaze on Mia, who was laughing at something Tyler said. "I've gotten myself into the best thing to ever happen to me, and I'm going to make it work, no matter what it takes."

Charley rested her hand on her heart. "Look at you. I barely recognize you."

Wade smiled. "This is the me I was always meant to be. I've been crazy about her since the first time I met her almost two years ago."

"And you never said a word."

"Hannah and Ella knew. I'm sorry I didn't tell you."

"Don't be. I know what it's like to want a little privacy in this family. It's hard to come by."

"Yes, and this was such a bizarre situation that I didn't want people to know. Mostly because I was convinced nothing would ever come of it. And now..."

"Now you're married to her."

"I still can't believe it."

A shriek from behind him had Wade spinning just in time for his cousin Izzy Coleman to hug him. "Holy crap! Someone has been keeping some big secrets!"

Wade managed to remain standing, but just barely. "Christ, woman. You nearly flattened me."

Izzy laughed. "Where is she?" As always, her camera was slung diagonally across her body, always ready to capture the moment.

"Charley's fiancé took off with her."

"Go get her back. I want to meet her."

"Hang on." Wade skated over to where Mia was now surrounded by Tyler, Will, Lucas, Landon, Max and Hunter. He pushed his way between Will and Lucas. "Show's over, boys." He took her by the hand and led her away from them. "Sorry about that."

"Don't be. They were fine. Very respectful."

"You're talking about *my* brothers? *Respectful?* No way."

"They were," she said, laughing.

Wade skated backward, towing her along with him as he brought her to meet Izzy. "This is my cousin, Isabella Coleman. We call her Izzy."

"I love your work," Mia said.

"Thank you so much."

"I have your photos in my house. Or, well, I did. Where I used to live."

"I'll get you some new ones for Wade's place. Your pick."

"That would be great, thank you. I love them."

"Come by the studio, and we'll make that happen."

"Thanks, Iz," Wade said.

"No problem."

"Wade," Landon called. "We're going to race. Come on."

"I'll sit this one out."

"Go ahead," Mia said. "If you want to…"

"I almost always win," Wade said. "I hate to embarrass them in front of their new sister-in-law."

Izzy laughed. "You'll soon find out there's no shortage of ego in this family."

HERE COMES THE SUN | 129

"It's not ego if it's true," Wade said.

"This I need to see," Mia said. "Go get 'em, tiger."

"I'll do it for you," Wade said solemnly.

Mia grasped the front of his jacket and laid a hot kiss on him. "Win for me."

He groaned. "Don't do that. You're making my legs weak."

"Come on, lover boy," Lucas called from about a hundred yards away. "Put your money where your mouth is."

"I'd like to put my mouth somewhere else," he muttered to Mia.

Her face turned bright red—and not from the cold. She gave him a push that sent him in the direction of his brothers.

"Make sure you're watching," he said, skating backward. "It'll happen fast, and you don't want to miss it."

"I'll be watching," Mia said.

"They're always like this," Izzy said. "Super competitive. I remember them arguing over who could climb the highest—always Landon. Ski the fastest—always Will. Run the fastest—almost always Wade. Drink the most—always Lucas. The competitions never end when there are seven boys in a family."

"Was your family like that, too?" Mia asked.

"Not quite as bad as the Abbotts. There's a big age difference between my older brothers and the younger ones. Grayson and Noah were always trying to one-up each other, though."

"I was an only child, so families like yours are somewhat fascinating to me."

"Cameron was like that when she first came around," Charley said. "Endlessly curious about the family dynamics."

"Is she from a small family, too?" Mia asked.

"Another only child," Charley said. "Her father is Patrick Murphy, the business tycoon."

"I had no idea!"

"You'd never know from meeting her that she comes from that kind of money," Izzy said. "She's super down-to-earth."

"We love her," Charley added. "Even if she hit Fred on the way into town."

"I met Fred earlier!" Mia said. "Wade forgot to tell you guys. We saw him with a baby moose."

"What?" Charley asked, her mouth falling open. "Fred has a *baby*?"

"We aren't sure whose baby it was, but it was following Fred when we saw him earlier."

"This is huge news," Izzy said. "It might even be bigger news than Wade's surprise wedding. No offense."

"None taken," Mia said, laughing.

"Here they come," Megan said.

From the far side of the lake, seven grown men raced across the ice, shouting and occasionally shoving one another.

Mia watched with the other women, her gaze fixed on Wade, who seemed to be running away with it. The next-closest to him was Max. "Where's the finish line?"

"The shoreline," Charley said. "First one to hit the grass wins."

"Sounds like you've seen this a time or two."

"A time or two thousand. They can't skate without racing. They can't do *anything* without racing."

Wade went flying by and dove into the grass on the side of the lake, pumping his fist, breathing hard and smiling widely when Max landed right behind him.

Hunter brought up the rear, and Megan went to him, wrapping her arm around his waist. "It's okay, old man. I still love you."

He playfully cuffed her chin while his younger brothers howled with laughter.

This family, Mia thought, *is amazing*. Fun and funny and competitive and... loving. They were obviously crazy about each other, even when they were competing. The good-natured jabs made her laugh while she waited for Wade to pick himself up off the ground and return to her.

He skated over slowly, hands on his knees. As he approached her, he straightened and unleashed that smile that made *her* legs go weak. "How was that?"

"My hero. I'm *so* proud."

Slinging an arm around her waist, he picked her up and kissed her before skating off with her still in his arms while the others whistled and hollered.

With her gloved hands on his face, Mia kissed him back, mindless of who was watching. After waiting what felt like forever to be able to kiss him anytime she wanted, she wasn't about to miss the opportunity.

"I'm so glad you're here," he said, his lips gliding over her face. "Having you here makes everything perfect."

"I love it here. Your family is amazing."

"They're on their best behavior because you're new. That won't last."

"I'll take my chances."

"You really love it here?" he asked, gently setting her down. "It's only been two days."

She reached up to kiss him again. "The best two days of my entire life."

Wade felt like he was floating on air as they skated for two hours before giving in to cold and hunger. Being with Mia, watching her interact with the people he loved the most, knowing he got to go home with her later and be with her... This was shaping up to be the best day of his life, even better than yesterday, and that had been a pretty great day.

They took off their skates and headed to the barn for dinner.

"There's going to be even more of them at my mom's," Wade said. "You know that, right?"

"How can there be more?"

Wade laughed. "I've been asking myself that question since the day I was born."

"Who haven't I met?"

"Hannah, her husband, Nolan, their baby, Callie, and Will's wife, Cameron. It's a freaking mob scene when everyone is home. I can loan you my earplugs if you need them."

"You don't really have earplugs."

"What if I do? You just wait. You'll be begging me for them."

"I wouldn't want to miss anything. Everything that goes on with this family is interesting to me."

"Oh God. You sound like Cameron. She says we're better than any sitcom she's ever watched."

"I think I'm going to like her."

"You will. Everyone does. You'd never know she grew up as a Park Avenue princess, as she says. Her dad is quite a guy. He's engaged to our office manager, Mary. Or I should say our ex-office manager. She got a much better offer from Patrick. Last I heard, they were living it up on the French Riviera."

"He met her through you guys?"

"Yep, and no one even knew they were together until they announced their engagement. It's a really cool story. His wife died giving birth to Cam, and he'd never been serious about another woman until Mary, who's a total doll. We all love her and miss her at the office. But Emma took her place, and she's great, too."

"I love that he was alone for so long and then met someone through his daughter's new family."

"Love is in the air around here lately. First Will and Cam, then Hannah and Nolan, Colton and Lucy, Hunter and Megan, Ella and Gavin, Grayson and Emma, Patrick and Mary, and the biggest shocker of all—Charley and Tyler."

"Why do you say that? She seems really nice."

Wade rolled his eyes. "Wait till you get to know her better. You'll see."

"I don't believe it."

He laughed. "Okay... But let me just say that the day Tyler came along and rescued us from her was one of the best days of my life."

"She's probably saying that about me rescuing her from you."

"Right," he said, scoffing. "Again, you're either with her or with me. You can't have it both ways."

"Hmmm, let me think about that."

He nudged her leg, making her laugh.

"I'm always with you, but I want your family to like me, so you'll have to let me be friends with Charley."

"I can live with that. Just don't let her ruin you. I like you the way you are."

They arrived to chaos at the big red barn. George and Ringo were chasing Colton's dogs, Elmer and Sarah, as Hunter's puppy, Horace, and his littermate, Hannah's puppy, Homer Junior, tried to keep up with the bigger dogs.

Nolan stood watch over the entire fiasco.

"That's a lot of dogs," Mia said.

"That's not even all of them. Will has Tucker and Tanner."

"I love dogs. I've always wanted one of my own."

Wade filed that information away. He'd love nothing more than to give her something she'd always wanted.

They parked behind Will's truck, got out and headed for the mudroom door, stopping so Wade could introduce Mia to Nolan.

"Great to meet you," Nolan said, shaking her hand. "And you," he said to Wade, "way to get the whole family talking."

"I like to be unpredictable."

Nolan snorted. "That's one word for it. But congrats to both of you. Hannah says this is what you've wanted for a long time."

"She's known about Mia since she started dating you."

"That's what she told me. Welcome to bedlam, Mia. My best advice is to keep your head down and avoid eye contact."

"Don't freak her out," Wade said, putting an arm around Mia.

"She can't go in there without proper defenses. Why do you think I volunteered to watch the pups?"

"By the way, if you need help at the garage," Wade said, "give my wife a call. She has mad skills."

"Is that right?"

"Basic skills," Mia said. "My grandpa was a mechanic."

"That's cool," Nolan said.

"Oh, and thank you for getting my car out of the snowdrift," Mia added.

"No problem."

"Ready for this?" Wade asked her, gesturing to the door.

"As ready as I'll ever be."

"Go with God," Nolan said gravely.

"Don't listen to him," Wade said, holding the door to the mudroom for her. "We're not that bad." Along the wall of the mudroom were ten hooks with names above them. Wade had watched as many of his siblings added a second coat to their hook, so it meant something to him to take Mia's coat and hang it with his on the sixth hook from the left.

"That's awesome," Mia said of the hooks.

"Feel free to use mine anytime you're here."

"I'll do that."

Smiling, he took her hand and led her into the kitchen, where Molly stood guard over a huge pot of chili on the stove. To the left was a smaller pot of the vegetarian version for him and Mia. His mom never forgot him. From adjacent rooms, he could hear the others talking and laughing as babies cried. Just another Sunday at the Abbott barn.

His mom raised her cheek to accept a kiss from him. "How was the skating?"

"It was great."

"I heard you kicked some butt in the big race."

"They never could catch me."

"This one," she said to Mia, "was quick like a ninja from the second he got legs under him. I couldn't turn my back, or he'd be gone."

"She dressed me up as a ninja for my second Halloween," Wade added.

"Are there pictures?" Mia asked.

"You know it," Molly said. "I'll dig them out for you."

"I don't like this," Wade said.

"Too bad," his mom replied.

"See how it is around here?" he asked Mia.

"I'm beginning to."

"Mia, why don't you give me a hand while Wade goes away so I can talk to you without him around?"

Mia covered her mouth, but her eyes danced with laughter.

"Mom…"

"Don't 'Mom' me. Get lost so I can get to know my new daughter-in-law the way I would have if you'd actually *dated* her before you married her."

"Dating is overrated," Wade said. "Marriage is the *bomb*."

"Go away."

He kissed Mia's forehead. "I'll be in there if you need me."

"She won't need you."

"Do not laugh," he said to Mia. "Under no circumstances should you find this funny."

Mia made a comical effort to hold back her laughter.

"Why are you still here?" Molly asked him.

"I'm going," he said, walking backward toward the dining room, "but if she's not here when I come back, I'm holding you responsible, Mom."

"Scram. And tell the others to stay out of here, too."

CHAPTER 14

"Happiness is not something that is ready made.
It comes from your own actions."
—Dalai Lama

"Honestly," Molly said when they were alone. "The drama." She smiled warmly at Mia. "Now, can I interest you in some hot chocolate, coffee or tea?"

"Hot chocolate would be lovely."

"Coming right up."

Mia watched her heat soy milk and add chocolate, stirring until the two came together in a frothy concoction. "I've always made it with water."

"Most people do, but warm milk is the secret." She poured the hot chocolate into a mug and topped it with whipped cream.

Mia took a sip. "It's delicious."

"Glad you think so." Molly stirred both pots of chili, and Mia noticed she used different spoons, which meant she didn't just indulge the vegan lifestyle, but understood it, too. That told Mia a lot about what kind of mother Molly Abbott was.

"Tell me about you," Molly said.

"Let's see... I grew up in Burlington with my mom and grandfather. She lives in New Mexico now with her husband and his family. My grandfather died when I was twenty. I was briefly married after my mom left, but that didn't work out. I moved to Rutland to live with a high school friend. A couple of years later, my friend got married, and I had a hard time making ends meet without her to share the bills. When I met Brody and he kept saying he wanted to take care of me and make things easier for me... At first, it seemed like a dream come true."

"Do you get to see your mom?"

"Not very often. She's busy with her life there, and I work a lot. Or I did until recently."

"Wade asked Hunter to find you a job in our company."

"Yes, he told me."

"What kind of job did you have in Rutland?"

"I worked in a restaurant as a waitress until I had to call out too many times due to injuries sustained at home. Then I worked for a short time in a store for a lot less money than I made waitressing."

Molly grimaced. "I'm so sorry you went through all that. How any man could do that to the woman he supposedly loves..."

"He never loved me. He wanted to control me. I've come to see there's a huge difference."

"Yes, there is."

"It's comforting to know I'll never have those worries with Wade."

"He's one of the best people I know. He'd do anything for anyone."

"He was a good friend to me when I needed one badly."

"That's nice to hear." Molly paused, choosing her words carefully. "You seem like a very nice young woman."

"Thank you."

"But I'd be lying if I said I'm comfortable with the way things happened with you and Wade. Obviously, he's very happy to have you in his life, and his happiness is my happiness. But if I find out that you're taking advantage of my son or less than sincere in your feelings toward him, I'll be relentless in my efforts to protect him."

Mia swallowed hard. "I understand."

"I hope you do. Wade has an army surrounding him, and we take care of our own."

Mia nodded. "I get it."

"I'm glad we understand each other."

"Mrs. Abbott…"

"Call me Molly. Please."

"Molly… I want you to know that I care very much about Wade, and I have for quite some time now. There were… complications… in my life in Rutland, or I would've come here a long time ago. My feelings toward him are very sincere."

"Thank you for telling me that. It makes me feel better. I don't mean to be unwelcoming to you, but the situation is somewhat unsettling."

"I know, believe me."

Molly rested her hand on Mia's arm. "I want you to be safe and to live without fear, but I want my son to be safe, too."

"I want that as much as you do. Thinking of him, knowing he was out there somewhere… He kept me going until I was able to escape from a nightmare."

"No one should have to be afraid in their own home."

"I blame myself as much as I do him. My mom had moved to the other side of the country, my grandfather had died. I was very much alone in the world when I met Brody, and I ignored signs I should've paid closer attention to. By the time I realized who he really was, it was too late to get away from him."

"Abuse is never the fault of the victim. You shouldn't blame yourself."

"I was stupid and naïve and in love with a man who lied to me from the day I met him. He's what's referred to as a malignant narcissist. I'd never heard that term before one of the women I worked with used it to describe a customer. I looked it up and found a description tailor-made to Brody. I'd recognize the signs now, but at the time, it was all new to me."

"I'm sorry you went through such an ordeal."

"Thank you, but I'm a much stronger person than I used to be. I think I'm better prepared to make a success of my relationship with Wade than I would've been before Brody showed me what I don't want."

Two women appeared at the doorway to the kitchen. One had dark hair and a baby in her arms. The other was blonde, with a small baby bump under her red tunic top.

"We stayed away as long as we could," the dark-haired woman said.

"You showed amazing restraint," Molly said wryly. "Mia, meet my daughter Hannah, my granddaughter, Callie, and my daughter-in-law Cameron."

Hannah came into the kitchen, handed the baby to her mother and hugged Mia. "I am so, so, *so* happy to meet you. Wade told me about you ages ago. It almost killed me to keep that secret."

"We aren't good at keeping secrets in this family," Cameron said, hugging Mia. "I'm so glad to meet you, too. I hear you're also an only child, so I can give you some pointers on surviving the Abbotts."

"I'll gladly take any help I can get."

"Show's over," Wade said when he joined them in the kitchen, extracting Mia from the center of the beehive and putting his arms around her. "Whatever they said or did, I'm sorry."

"No need to be sorry," Mia told him. "Everyone has been very nice."

"We're always nice to new people," he said. "It doesn't last."

"Yes, it does," Cameron said. "I'm living proof of that."

The baby began to fuss, and Hannah reached for her daughter.

"Hey, Han, did you hear that we saw Fred earlier with a baby moose?" Wade asked.

Hannah looked so shocked, she nearly dropped her own baby. "*What?* Fred can't have babies! He's a boy moose."

"Do we know that for sure?" Wade asked.

"He had antlers," Hannah said. "Didn't he?"

"I don't recall ever seeing him—or her—with antlers," Molly said.

"Dude would know," Hannah said.

"Gertrude 'Dude' Danforth is Butler's version of Snow White," Wade explained to Mia, "because of her close relationships with animals of all kinds. Many believe she's the one who domesticated Fred, but she doesn't talk about it."

"She also dates Skeeter, who works for Nolan," Hannah added. "The ultimate odd couple."

Wade groaned. "Dude is about six feet tall and two feet wide, and Skeeter is... well, Skeeter."

"They're *madly* in love," Hannah said, giggling.

"Who's madly in love?" Nolan asked when he came in with the pack of dogs in hot pursuit. They tore through the kitchen on their way into the dining room.

"Skeeter and Dude."

Nolan held up a hand. "Don't. I have to hear *all* about it at work. I don't need to hear about it on a Sunday."

"He's traumatized," Hannah said, bouncing Callie on her hip. When the baby saw her daddy, she let out a happy squeal.

Nolan took her from his wife and lit up with delight at the sight of her.

Mia sighed, wondering what it might be like to see Wade with a child of theirs.

As if he could sense her thoughts, he tightened his hold on her. "Come see my old room."

"Everyone knows that trick," Hannah said.

"What trick?" Wade asked, taking Mia's hand to lead her out of there before Hannah could reply.

"This house is beautiful," Mia said as they went through the dining room to the stairs.

"It was a wreck when they first bought it. They camped on the property for months when they were renovating it. My dad loves to tell everyone that Hunter and Hannah were conceived in a tent and raised in a barn."

Mia laughed. "That's awesome."

"Being raised in a barn gets you a pass on a lot of bad behavior, which is necessary when you're one of ten." He opened a door on the right side of the hallway and ushered her inside before closing and pressing one of three locks on the door. "This is where the magic happened."

The room was so small, she could almost touch both sides if she extended her arms.

"It was a closet that I turned into a bedroom, so I didn't have to share with Colton. It wasn't much, but it was all mine."

"And that was important to you."

"It wasn't easy being a solitary creature in this family. Having my own room saved my sanity."

"You really needed *three* locks?"

"My younger brothers were amazingly accomplished at picking locks. I kept adding them until I found one that worked." Wade put his arms around her and held on tight. "Has it been days since I could hold you like this, or does it just feel like it?"

She snuggled into his embrace. "Only a few hours."

"Seems like an eternity. What was I thinking, sharing you with my family on the second day of our marriage?"

"I'm enjoying your family very much."

"What did my mom have to say to you?"

"We had a nice chat."

He drew back so he could see her face. "That's all it was? A nice chat?"

"Uh-huh." Mia didn't think Molly would appreciate her sharing the warning she'd levied. "It's all good."

"If anyone gives you a hard time, or makes you feel uncomfortable, I want you to tell me."

Mia rubbed against him. "You're the only one who has made me uncomfortable so far—in the best possible way."

Wade groaned. "Don't do that to me here."

"What did I do?" she asked, looking up at him with an innocent smile.

He kissed her fiercely, his lips and tongue hungry as he devoured her.

Mia clung to him, trying to get as close as she could. Then she was falling as he lowered them to the bed and came down on top of her. "Wade," she gasped. "We can't."

"We can be quick."

"No, not here. They'll know."

Groaning again, he dropped his head to her chest and took a series of deep breaths while she ran her fingers through his hair. "We're going to eat and run, you got me?"

"We're not going to be rude," she said, loving the slide of his silky hair through her fingers.

"Screw that. It's my family. We can be rude if we want to."

"You can be rude, but I won't be. I'm the new girl. I want them to like me."

"They do like you."

"Not yet. Even though they've been very nice and welcoming, they're probably still wary, which is understandable under the circumstances."

"It's not understandable, and who's wary?"

"How would you feel if one of your younger brothers came home with a woman none of you had ever met and said he was going to marry her—right away—to help her out of a jam?"

To his credit, Wade pretended to give that some thought. "I wouldn't love it, but I'd respect his choice."

"Would you? Or would you be leery until his choice proved she's worthy of your respect?"

Sighing, he rested his forehead against hers. "I guess I'd be suspicious at first."

"They want what's best for you. I understand that."

"*You* are what's best for me, and we're going to show them this is the real deal."

"That's not going to happen overnight."

"That's okay. I'm not going anywhere. Are you?"

"No, but—"

He kissed the words off her lips. "No buts. We're in this for keeps, and in a couple of months, when you're firmly entrenched in the Abbott family, no one will remember they hadn't met you before we got married."

"If you say so."

Someone pounded on the door. "Mom says if you're having sex in her house, she'll cut your balls off."

Landon.

"Mom did not say that, so fuck off."

Landon laughed at his own joke, but he went away.

"Sorry about that," Wade said. "Do not laugh. It's not funny."

"It really is."

"Not if you've been putting up with their crap for twenty-six years. There's nothing funny about it."

"I'm new, so it's still funny."

Wade scowled at her. "You're not allowed to think they're funny."

"Got it," she said, affecting a solemn expression. "Younger brothers not funny. Any other rules I need to be aware of?"

"Charley's not funny either."

"Okay…"

He took her hand, helped her up and unlocked the door. "Let's go eat so we can get out of this madhouse."

"But it's just getting interesting."

CHAPTER 15

*"Happiness is having a large, loving, caring,
close-knit family in another city."*
—George Burns

Even with his brothers busting his balls, nothing could put a damper on Wade's good mood. For so long, he'd wished Mia could be with him on days like this, regular days in which nothing out of the ordinary took place. Skating with his siblings, dinner with the family... This was his life, and she was now part of it and seeming to enjoy her first exposure to the crazy Abbotts. And after dinner, he got to go home with her, sleep with her, make love with her.

This had been the best weekend of his life, and it wasn't over yet.

At dinner, Wade sat between Mia and Max, who held baby Caden while he tried to eat with one hand.

"Let me take him," Wade offered.

"I won't say no to that," Max said, handing over the baby.

"What a cutie," Mia said.

Caden grasped the finger she offered and tried to put it into his mouth.

"He's teething," Max said. "Everything goes in his mouth."

"Hey, buddy," Wade said, bouncing Caden on his lap. The baby's hair and eyebrows were so blond, they were nearly white. He had big light brown eyes like Max's and a gummy smile that made Wade melt every time he looked at his nephew. Caden had been a revelation to him. He'd never given much thought to having kids of his own until Caden arrived and made him wonder what it might be like.

"Can I hold him?" Mia asked.

"Sure, go ahead," Max said.

Wade handed him over.

"Hey, pal, I'm your new aunt Mia."

Caden grasped a handful of her hair.

Wade carefully extracted her hair before Caden could yank on it. Seeing her holding the baby filled him with yearning for things he hadn't wanted before he had her. What might it be like to have a family with her? He'd spent so much time wishing to have her in his life, and now that she was here, he wanted everything with her—and he wanted it right now.

"Do you like kids, Mia?" Charley asked.

Wade glared at his sister.

"What?" Charley asked. "I'm just trying to get to know my new sister-in-law."

"I love them," Mia said, smiling at Caden as she entertained him.

"Charley says she doesn't want kids," Ella said. "Can you imagine growing up in this house and not wanting kids?"

Charley rolled her eyes at her sister. "One madhouse per lifetime. That's my rule."

"Children aren't for everyone," Molly said. "Good thing for all of you that your dad and I had no such reservations."

"Evidence indicates you had *no* reservation," Colton muttered, setting off a wave of laughter.

"What can I say?" Molly flashed a wicked grin. "Your dad is irresistible."

"Ugh," Wade said as the others groaned loudly. "For God's sake, can we *please* not show Mia how bad we can get on her *first* day with us?"

"She may as well know what she's getting into from the get-go," Hunter said. "This is us on best behavior."

"Don't behave on my account," Mia said. "I'm finding you all very entertaining."

"I like her *so* much," Hannah said.

"The thing I don't understand," Lucas said, "is what the hell a nice girl like you sees in Wade. He's a vegan and he climbs rocks without ropes and he likes *yoga*." Lucas made a face. "He's so *weird*."

Mia smiled at Wade. "I'm just as weird as he is. I'm a vegan who loves yoga. I like to climb, but I need ropes."

"That's fine with me," Wade said, winking at her. "I'm happy to share my ropes with you."

"Ewww," Landon said. "Don't be gross in front of Mom."

"Why not?" Wade asked. "She was just gross in front of us."

"Nothing gross about it," Molly said, smirking.

"I can't deal with this family," Will said, while Cameron lost it laughing.

"Let's change the subject, shall we?" Lincoln said.

"Do we hafta?" Molly asked her husband. "They're so adorable when we talk about how we came to have ten kids."

"We'll talk about our favorite subject later," Linc said, winking at his wife.

"Oh goodie," Molly said. "We've been trying for number eleven for *years* now."

"Jesus," Wade said. "I'm so sorry."

Mia wiped laughter tears from her eyes.

"What have I told you two about talking about such things in front of the children?" Elmer asked as he came into the dining room, his cheeks red from the cold.

"Sorry, Dad," Molly said.

"She's not sorry, is she?" Elmer asked, taking a seat between Colton and Charley and accepting the bowl of chili Molly handed him.

"She's definitely *not* sorry, Gramps," Colton said.

"Sorry not sorry," Molly said in a taunting tone.

"Mia, honey," Lincoln said, "I apologize for my inappropriate wife and children."

"No apology needed. I haven't laughed this hard in years."

It was good for her, Wade realized, to have some levity in her life, and if his family gave that to her, he'd forgive them for being obnoxious during her first family dinner as an Abbott.

"Hunter tells me you might be interested in a job within the company," Linc said.

"I would love that. I like to be busy."

"Do you have any thoughts about what might interest you?"

"The warehouse sounds like fun," she said. "I love to organize things. I don't have any relevant experience, but I'm a fast learner, and I'd love to help if I can."

"We need all the help we can get coordinating the warehouse and catalog effort," Lincoln said. "We'd be happy to add you to the team. Come into the office tomorrow, and we'll get the paperwork taken care of."

"Thank you so much."

"Ours is a family business, and you're family now."

She smiled at Wade, clearly thrilled with his father's warm welcome.

Caden started to fuss, so Mia pushed back her chair and stood to walk around with him so Max could finish eating.

Lincoln caught Wade's eye and gave him a thumbs-up.

Having his father's approval meant the world to him.

It was already getting dark when they left his parents' home a short while later to head home.

"What a fun day," Mia said.

"Glad you thought so. They can be a bit much."

"Nah, they're fine. It's all in good fun."

"They like you."

"You think so?"

"I know so. They wouldn't have been so... *themselves*... if they hadn't. They would've been quieter, more reserved."

"I can't imagine them quiet or reserved."

"You won't see them that way, because they like you."

"I'm glad they do, but the most important thing is that *you* like me."

"I like you very, *very* much."

She reached for his hand and curled her fingers around his. "This was the nicest day I've had in a really long time. Thank you."

"Please don't thank me. Having you here with me is the best thing ever."

They pulled up to the house, and the headlights illuminated a stack of boxes sitting on the front porch.

"Looks like your things have been delivered. That was fast."

"It seems like a lot."

"Don't worry. We'll make it all fit."

"I know how much you like having your own space. If having a roommate gets to be too much for you, you have to tell me."

"Mia... You're not my roommate. You're my wife, and I'll happily find space in my house for you and your stuff. Come on, let's get you moved in."

Working together, they brought in the boxes and got busy unpacking them. Wade cleared out two drawers in the dresser for her to use and moved half of his stuff from the bedroom closet into the one in the hall so she would have room for her things.

Mia was in their bedroom unloading a box when she let out a cry of distress.

Wade went in to see what was wrong.

She held a piece of paper with bold red ink that said: *You won't get away with this. If you think you've seen the last of me, bitch, think again.*

"Call Larry," Wade said. "Right now."

Nodding, Mia picked up the bedside phone and dialed Larry's number. She put the phone on speaker so Wade could hear, too.

Wade kept his hands on his hips as he listened to her relay the contents of the note to the prosecutor and how it was hidden in her things so she was sure to find it but no one else would see it.

"This is grounds for further charges," Larry said. "Put the note in a plastic bag and seal it. I'll send someone by to pick it up in the morning."

"Okay. Is he... Is he in jail?"

"He's in custody. I personally broke the news to him that you'd gotten married, and to say he didn't take it well is putting it mildly."

Mia sat on the bed. "What about his friends? Will they find out?"

"They may, but they know we're watching them very closely. They'd be foolish to go anywhere near you, and besides, we didn't give him any info about who you married or where you are."

"Okay," she said, her shoulders sagging in a way that had Wade walking around the bed to sit next to her.

He hated to see her dragged back into the Brody drama when she'd been having such a good day.

"I'll be in touch soon," Larry said before they ended the call.

Wade took the note from her and put it facedown on the bedside table and then wrapped his arms around her. "Don't let him ruin this day for you. He's not worth it."

"I know."

"He's in jail where he belongs, and tonight he gets to stew over the fact that you've married someone else."

"He must be so mad." She shuddered.

"That's no longer your problem. You're safe now, Mia. He can't touch you."

Nodding, she said, "I know that, but old habits die hard. I hear he's angry, and I'm fearful."

"Someday you'll get to a place where the sound of his name won't have any impact whatsoever."

"That'll be nice. The sooner the better."

"Let's finish the unpacking tomorrow." He kissed her cheek. "I want to snuggle with my wife."

"Your wife would like that very much."

"I'll even give you first dibs on the bathroom."

"You're the best husband I ever had."

"I plan to be the *only* husband you have for the rest of your life."

She offered a small smile and got up to get ready for bed.

He hated to see her undone by Brody. Even when the guy was in jail, he was still like a third person in their marriage and would be for quite some time while the legal proceedings unfolded. Wade got a plastic bag from the kitchen, put the note in it and moved it to the table by the front door.

Returning to the bedroom, he unbuttoned his shirt and tossed it in the laundry basket. He stripped off his jeans, added them to the laundry pile and then went to put some more wood on the fire to keep the house warm overnight.

As he walked into the bedroom, Mia came out of the bathroom wearing one of the nightgowns he'd gotten her at the store. He'd seen it a million times hanging on a rack, but it had never stirred him the way it did now.

"That looks beautiful on you."

"Thank you. I love it."

"Mmm," he said, sliding his arms around her. "I love it, too. You're so incredibly beautiful, you take my breath away."

She tipped her head slightly to encourage the kisses he was leaving on her neck. "Wade…"

"What, honey?"

"I feel like I'm living in a dream—you and your family and this town and your moose. All of it…"

"I'm living a dream come true. That's what having you here is to me."

"It can't be real."

"It's incredibly real, and it's going to stay that way."

"Nothing good ever lasts for me. Something always goes wrong."

"That's not going to happen this time."

"How do you know?"

"We both want this to work, so we'll make it work."

"Is it really that simple?"

"For me it is. I've never wanted anything more than I've wanted you as long as I've known you, and now that I have you…" He tipped her chin up to receive his kiss. "I'm never letting you go."

Her arms curled around his neck, and her mouth opened to his tongue. After that, there were no more words as Wade set out to show her how he felt about her. He eased her down onto the bed and took a second to look at her hair spread out on the quilt, her lips swollen from their kisses and her face flushed with desire. He would never get tired of looking at her.

"What?" she asked, her brows knitting.

"I like looking at you."

She smiled. "I like looking at you, too. I never pictured you with shorter hair, but I really like it."

"I got tired of my sisters making fun of my man bun. Figured I'd see how short felt for a while. I can grow it back if you prefer it long."

She combed her fingers through it. "I like it both ways." Her touch sent a shiver of longing through him, which had never happened with any other woman. All she had to do was look at him, and he wanted her.

"Every time we saw each other, I'd want to cry when I had to leave you." He kissed her collarbone and shoulder, taking the strap holding up her gown with him as he made a path to her arm. "I wanted to pick you up and put you in my truck and take you home with me."

"You have no idea how much I wish you had done that."

He took her nipple into his mouth, making her gasp. "Me, too."

"When I came here, I didn't know for sure that you'd still want me. That you'd still feel the way you did before."

"I felt *all* the things for you from the beginning, but I thought you were married. It killed me to think of you with some other guy, especially when I suspected he wasn't nice to you."

"You were what I wanted then, and you're what I want now."

He moved from one breast to the other, teasing her nipple with his lips and tongue. "We need a honeymoon." He drew her nipple into his mouth and ran his tongue back and forth before releasing it. "I want to spend days doing nothing but this."

"Yes," she said, sounding breathless as she fisted a handful of his hair. "I want that, too."

"I need a week, maybe two, to deal with work, and then we'll go somewhere." He worked a hand under her nightgown, pulling it up as he caressed the back of her smooth leg. God, she made him crazy. Everything about her did it for him—her sweetness, her strength, her soft skin, beautiful face and sexy smile. He loved her laugh and the way her eyes sparkled when she was excited about something. He liked talking to her, kissing her and—

She raised her hips, seeking him, making him feverish with need for her.

He forced himself to slow down, to savor when he wanted to devour. She was his wife now, his precious, beautiful wife, and she deserved only tenderness, especially after what she'd endured in the past. Moving his hand up, he discovered that she wore nothing under the gown and moaned when his fingers encountered proof of her arousal.

"Mia, God... If you knew how much I want you..."

"I want you just as much."

He pulled back from her, helped her out of the nightgown and, sliding his hands under her, cupped her ass and brought her to the edge of the mattress. Then he dropped to his knees next to the bed and buried his face in her sweetness.

Mia, Mia, Mia... He'd dreamed about her, about being able to touch her this way. So many nights he'd woken from dreams about her, hard and throbbing for her, and now... Now, he could touch her and make love to her anytime he wanted. He wanted to show her in every way he could think of that she was his and he was hers.

"Wade, no. Don't do that."

"Why not?"

"I don't like it."

Wade wasn't sure he believed her, but he would take that up with her some other time. For now, there were other things they could do that he hoped she would like. Freeing himself from the flannel pajama pants, he pressed his cock to her entrance. "Is this okay?"

She nodded, her eyes big with wonder and desire and what might be love. God, he hoped so.

Her legs curled around his hips and her arms came around his neck, anchoring him to her as he made love to her.

Nothing in his life had ever been better than being with her this way. He could die right now, and he'd go happy because of her.

Mia's hands moved in caressing circles on his back, moving down until she grasped his ass to hold him inside her while she came.

The tight squeeze of her muscles caressing his cock shredded his control, and he came hard, the pleasure so intense, he saw stars. After only a few days, he was so addicted to her, he couldn't conceive of a day without her in his arms, his bed, his life.

"It's too soon and everything is so new," he said, "but I can already tell you that this, you... You're the best thing to ever happen to me."

"Me, too. The very best thing ever."

CHAPTER 16

"Happiness is a butterfly, which when pursued, is always just beyond your grasp, but which, if you will sit down quietly, may alight upon you."
—Nathaniel Hawthorne

Wade's alarm went off at the usual early hour the next morning, and he reached over to shut it off before it woke Mia. He had to go to work today. No way around it. The rep from the intimate line company was coming in to start their training, and he had to be there for it as much as he did not want to be—for more than one reason.

His body ached from making love with Mia for half the night, and exhaustion tugged at him. Normally, he got up to meditate and practice yoga, but today he reset the alarm for another half hour and snuggled up to his wife.

His wife. Day three, and the words still brought a smile to his face. Mia was his *wife*. And he could hold her and touch her and sleep naked with her after making love to her.

With her back tucked up to his front, he ran his hand over her arm and cupped her breast, dragging his thumb over her nipple.

She moaned and wiggled, her ass pressing against his cock.

Her hand covered his on her breast, and her legs moved restlessly.

How was it possible that he wanted her again after having her three times during the night? "Easy, honey. I've got you."

She strained against him. "Wade…"

"Like this." He eased her onto her belly. "Is this okay?" he asked, cognizant of the abuse she'd suffered at Brody's hands. He never wanted to do anything that reminded her of him.

"Yes," she said, fisting a handful of sheet.

He rose to his knees, shoved a pillow under her hips and spread her legs farther apart. "I wish you could see what I see," he said, squeezing her supple ass cheeks.

"What do you see? Tell me."

"I see my beautiful wife, her sweet ass and her long, gorgeous legs. I see her desire for me…" He slid his fingers into her, curling them to press against the spot that made her gasp. "I see everything I've ever wanted right here in my bed." Taking his cock in hand, he withdrew his fingers and pushed into her. "Are you sore, honey?"

"A little, but don't stop. Please don't stop."

Her words were like gas on the fire that burned so brightly inside him. Making love to her beat the hell out of his regular morning routine. In fact, if he could start every day just like this, that'd be fine with him. Work was the furthest thing from his mind as he pushed into her and then withdrew almost completely, before going deep again.

She met every deep stroke with the push of her ass against his belly.

He grasped her hips and kept up the slow pace for a long time, so long he lost track of time and place and anything that wasn't her, spread out before him, the sexiest thing he'd ever seen. Reaching under her, he pressed his fingers to her clit. He'd barely touched her when she exploded, her body going rigid beneath him and shattering his control.

Wade came down on top of her, his body molded to hers as they tried to catch their breath. He kissed her shoulder. "Morning."

Releasing a huff of laughter, she said, "Morning."

"Best start to a day ever."

"Mmm, definitely."

"I hate that I have to go to work." More than anything, he hated that he had to leave her home alone.

"It's okay. I have a lot of unpacking left to do."

"We're training on the new product line after lunch if you want to come in for that, as long as you're coming to fill out paperwork anyway. You might find it... interesting."

"I'd love to. Are you sure it's okay?"

Wade tried to picture himself paying attention to a presentation about sex toys with her in the room. "I'm sure." He'd been dreading this day for months, but if it meant he didn't have to wait all day to see her, he could handle having her there. "My siblings are apt to be immature jackasses."

"I have no doubt it'll be a highly entertaining afternoon."

Reluctantly, Wade withdrew from her. "I have to get going, but I really don't want to."

She turned her head toward him and pushed the hair back from her face. "I wish you didn't have to either."

"You'll be careful here alone, right?"

"I'll be fine. No one knows where I am."

"Or so we think."

"One thing about Brody's crew you need to know—they're not the sharpest tools in the shed."

"Still... I'm not taking any chances with your safety. We need a dog. A big, snarly dog. I'll check with Dude today about whether she's got anything that fits the bill."

"I want a cute dog, not a snarly dog."

"I'll get you a cute dog who'll also rip out the throat of anyone who tries to harm you. How's that?"

"That'd work."

"Stop looking so sweet and sexy so I can leave you."

She made a scowl face that only made her more adorable to him. "Go away and leave me alone."

"Don't wanna." He ran a hand from her shoulder to her back and down to squeeze her ass. Then he dragged himself out of bed and into the shower, dreading the long day that stood between him and more time in bed with her.

Wade was twenty minutes late to the Monday-morning staff meeting, and every eye in the room turned to him when he came in and took his usual seat, avoiding the curious stares of his siblings and father.

"As I was saying," Lincoln continued with a pointed look for Wade, "Amanda will be here at one for the meeting."

"You didn't invite Landon and Lucas to the training, did you?" Will asked.

"Hell no," Lincoln said emphatically.

"Oh, good," Will said as the others laughed.

The thought of those two buffoons involved in sex-toy training gave Wade angina.

"Listen, folks, I know you all weren't in favor of this new line, but I hope you'll give Amanda a warm welcome and make her feel at home here."

"Of course we will, Dad," Ella said. "Our issue is with you, not her."

Everyone laughed at that.

"What she said," Hunter replied dryly, using his thumb to point at Ella.

"Fair enough," Lincoln said with a good-natured smile. "Someday, you won't have the old man to kick around anymore."

"We'll still kick you around long after you're gone," Will said. "Don't worry."

"On that note," Lincoln said, "this meeting is adjourned."

"Thank God," Wade muttered to snickers from Ella and Charley, both of whom followed him into his office.

Charley shut the door behind them. "So, how's it going?"

"Fine."

"How's Mia?" Ella asked.

"Great. How's Gavin?"

"You know he's fine because you saw him yesterday."

"And you know Mia is fine because *you* saw *her* yesterday."

"Come on, Wade," Charley said. "Don't be a pain in the ass. You know what we're asking."

"I learned everything I know about being a pain in the ass from you."

Ella snorted while Charley glared at her.

"What?" Ella said. "He does have a point."

"What I want to know," Charley said, "is whether this is a real marriage or a sham to keep the ex away from her."

Wade stared at her, incredulous that she'd ask such a question. But Charley had never been one to pull punches. "Define *real*." He thought about the passionate night they'd spent together. That was the most "real" thing he'd ever experienced, and he couldn't wait for more of it.

"Like do you, you know, sleep together and stuff?"

"Charley!" Ella said. "I never agreed to ask him that kind of question when you dragged me in here."

"A. I didn't drag you. B. You said you wanted the deets. We're getting the deets." She turned her attention to Wade. "Well?"

"Not that it's any of your business, Charlotte, but it's a very real marriage in every sense of the word. How's yours going?"

She shifted from one foot to the other, seeming uncomfortable, which was the least of what she deserved. "We don't need to get married. We're perfectly happy the way we are."

"Excellent. Once you're married, you can ask how my marriage is going. Until then, butt out."

"Mia seems really nice," Ella said, striking a more conciliatory tone.

"She *is* really nice."

"And you're happy?" Ella asked.

"As happy as I've ever been." That much was the truth.

"What happens later when the ex is no longer a threat?" Charley asked.

"What do you mean?"

"Will you guys stay together?"

Ella scowled at her, but then she looked at Wade, wanting an answer to the question.

"That's the plan." It was his plan anyway, and he could only hope it was hers, too. "We're married. That means for better or worse, until death do us part."

Charley's mouth twisted to the side, which meant she was trying not to say something she knew she shouldn't say.

Sighing, he gestured for her to go ahead, knowing he couldn't stop her.

"It's just that I want to believe she's with you for the right reasons," Charley said tentatively. "However, I can't help but wonder if her motives are pure."

He bit back the urge to snap at her, because he knew she was looking out for him. Sometimes he wished his family cared a little less than they did. "Her motives in coming to me included escaping a violent relationship with a man who made his living selling heroin. He was pressuring her into marrying him so she wouldn't testify against him, because he knows she can bury him."

"And I get that," Charley said. "I just hope that's all it is."

"What's that supposed to mean?"

"Do you know for sure that she's told you everything you needed to know before taking this gigantic leap with her?" Ella asked gently.

Ella's words struck at his deepest insecurities where Mia was concerned. That she hadn't told him, before they were married, that she helped to build the case against Brody had rattled him. He'd never deny that. It had made him wonder the same thing Ella and Charley were asking—was there more? She'd assured him he knew everything, but how did he know that for sure?

"I appreciate your concern," he said. "I really do, but I know everything I need to know."

"Fair enough," Ella said. "We'll leave you alone, then."

"But I have other questions," Charley protested.

"Too bad." Ella pushed her through the door and rolled her eyes at Wade over her shoulder.

Thank God for Ella, Wade thought, and not for the first time. The two of them had always been close and had often "run away" together when their big, boisterous family got to be too much for them. He recalled having similar concerns when she first got together with Gavin, who'd been a hot mess since his brother Caleb had been killed in Iraq.

Wade hadn't wanted his beloved sister taken down the rabbit hole Gavin had been in for years at that point, but Ella had her heart set on him, and the two of them seemed exceptionally happy together. And Gavin… He was a new man. The changes in him since he'd been with Ella were apparent to everyone who knew him. No one deserved to be happy more than Gavin, who had suffered so terribly over the loss of his brother.

The questions from his sisters had left Wade feeling drained by worries he'd pushed deep into the back of his mind after Mia appeared on his doorstep, half frozen, badly beaten and in need of his help.

He had a ton of work to do, new product proposals coming out his ears and the training to endure that afternoon. But he couldn't focus on any of that when the concerns raised by his sisters refused to be ignored. He opened a browser window, set it to private and did a search for her.

The first few results were for a Mia Simpson in Washington state. Then he clicked on a link to the restaurant in Rutland where she used to work. She was shown in a photo of the staff. Wade zeroed in closer on the picture. Mia wore a crisp white shirt and black apron as she smiled for the camera, but he thought he saw a bruise on her neck. He couldn't be certain, because the photo was grainy, but it looked like a bruise to him.

How, he wondered, had she explained the bruise to her coworkers? Had they suspected she was being abused? Had they tried to help her? He thought about the people who'd tried to help her and had borne the brunt of Brody's retaliation. Had others been afraid to get involved, as people so often were, especially when the alleged abuser was someone well known in a community as Brody had been in Rutland?

Wade devoured the reports of Brody's arrest, the disbelief among family and friends who'd grown up with him, the certainty that there had to have been a mistake. "Brody would never do something like this," one high school friend told the *Burlington Free Press*, which had front-page coverage of the drug bust that had brought down Brody's organization. "He was a youth football coach. He's the last person who'd ever sell drugs to kids."

"You just keep thinking that," Wade muttered as he read one testimonial after another to Brody, the homegrown hero. No wonder Mia, who'd grown up in Burlington, had been so afraid to ask anyone in Brody's hometown for help—and no wonder she was afraid of what might happen to her when word got out that she'd helped the police make their case against him.

"Someone needs to look at the girlfriend," one of the homers said in the news story. "No one knows where she came from, and Brody was never in any trouble before he met her."

Wade's chest felt tight as he read the statements about Mia. The paper had reported that she was never under any suspicion and had been cooperating with the investigation.

He downloaded the PDF of the indictment against Brody and read every word of the charges that had been filed against him. He read that, in addition to the Vermont State Police, the Drug Enforcement Administration and FBI had been involved in the bust.

"Jesus," he whispered as the full scope of the investigation and the case registered with him. Brody and nine of his associates faced federal and state charges. On the front page of that day's *Rutland Herald* was a story about Brody being taken back into custody on domestic assault charges. Mia's name wasn't mentioned. She was referred to as a woman who resided at his home.

Wade clicked on the hundreds of comments posted below the *Herald's* online article.

The girlfriend is bad news. I've said it from the start—he wasn't in any trouble until she came along.

Brody wouldn't harm a fly. I don't believe this for a second.

How can they lock him up when she's the one who got him into trouble in the first place?!? Further proof that our justice system is totally F'd up.

He'd never hit a woman. I've known him my entire life, and I'd stake my own reputation on that. It's total bullshit. Who is SHE? Do we know??

Wade scrolled through a hundred comments without seeing even one in support of her. Too bad he didn't have photos of her bruises handy so he could post them to show she wasn't lying. Brody had beaten the hell out of her.

Or someone had...

Wade hated that nagging voice in his head that had him questioning whether she'd told him the truth about who hurt her. He'd sat by her side when she reported the same information to the prosecutor, so if she was lying, that meant she'd also lied to law enforcement, which was a crime.

She hadn't lied. Brody had been roughing her up for a long time. Wade had seen proof of that himself more than once during the first year he knew her, when they would meet for coffee and he would notice bruises on her arms that looked like fingerprints. Once, he'd asked her about them, but she'd said they were nothing. He hadn't asked again.

His mind went a little crazy imagining a scenario in which she'd preyed on his obvious interest in her, giving him just enough information about her situation to ensure that he'd continue to worry about her, even after she ended all contact with him. Had that been a strategic move on her part? Stop contacting him, knowing it would freak him out so when she came running to him, he'd do anything for her?

He dropped his head into his hands, hoping it would stop the sick feeling swirling inside him. If he allowed his thoughts to stray in that direction, he'd have to entertain the possibility that the woman he loved was a heartless monster who had played him for a total fool. So, he wasn't going there. She wasn't a heartless monster. She couldn't be. If she was, he'd never trust anyone again.

He clicked on another article, one that had him sitting up straighter.

Girlfriend of Accused Drug Kingpin Ties the Knot

Mia Simpson, 29, the girlfriend of accused drug ring leader Brody Dennison, 36, of Rutland, got married over the weekend to Wade Abbott, 31, of Butler. Mr. Abbott is a co-proprietor of the family-owned Green Mountain Country Store in Butler.

Sources tell the Herald *that Simpson, who accused Dennison of domestic abuse, resulting in his bail on the drug charges being revoked, was under pressure to marry Dennison so she couldn't be compelled to testify against him in his upcoming federal trial.*

According to another source, who wished to remain anonymous, Simpson has known Abbott for two years. Calls to Simpson and Abbott have gone unanswered, but the Herald *will continue to reach out to them for comment.*

Wade was reeling. How could they know all that? Who would have told them? No one knew but the two of them and members of his family, who would never breathe a word of it to the media. It was too soon for the marriage license to have shown up anywhere online. That would take days.

The prosecutor and state police knew, but they wouldn't speak to the media about it, would they?

The only other person who knew was Mia, and she'd been with him all weekend.

Except when he was in the shower.

CHAPTER 17

"Happiness is not a matter of intensity but of balance,
order, rhythm and harmony."
—Thomas Merton

I can't think like this. I can't, or I won't be able to function.

Running his fingers through his hair repeatedly, Wade tried to control his racing thoughts so he could try to focus on work. But the erratic thoughts wouldn't be controlled or contained. This couldn't be happening. What if their marriage was nothing but a great big lie? He thought about their lovemaking and decided if she was lying to him, she was one hell of an actress.

Another thought occurred to him. He'd had unprotected sex for the first time in his life. She'd said she was on the pill, but what if that was another lie intended to further trap him?

Wade picked up the phone and buzzed Ella's extension.

"What's up?"

"Can you come in here?"

"Yep. Be right over."

As he waited for her, he forced himself to take deep, meditative breaths. There had to be a reasonable explanation for everything. There had to be.

Ella knocked, came in and closed the door behind her. She took one look at him and said, "What's wrong?"

"I'm not sure. I'm kinda freaking out."

"About?"

"Mia."

"What about her?"

Wade gave his sister an abridged rundown of the things he'd found online. "Who could've told the *Herald* we got married? None of our family would do that, and the prosecutors wouldn't. The only other person who knows is Mia."

Ella's eyes went wide with shock. "You think *she* gave them the story?"

"I don't know what to think about any of it. The stories online are crazy, El. People in Rutland say Brody was never in any trouble until she came into his life and that he wouldn't harm a fly, let alone a woman."

"And you believe them over her?"

"I don't want to, but after what happened the other day, I'm not sure what to believe."

"What happened the other day?"

"I heard from the prosecutor—and not her—that she helped to build the case against Brody. She's the one who reported him."

Ella sat in the visitor chair on the other side of his desk. "Holy crap. And she didn't *tell* you that before you married her?"

He shook his head. "She said she didn't think it mattered."

"Ahh, not sure I agree with that. It's a whole different story to be associated with someone who did something illegal. It's another thing altogether to have had a hand in getting him arrested."

"My feeling exactly. People in Rutland think she had something to do with the drug ring, and she's the reason he got in trouble, which is ridiculous." At least, he hoped it was...

"Do you?"

"No, of course not," he said, but with less conviction than he would've had an hour ago. "I don't know what to do with this info, El. Do I ask her if she told the *Herald* about our marriage?"

"I suppose you have to."

"And now it's out that she's here, which is the last thing we wanted." He sagged into his chair and tried to get his head around the implications.

He was thankful the state police were watching her and his house, so he felt confident she was safe anyway. "When she showed up the other night, beaten, frozen and scared, and asked me to marry her, I never hesitated. Not for one second. What if I was wrong, El? What if this whole thing is a ploy to get her out of something bigger than both of us?"

"*Whoa*, Wade, take a deep breath. You're getting way ahead of yourself. First thing—call Aunt Hannah and find out if the marriage license has been filed yet. Do that. Right now."

Wade picked up the phone and dialed the number he knew by heart. His aunt answered on the second ring.

"Hi, it's Wade."

"Hi, honey," Hannah said. "How's married life treating you?"

"Not bad. I have a question—how long does it take for a marriage license to show up online?"

"Usually a couple of days, but I took care of it Saturday because I was snowed in. Why?"

"No reason. I was just wondering how that worked. Thanks for the info."

"Anytime."

"Have a good day."

"You, too, honey."

Wade put down the phone. "She did it Saturday."

"So, it's possible the *Herald* got the info from publicly available records. Remember how Cam set up alerts for the store name, our names and anything having to do with the business so we would know if we were mentioned somewhere online?"

Wade nodded.

"The media covering the drug case probably has alerts set up for her name, Brody's and anyone associated with the case, so if anything is reported about them, they get a notification. When the marriage license went live, that would trigger the alert attached to her name."

"I can see how that would happen, but how would they find out Mia and I have known each other for two years?"

Ella's brows knitted as she pondered that. "That I don't know. You should ask her who else knew about you two."

"I only told you and Hannah, and I inferred to Gramps that I'd met someone a while ago, but it wasn't going anywhere."

"Maybe she confided in someone in her life, and that person is talking to the media."

He hated the thought of asking her, but he had to know.

The extension on his desk buzzed with a call from Emma. "Hey," he said. "What's up?"

"Hi, Wade. Mia is here for you."

"Thanks. I'll be right out." His stomach swirled with what felt like a thousand butterflies—and not the good kind, not the kind he normally experienced when Mia was nearby.

"Deep breath, Wade," Ella said. "Don't jump to any conclusions until you have all the facts."

Nodding, he took two deep breaths and released them. Deep breathing usually did wonders for him whenever he felt anxious. It didn't help at all in this case. If he'd made a huge mistake with her, he would never get over it or trust his own gut again.

"Thanks."

"No problem."

"You won't say anything—"

"Wade, give me a break. I'd never repeat a word of what you said to anyone, not even Gavin."

"Thank you."

She squeezed his arm. "I'm going to hope and pray that she's as sincere as she seems."

"Me, too." The alternative didn't bear thinking about.

Mia waited for Wade in the reception area and chatted with Emma, who was very nice and welcoming.

"I'm new around here, too," she said. "We should form a support group."

Mia laughed. "I have a feeling that might be a good idea."

"This family is formidable."

"The sheer numbers are overwhelming."

"That they are. Wait until you see all eighteen of them together in one place." Emma shuddered. "The volume alone would deafen you."

"Yikes. I'm an only child. I have no experience with such things."

"You sound like me back in the day," Cameron said when she came out of an office across from Emma's desk. "Sorry to eavesdrop, but I couldn't help but overhear."

"No problem," Mia said. "I need all the pointers I can get about fitting in around here."

"The key," Cameron said in all seriousness, "is to never let them see you sweat. The minute they sense fear, all hope is lost."

Emma giggled behind her hand. "That's very true," she said. "Lucy told me the same thing when I started seeing Grayson."

"Remind me again," Mia said. "Lucy is your sister?"

"Right," Emma said. "She's engaged to Wade's brother Colton."

"The maple syrup guy," Mia said.

"Yep. That's him. He's got my city slicker sister living up on a mountain. She calls it the penthouse because it's the only place in the area with reliable cell service. She runs her business from that mountaintop."

Mia made note of the information. At some point, she needed to check her phone for messages. Maybe Wade would take her up to Colton and Lucy's so she could do that.

Wade came out of his office, and her heart did a funny swooning thing in her chest. She had a bad case if the mere sight of him caused that.

"Hi," she said, suddenly feeling shy about coming to his office and interrupting his workday.

"Hey. What's up?"

"I thought I'd come in early to see if I could take you to lunch before the meeting. I also have to take care of the employee paperwork."

Wade checked his watch and seemed surprised by the time.

"Unless you're too busy. If you are, that's no problem."

"I'm not too busy. Let me grab my coat, and we'll go across the street to the diner."

"Sounds good."

After he went back to his office, Cameron leaned in to whisper, "You two are super cute together."

"You really think so?"

"Uh, yeah? Everyone does."

"That's nice to hear. I think *he's* super cute."

Cameron and Emma laughed.

"I feel the same way about his brother," Cameron said.

"I feel the same way about his cousin," Emma added.

Their humorous commentary made Mia feel welcome, and she hoped they would both become her friends over time. She'd missed having girlfriends over the last couple of years, when Brody had tried to control everything she did. Her world had become very small, and the isolation had made her wary of new people. But these people... They were lovely, and she already felt at home with them.

Her sexy husband came out of his office wearing his coat and gestured for her to lead the way downstairs.

"I'll see you at the meeting," Mia said to Cameron and Emma.

"We'll be there, much to our dismay," Cameron said. "I wish I wasn't pregnant. If there was any day for a liquid lunch, this is it."

"I'm just the office manager," Emma said, "so I get a pass on the meeting, thank God."

"Don't listen to them," Wade said as they headed down the stairs. "The presentation won't be that bad."

"Yes, it will!" Cameron called after them.

Mia laughed. "Is it wrong of me to be excited to see how this goes?"

"It's very wrong of you," he said, but the statement lacked the humorous tone she'd come to expect from him when they were being silly together.

Outside, she took a closer look at him and noticed he seemed tense. "Is everything okay?"

He hesitated before clearing his throat. "The *Rutland Herald* had a story about our marriage this morning."

Mia felt like she'd been punched. "What? How did they find out?"

"My aunt is required to make the license publicly available."

"Oh my God. I never thought of that. I'm sorry, Wade. I know how private you are, and to have it blasted all over the news..."

"They reported where I live, which means everyone knows where you are, too."

Mia wrapped her arms around her torso as she absorbed the latest blow. "I thought we'd have more time before that info went public."

"There was something in the story that I found odd."

"What?"

"It said we've known each other for two years. How would they know that?"

"I don't know." She took a closer look at him and saw something hard in his eyes that she'd never seen before. He always looked at her with such affection. "Are you accusing me of something, Wade?"

"Did *anyone* in your life know about me?"

"No! I was too afraid to say anything about you. I was always worried about Brody going after you. That's why I stopped contacting you. I told you that."

"The only people in this world who know we've known each other two years are you, me and my sisters Hannah and Ella, who didn't even tell their partners about you, let alone the media. And I sure as hell didn't tell them."

"I didn't either! When would I have done that? I've been with you around the clock until this morning."

"I'm not saying you did, but—"

"You thought it, though, didn't you? You thought maybe I snuck a call to my buddies at the *Herald* while you were what? In the shower? Bringing in wood?"

"No," he said. "I didn't think that."

"Don't make it worse by lying to me, Wade." She started to walk toward the parking lot, no longer interested in lunch.

"Mia! Wait. Don't go. I'm sorry. I saw that story, and I didn't know what to think."

"So you automatically assumed the worst of me. Good to know."

"Please be fair and try to see this from my point of view. You're involved in a very complicated situation, and I'm just trying to understand the various elements of it."

"And you're trying to decide whether you can trust me. I get it."

"I want to trust you. I want that more than anything."

"But you aren't sure if you can, right?"

"No, that's not right. Trust is something people develop over time. We haven't had the time for that. Not yet anyway, but we'll get there."

"Just so you know, I trust you with my life. That's why I came here when I could've gone anywhere."

Wade exhaled and looked down at the ground. "That means everything to me."

"Does it? Do you have any idea what it took for me to get in the car and point it in your direction, not knowing whether you'd be happy to see me after a year of silence, or if you had someone else, or if you even still lived here?"

"No, I guess I don't know what it took."

"It took everything I had, every ounce of faith I'd ever had in you and in *us* to come here."

"I'm glad you came to me."

"Are you? Or are you starting to wonder if you've made a huge mistake?"

"No," he said, putting his arms around her. "I'm not thinking I made a mistake."

She placed her hand on his chest to keep some distance between them. "If you feel that way, all you have to do is say so. I'd never hold you to our marriage if you don't want it."

"I want it. I want you. You know that, but I also want all the information there is. You need to think about who else might've known about you and me. Maybe it was someone you never told, but the person found out somehow."

She shook her head, feeling genuinely baffled. "I don't know of anyone. I swear."

Wade kissed her forehead and then her lips. "Okay, then. Let's get lunch."

"I've lost my appetite."

"You'll get it back as soon as you have a taste of Megan's veggie burger. She makes them just for me, and they're so good." He put his arm around her and directed her toward Elm Street, which they crossed on the way to the diner.

Mia's body was rigid with tension. What would she do if he turned his back on her? After only a few days here, the thought of leaving him and Butler and the wonderful Abbott family made her as sad as she'd ever been.

"Hey," he said, nudging her with his hip. "It's not always going to be easy, but we'll figure out this marriage thing, okay?"

"It's not going to work if you don't trust me."

"I know."

"I've told you everything you need to know about me, Brody, the case, my life in Rutland, my life before Rutland. I've been honest with you about everything."

"Okay."

"So that's it?" On the sidewalk outside the diner, she turned to face him. "You're going to trust me now?"

"I'm going to trust you."

"I didn't just come here because I needed protection from Brody."

"No?"

She shook her head. "I came because of *you*, because of what I've felt for you for such a long time." Tears filled her eyes. "It was more about you than anything else."

He put his arms around her and held her close to him. "I felt all the same things. I still do. I've never been happier to see anyone in my life than I was to see you on my doorstep the other night."

"Even half frozen and black and blue?" she asked, seeking a bit of levity.

"Even then." Wade kissed her and wiped away a tear that slipped down her cheek. "After lunch, I'll call Grayson and ask him to get in touch with the reporter at the *Herald* and see if he can find out where that info came from."

Nodding, she looked up at him. "Are we okay?"

"We're great. I'm a big fan of open communication, but I wasn't sure how to bring this up with you."

"Whatever it is, just say it. Don't stew over things. Put them out there."

"I will. I promise."

"Did we just have our first fight?" she asked, smiling.

"Nah, that wasn't a fight."

"I don't want to fight with you. I've had enough fighting to last me a lifetime."

"I know, honey. No more fighting."

She loved how he kept his hand on her lower back as they went up the stairs and into the diner, where everything came to an abrupt halt when they walked in.

Wade helped her out of her coat and hung it on the same hook as his. "Hey, everyone, this is my wife, Mia. Feel free to say hello, but do me a favor and try not to stare."

People offered murmured greetings as they went over to a table where Hannah sat across from Nolan, who held baby Callie on his lap. They moved in to make room for Wade and Mia.

"Did my brother just make a *public* declaration?" Hannah asked incredulously.

"Shut up, Hannah," Wade grumbled as he slid in next to his sister.

Mia felt her face go hot with embarrassment. It would take a while to get used to the sibling dynamics in the Abbott family.

"I'm seriously impressed," Hannah continued, clearly not taking Wade's advice to shut up. "My Wade Abbott doesn't make speeches."

"He doesn't usually muzzle his sisters either," Wade said, "but he's always willing to make an exception."

Nolan snorted with laughter.

"Don't laugh at him," Hannah said. "You know the rules. You're either with them or you're with me—and if you're with them, you don't get any—"

Wade put his hand over her mouth. "I have no desire to know how that sentence ends."

"I think it involves desire," Nolan said.

Hannah nodded.

Mia laughed.

"What a shit show this family is," Wade said, dropping his hand from Hannah's face.

"You're just realizing that now?" Nolan asked.

"Nah, I've known it for thirty-one years, but it's been extra shit-showy recently."

"Gee, I wonder why?" Hannah asked, batting her eyelashes. "Could it be because you came home with a brand-new wife that none of your family members had ever met?"

"Do we have to do this in front of said wife?" Wade asked.

"She's an Abbott now." To Mia, she added, "Consider this orientation."

"I hate my life," Wade muttered.

"No, you don't," Mia said with a meaningful smile that set Hannah off into hysterics.

Wade reached across the table for the baby. "Come see Uncle Wade and save me from your mean old mommy."

Nolan handed her over, along with a cloth diaper. "Watch out. She just ate, so she's apt to be explosive."

"That's okay," Wade said, expertly handling the baby, who looked up at him with big brown eyes full of wonder.

Mia knew that feeling. He had the same effect on her. Watching him with the baby did funny things to her insides. Was it possible for ovaries to melt? If so, hers were tingling. She'd never had a strong desire to be a mother, but seeing him holding a baby stirred something new in her, something she'd never felt before it was possible that he might be the father of her children.

Whoa. Talk about getting ahead of yourself, she thought. *He barely trusts you, and you're picturing him with your children. One step at a time.* Their conversation had left her feeling rattled and out of sync with him for the first time. One of the things she'd always liked best about him was how easy their relationship was. Of course, it was easy then—they'd been casual friends who occasionally met for coffee. Now they were married, she was embroiled in Brody's case, and she and Wade had never even been on a date.

That gave her an idea… They needed to go on a date. Maybe if she planned something romantic for them, he would understand how badly she wanted their relationship to work, despite the odds stacked against it.

She would show him he could trust her and that her affection for him was the most honest thing in her life. No matter what she had to do.

CHAPTER 18

"Happiness is only real when shared."
—Christopher McCandless

Wade bounced Callie on his knee and kept his focus on the baby so he wouldn't be tempted to stare at his gorgeous wife. People were already talking about them. He didn't need to add fuel to the Butler fire by being obviously smitten in public. He'd gone from uncertain to reassured by their conversation in the parking lot. She'd been straightforward and forthcoming and had vowed to be entirely honest with him. He couldn't ask for anything more than that.

Someone had told the paper about them. He'd get Gray to find out who. She swore it wasn't her, and he believed her. What point would there be to her blowing their cover when that info could put them both in danger?

He was used to living a fairly simple life, so the complications that came with her would take some getting used to. Like he'd told her, trust wasn't formed overnight, but she'd promised to be honest with him, and that was all he could ask for.

That was certainly better than thinking she'd played him for a fool.

Watching her interact with his sister and brother-in-law put him back on an even keel. She laughed and joked with Hannah and held her own with Nolan when talking about cars and the things her grandfather had taught her.

Megan came to take their order, apologizing for making them wait.

"No worries," Hannah said. "Better us than real customers."

"True," Megan said, grinning. "What can I get you?"

Hannah and Nolan ordered turkey clubs.

"I hear the veggie burgers are the best," Mia said.

"You know it," Megan replied. "I make them special for my special brother-in-law."

"I'd love to try one," Mia said.

"Coming right up." She took the menus off the table and left to get the drinks they'd ordered.

"You don't have to order?" Mia asked Wade.

"Nope. She knows what I want. I'm a regular."

"I go back and forth between the club and the grilled cheese when she has tomato soup," Hannah said.

"Ohhh, I love tomato soup," Mia said.

Wade added that to the growing list of things he was learning about her.

"She usually has it on Fridays," Hannah said. "How sad is it that I have the diner schedule memorized?"

"Very sad," Wade said.

"Try being home with a baby all day. The diner is the hub of my social life." Hannah ran a hand over the baby's cap of dark hair. "But I wouldn't have it any other way, would I, pumpkin?"

Hannah had waited a long time to be a mom and lit up with joy whenever she looked at baby Callie. Wade admired his oldest sister more than just about anyone he knew. After what she'd been through losing Caleb so tragically, it would've been easier for her to avoid new love. She'd taken a chance with Nolan and now had everything she'd ever wished for, but she and Nolan still managed to honor Caleb in so many ways, especially in the touching name they had given their daughter.

Wade looked up to find Mia watching him intently as he entertained the baby. He wondered what she was thinking.

Megan brought their food, and they dug in.

"Good, right?" he asked Mia when she tried the veggie burger.

"Delicious. Best one I've ever had."

Wade continued to hold Callie so Hannah could eat. He juggled the baby and his veggie burger while dodging Callie's efforts to grab everything she could reach.

"Damn, she's quick," Wade said.

"She's got great hands, like her daddy," Hannah said, smiling suggestively at her husband.

"Eww," Wade said. "Gross. Not in front of the baby."

"Oh, the things she's already seen," Hannah said, shivering dramatically.

"Hannah," Nolan said, his face flushing with embarrassment. "For Christ's sake. Knock it off."

"Oh stop. Don't be a prude. Everyone knows we're married, which means we *do it* as much as we can."

Nolan waved a hand at Megan. "Check, please."

"Is Hannah talking about sex again?" Megan asked as she put their check on the table.

"She's *so* inappropriate," Nolan said, tossing cash on the check before Wade could grab his wallet. "Like her mother."

The baby lunged for the sweet potato fries Megan had added to the menu at Wade's request.

"You love when I'm inappropriate," Hannah said.

"I'm going to lock you up and throw away the key if you don't stop embarrassing me every chance you get," her husband replied.

"Ohh, can we play that game tonight?"

"Mia, you're going to have to let me out of this booth before my wife succeeds in completely mortifying me."

Laughing, Mia got up to let Nolan out and gasped, which had them all looking at the sight outside the diner—Fred strolling down Elm Street with the little moose calf trailing behind him.

Hannah let out a shriek that startled her daughter. "Let me out, Wade!"

Wade slid out of the booth, and Hannah rushed by him.

"Oh, for God's sake," Nolan said as he went after her.

"Hannah thinks she's a moose whisperer," Wade said, bouncing the baby gently to settle her. "Your mommy is a loon."

"She's going right up to him!" Mia said.

"She does that. I'll stay with the baby. Go watch Nolan lose his shit. It's always entertaining."

Hannah approached Fred and the little one, holding out her hand to Fred, who usually nuzzled her palm. Today, he didn't seem as happy to see her as he usually was, which only added to Nolan's anxiety.

"Hannah," Nolan said from behind her, his heart in his throat as he watched his tiny wife approach the gigantic moose. "*Freeze.*"

"I just want to see the baby." She took another step toward Fred and the calf, who tucked in closer to Fred. "Hi, little one. What's your name?"

"Do you honestly expect an answer?" Nolan asked, exasperated.

Things had come to a halt on Elm Street while everyone watched Hannah and Fred, just like always when Hannah decided she needed to get up close and personal with the town moose, who was still, as Nolan liked to tell her, a wild animal.

"Are you a girl moose, Fred?" Hannah asked.

"Nope, he ain't," a voice said from behind them.

Dude and Skeeter joined them.

"Then what's he doing with a baby moose?" Hannah asked.

"Hard tellin'," Dude said. "Perhaps the baby lost his mama and attached himself to Fred. He doesn't look too happy about it."

"How can you tell?" Hannah asked, her brows furrowing adorably.

"He seems tense and troubled," Dude said.

To Nolan, he looked like a moose—a very big moose. How could she tell he was tense or troubled?

"It's in his eyes," Dude said.

Nolan didn't see it, but they didn't call her Snow White for nothing. "Um, Hannah, we have our own baby to think about. Wade is probably ready for some relief."

"I just want to pet the little guy." Before the words could register with him, she was moving around behind Fred to where the baby moose was huddled.

"Hannah!" In the span of a second, a thousand horrible outcomes ran through his mind, including his precious wife being kicked by a moose. He went after her, took her by the arm, drew her back against him and out of harm's way.

"Let me go, Nolan. I want to see the baby."

"You're not going near that moose, so cut it out."

"You ruin all my fun."

"Pardon me if I like you alive."

Fred ambled off toward the far end of town, and the little guy scrambled to keep up with him.

"That poor baby has lost his mother," Hannah said.

He could see she was on the verge of tears.

"Fred will take care of him," Dude said.

"But he doesn't want to," Hannah said.

"Doesn't mean he won't."

"Maybe you could get him for me," Hannah said to Dude. "I'd take care of him."

"No way, Hannah," Nolan said. "Absolutely *not*."

Hannah elbowed him in the gut. "Don't tell me what to do. You're my husband, not my keeper."

"You need a freaking full-time keeper."

"I do not. I feel sorry for that poor baby. If that makes me a bad person, so be it."

"You're not a bad person, but there's a good chance you're becoming a lunatic over that moose."

"Fred and I are old friends. We go back further than you and I do, so you might want to keep that in mind. If it comes down to a choice, you might not come out on top."

"Seems to me," Skeeter said to Nolan, "you might want to quit while you're ahead."

"The day I take marriage advice from you is the day they put me in the loony bin," Nolan said.

Dude, taller than her beloved by at least a foot, put her arms around Skeeter and nuzzled him into her formidable bosom. "You could take a page from my lovey's book. He's the most romantic man who ever lived."

Skeeter all but cooed from the compliment.

"I can't deal with this day," Nolan muttered, taking Hannah with him when he walked toward the diner.

"Dude," she said, "call me about the baby moose."

"I will," Dude said.

"You won't," Nolan said, scowling at Dude.

"Don't listen to him," Hannah said over her shoulder. "I don't."

Nolan gave her a playful spank on the ass and sent her up the stairs to the diner. "Go get our daughter while I go back to work—and stay away from that moose."

She turned on the stairs and planted a loud kiss on him. "Yes, dear."

"Don't humor me, Hannah. I mean it. No moose."

"Okay."

To Mia, who was standing on the sidewalk, he said, "She's humoring me. Let me know if you hear her talking about taking in that baby moose."

"She's not going to side with you. She's *my* sister-in-law."

"She's *our* sister-in-law, and even she can see that you're half nuts getting that close to a fully grown bull moose."

"He's my friend!"

"He's a *moose*, Hannah!"

"Go to work, Nolan." She patted him on the face and went into the diner, letting the door slam shut behind her.

"She's going to be the death of me," Nolan said to Mia.

"Umm, she is rather passionate about Fred."

"You have no idea. Sorry for the spectacle, but they tend to happen from time to time in this family."

"I'm starting to realize that."

"Let me know if you need a place to hide out from the madness. I can always use an extra set of qualified hands at the garage."

"I might take you up on that. I miss my grandpa and his garage."

"Come by anytime."

"I'll do that, thank you. I forgot to ask what I owe you for getting my car."

"No charge for family."

"How do you stay in business with that policy? The family is huge."

"Fortunately, I'm not related to everyone in this town, despite how it seems."

"Well, thank you again. I appreciate it."

"No problem. Enjoy the rest of your day."

"You do the same."

He headed back to the garage, intending to have a word with Skeeter, the most romantic man alive—*ugh*—about keeping Dude and that baby moose far, far away from his wife.

Mia returned to the booth where Wade was helping Hannah zip her daughter into her snowsuit.

"Come on, sweetheart," Hannah said, lifting the baby from her brother's arms. "Let's go home so you can take a nap and I can research the care of baby moose."

"Nolan is going to kill you, Hannah," Wade said.

"No, he won't. He's all talk. He doesn't scare me."

"What the hell do you want with a baby moose anyway?" Wade asked.

"The poor thing's mother is lost. That baby needs a mother, not a man moose who doesn't want him."

"You do realize it's possible you've gone completely around the bend, right?"

"Because I love animals and moose in particular? Call me crazy, but I want that baby."

Wade held up his hands in surrender. "I can see there's no point in trying to talk some sense into you."

"No point at all." Hannah shouldered her diaper bag. "See you guys later."

"I never got to thank Nolan for lunch," Wade said.

"Yes, me, too," Mia said.

"I'll tell him."

She and Callie took their leave, and Mia slid in across from Wade.

"Is that Dude out there?" Wade asked.

"Is she the tall lady with the little boyfriend?"

"That's her. I'll be right back." Wade ran outside to talk to Dude while Mia watched and wondered what he was doing.

He came back a few minutes later.

"What was that about?"

"Seeing a woman about a dog. She said she'll keep her eyes open for us. I asked for cute but fiercely protective. She said it could take a month or two to find the right dog."

"Oh, I can't wait!"

"I love to see you so excited."

"Having my own dog would be super exciting."

"We'll make that happen as soon as we can. Dude is very good at matching animals with people. So Hannah, Nolan and the moose. Entertaining, right?"

"Extremely." She couldn't get over the way Hannah had spoken to her husband. If she'd ever been that sassy with Brody, he would've backhanded her.

"What're you thinking?" Wade asked.

"I was thinking about how she talked to him and how he just rolled his eyes and put up with it."

"That's how they are with each other. He worships the ground she walks on, and despite what he says, if she wants that baby moose, he's not going to stand in her way. But he will tell her all the reasons why he thinks it's a bad idea."

"It's just very... refreshing."

"That's the way it should be, Mia. No one should have to worry about saying or doing the wrong thing and being physically harmed for being themselves."

"You're right. No one should worry about that. It's going to take some time for me to not be afraid of what's going to happen when I see a woman talk back to the man in her life."

"You'll never see the men in my family treat their women with anything but love and respect, even when they're exasperated or angry."

"I like it here," she said. "It's the nicest place I've ever lived."

"I'm so glad you feel that way."

"Could I ask a favor?"

"Anything you want."

"Could I borrow the Wi-Fi in the office to check my messages?"

"Of course. No problem. I'll set you up when we get back. And Hunter has the paperwork for you to fill out to get you on the payroll."

"I'm so excited to find out more about the company. You said your mom's parents founded it, right?"

"Uh-huh."

Mia dipped one of the tasty sweet potato fries in ketchup. "So how did your dad end up running it?"

"When my Gramps retired, he made Dad the CEO. He's a graduate of Yale's business school, and the business has really grown under his leadership. However, walk a fine line between modernizing and keeping the old-time feel of the place intact."

"It's really cool that you and your siblings are third-generation proprietors."

"We've very proud of that. Some of the employees, like Evelyn, have been with us longer than I've been alive. It's a family business in more ways than one." Wade checked his watch. "And now I have to get back for the training this afternoon. You don't happen to have a Xanax handy that I could take beforehand, do you?"

Mia laughed. "Sorry."

"This is going to be a nightmare of epic proportions. I'm warning you now... If you want to reconsider attending, I wouldn't blame you."

"I wouldn't miss this for the world."

"I had a feeling you were going to say that."

CHAPTER 19

"Health is the greatest gift, contentment the greatest
wealth, faithfulness the best relationship."
—Buddha

Wade walked into the conference room and wanted to turn around and walk right back out. The table had been set with placemats as if they were hosting a dinner party. On each placemat was a wide array of products, things normally used in the privacy of one's bedroom and not laid out like a sexual buffet on the conference room table.

Will came in after him, took one look and groaned. "Do we *hafta?*"

"Dad says we hafta."

"Maybe we should look into a nursing home for him. He is getting on in years."

"I heard that, William," Lincoln said when he came in. "And good luck with that plan."

"I can't sit in a room with my sisters and talk about sex toys," Will said.

"Yes, you can. Think of them the same way you would anything else we carry—foot fungus cream or hemorrhoid remedies or yeast infection cures."

"We don't have to have special training for any of those products," Will said.

"Um, I did," Wade said.

"Not with *Charley* in the room," Will said.

"True."

"This product line has nothing to do with me," Will said. "It's not Vermont Made. Why do I have to be trained on it?"

"Very good question, Will," Hunter said when he joined them. "I'm an accountant. Why do I need to know about this?"

"Because we're going to have to train the sales team on the floor and at the distribution center," Linc said, "so we need to be able to answer their questions. And we don't ask anything of our employees that we aren't willing to do ourselves."

Most of their "sales team" were grandmothers who'd worked for the company for decades. The thought of indoctrinating them on this product line had given Wade nightmares for months. Fortunately, the contractor from the company that produced the line would be doing most of the heavy lifting. But he had to be in the room. He didn't want to be in the room.

"I don't work with the sales team," Hunter said. "They won't be asking *me* questions, so I don't need to be in this meeting."

"I never realized I'd raised such a bunch of prudes," Linc said. "Where did your mother and I go wrong?"

Molly breezed into the conference room. "Are they being prudes, love?"

"You warned me they would be," Linc said, accepting a kiss from his wife, who marched right over to one of the place settings and began picking up and examining the various objects. She pushed a button on one of them, and it roared to life, making her laugh.

"I can't," Hunter said, staring at their mother, eyes agog. "I just can't."

"Oh, sit down and be quiet," Molly said. "These things are going to generate revenue unlike anything we've ever seen. Think about the money you'll get to count, Hunter. That always makes you happy."

"Put that thing down, Mom," Will said, "and never touch it again."

Elmer came bustling in, stopping short at the sight of his daughter holding a phallic object. "Oh. Well. Here we go, then."

"What," Will said, "is *he* doing here?"

"I'm the reason *you're* here, young man, so I'll remind you to mind your manners."

"Are you providing counseling for those of us who're going to be traumatized by this?" Will asked his father.

"Sit down and chill," Linc said. "It won't be that bad."

Elmer hit the power button on one of the devices, and it launched right out of his hand.

"It will be that bad," Will said, slumping into a chair with Hunter next to him.

"Did they bring blindfolds?" Hunter asked. "That'd help."

Emma came to the door, saw Molly holding one of the vibrators and cleared her throat. "Um, Wade, Amanda said to tell you she's ready whenever you are."

He'd never be ready for this. "Thank you, Emma."

She scurried away, not that he could blame her. "We need to give Emma hazardous duty pay for having to see Mom manhandling a vibrator."

Will glared at him. "Don't ever again use the words 'Mom' and 'vibrator' in the same sentence, do you hear me?"

"Honestly, Will," Molly said. "You're a married man, and the thought of your mother looking at a vibrator makes you squeal like a little girl?"

"I did not *squeal*," Will said indignantly.

"Whatever you say," his mother replied. "Maybe you should take some of these home and give them a whirl. You'll find out why they're so popular."

"I'm going to quit my job if you don't make her stop," Will said to his father.

"I'll go with him," Hunter said.

"Ease up on the boys, Mol. I can't afford to lose them right now."

"The *boys* are actually *men*, and they should act like it."

"I agree, but we don't want them to quit, do we?"

"Nah, I guess not." She put down the vibe and smiled at her sons. "Better?"

"Much," Will said.

"I'm going to get Amanda," Wade said. "Are we ready for this?"

"As ready as we're ever going to be," Hunter grumbled as he pushed his placemat full of toys toward the middle of the table.

"I can't wait to hear what she has to say about these doodads," Elmer said.

Will groaned loudly.

Wade went to get Amanda in his office, where he'd told her to make herself comfortable while she was in town. She had set up on the small table where he kept products under consideration for the store. His table was now littered with sex toys. He'd be seeing them in his dreams at this rate.

"We're all set," he said to her.

She finished typing something on her laptop and closed it. "Great! I'll be right in." Amanda had shoulder-length dark hair and a smile that lit up her green eyes. What had struck Wade from the time they'd first met and in all their subsequent dealings was that she spoke of her company's line without a hint of embarrassment.

He hoped his family could follow her lead and keep it together during this meeting. "I just want to apologize in advance for whatever's about to happen in there," Wade said.

Amanda laughed. "Don't worry—I've seen it all. Nothing can surprise me."

"Please don't underestimate the Abbott family when it comes to opportunities for irreverence."

"I've been warned. It's all good."

"I'll meet you in there." Why did he feel like he was about to face a firing squad in this meeting?

Mia came out of Hunter's office, where she'd been completing employment paperwork.

"All finished?" Wade asked.

"Yep, and I checked my messages. Nothing critical. Larry emailed to let me know that Brody has been arraigned on the domestic violence charges."

"That's good news." He thought of the article he'd read in the paper and the comments that made Mia out to be the bad guy in her relationship with Brody, but didn't share that information with her. What did it matter what people in her former town were saying about her? She didn't need to know that.

"Is it time for the meeting?" she asked.

"Unfortunately, yes." Wade glanced at the conference room, where Ella, Charley and Cameron were now examining the products. "I want to go home."

Mia took him by the arm and directed him toward the firing squad.

"Look at this one," Cameron said, holding up a purple device with a long thin wand. "What does it do?"

"That's a prostate massager," Amanda said when she came into the room, carrying her laptop and a bottle of water. "Push the button on the base."

Cameron did as directed, and the device came to life, swirling and vibrating and pulsating.

Dear God…

"Men who've suffered from prostate cancer or other urinary and prostate issues sing the praises of that little baby." Amanda never blinked an eye as she talked about the device the way someone else would describe moisturizer.

Wade directed Mia around the table and sat next to her. Maybe if he didn't have to look directly at her, he could get through this.

Amanda fired up her PowerPoint presentation and skipped ahead to the slide showing animated pictures that demonstrated how the prostate massager was inserted and how it worked.

Wade looked away.

"Oh *my*," Molly said, clearly fascinated. "And men like that?"

"They *love* it," Amanda said.

Molly gave Lincoln a wolfish look that made Wade want to jump out the window—anything to get out of that room.

"Is everyone here?" Amanda asked Wade.

"Unfortunately, yes."

"Excellent, then I'll start at the beginning." She went through a refresher on her company and how they'd gotten into the business of supplying intimate aids to those suffering from various forms of sexual dysfunction, whether it be from age or health problems or loneliness. "Our focus groups indicate that loneliness is actually a very big concern for the senior population, especially after an individual is widowed. They are used to sexual companionship that is lost when their spouse passes away."

"I can certainly attest to that," Elmer said, picking up the prostate massager for a closer look while his grandchildren directed their gazes toward the ceiling.

"One of the key things we try to impart in our training is how important it is to be empathetic toward customers who are interested in this line. Often it takes a tremendous amount of courage for them to walk into a store and ask for something like this. We want to make them feel welcome and supported, and I'll emphasize that point when we train your sales team."

She was so matter-of-fact about it all that Wade found himself listening with interest to her presentation and thinking about how to train the sales team on the floor to best support the products—and their customers. Many of their salespeople would be embarrassed at first, but perhaps, over time, they'd become as accustomed to talking about these products the same way they were about other things that most people didn't talk about freely.

Then Amanda encouraged everyone to pick up the products, turn them on and become familiar with how they worked. "You should feel free to take any of them home to get better acquainted with them."

"Did we miss it?" Lucas said as he and Landon rushed into the room, still wearing turnout coats and covered in soot from head to toe. Their faces were so black that their eyes stood out in stark contrast. "We had a fire in Burke. We just got back. We aren't too late, are we?"

"Oh my God," Hunter muttered, glaring at their father. "You said they weren't invited."

"They weren't," Linc said.

"Hey," Lucas said to Amanda. "I'm Lucas. This is my brother Landon. We don't work here, but we're *very* interested in the new product line."

"Excellent," Amanda said. "Have a seat and feel free to check out the products. I'm happy to answer any questions you might have."

"We might need a private lesson later since we missed the beginning," Landon said.

"I'd be happy to meet with you afterward," Amanda said.

"That's *not* happening." Wade pointed his brothers to seats at the far end of the table. "Sit down and shut up. Don't say a single word to her or anyone else."

"We're so misunderstood in this family," Landon grumbled.

"You're perfectly understood," Will said, "which is why you weren't invited to this meeting."

"And you stink," Hunter said, waving a hand in front of his face as he grimaced with disgust.

"We didn't want to take the time to shower and maybe miss even more than we already did," Lucas said. He picked up a large purple dildo and held it up for his twin's inspection. "Not quite as big as me, but it'll do in a pinch."

"Mom!" Wade said. "Make it stop."

"Boys," Molly said, "behave or get out. I mean it."

"We are behaving," Landon said indignantly. "We're just curious. That's allowed in this company, isn't it?"

Wade realized Mia was rocking with silent laughter. She laughed so hard that tears ran down her face. Her laughter made him smile, and he had to fight back the need to join her. His younger brothers were always ridiculous, but never more so than in a room full of sex toys. Wade loved to see her laugh.

"Amanda," Linc said, "I apologize for my younger sons. We did what we could, but they came out this way. Please proceed."

Despite the grime that covered them, Amanda seemed somewhat captivated by the younger Abbotts and kept glancing at them as she continued her presentation, which went into intricate detail about what each object was intended to do and how it worked. An hour later, Wade knew more about sex toys than he'd ever wanted to and could speak intelligently about them to the store's employees, which had been the point of the dreaded meeting.

"Now, let me take any questions you have."

The comment was met with silence.

Lucas and Landon raised their hands simultaneously.

"You two don't get to ask questions," Wade said. "You don't actually work here."

"No, but we represent the family in the community through our generous work as volunteer firefighters, and people are bound to ask us about the new product line," Landon said in all seriousness.

Wade rolled his eyes.

"You want us to be able to answer questions, don't you?" Lucas added.

"Actually, that's about the *last* thing we want," Wade said.

Hunter and Will nodded in agreement.

"Let them ask," Charley said. "How bad can it be?"

The others looked at her in horror.

"Are you seriously asking that?" Wade asked.

"I was wondering if you're available to give private demonstrations to customers who might want to know more about the line," Landon asked.

Amanda's composure seemed to desert her. "I, um…"

"You don't have to answer that," Lincoln said, glaring at Landon.

"I don't mind," she said. "We offer workshops to people looking for more information, and that's part of the package. I look forward to the opportunity to speak one-on-one with people in the community about the product line and how it might benefit them."

"I'm really interested in those workshops," Lucas said solemnly.

"I'm going to have them killed," Wade muttered.

Mia shook with laughter.

"I'll make sure you're notified when they're being offered," Amanda said.

Wade couldn't tell if she was intrigued or horrified by them. Some women tended to go stupid in the head in their presence, which only made them more unmanageable.

The meeting wrapped up at the end of the second hour. Will and Hunter got up and left the second they could. Ella, Charley and Cameron thanked Amanda for the in-depth presentation and made a date to meet in the morning to plan the orientation of the sales team, which was Ella's job.

Wade would help because the product line fell under his department, but Ella would head it up. Thank God. She had a gift for dealing with the lovely ladies who worked for them, and she'd know just how to handle their training.

Lucas and Landon lingered, clearly hoping for a private word with Amanda.

"Move along, gentlemen," Wade said. "Show's over."

"We want to thank her personally," Lucas said. "She did such a great job of explaining everything in terms we could easily understand."

"Yeah, like 'orgasm' and 'erection' and 'clitoris,'" Landon added. "Those are some of our most favorite words."

"Don't forget 'prostate,'" Lucas said. "That's the best word *ever.*"

"Leave her alone," Wade said. "She's just doing her job and doesn't need to be harassed by you guys."

"We've never harassed a woman in our lives," Landon said. "We don't have to."

That was a fact and a big part of the reason they were such menaces. Women had fallen all over them from the time they were teenagers, and the attention had never abated.

Lucas pushed past Wade to speak to Amanda. "Could I interest you in dinner at the inn tonight?" he asked.

"That's where I'm staying," she said, appearing flustered.

"Perfect. I'll come by around seven? And I promise to shower first."

"Don't mind if I join you," Landon said.

"I do mind." Lucas glared at his twin. "I asked first."

"Fine. I'll ask second. Tomorrow night? Same time?"

"I, um…"

"You don't have to say yes to either of them if you don't want to," Wade said.

"No, that's okay," she said. "Sounds fun. I'll see you tonight and you tomorrow night."

"Excellent," Lucas said, smirking at Wade. "See you then, Amanda."

"I was going to suggest we need a date of our own tonight, since we've never actually been on one," Mia whispered to Wade. "Now I know where I want to go."

"That's a very good idea," he said, "in more ways than one." And he wished he'd thought of it. They'd known each other almost two years but had never been on an official date. Tonight, they would rectify that. "Let's go home."

"Now?"

"Right now." He rarely took time off or left early, and if there was any day to claim some time for himself, it was two days after he got married. "I didn't get to work out this morning, and I'm feeling the need to stretch."

"Me, too. Maybe we can work out together?"

"I'd love to." He took her hand to lead her from the conference room, releasing it only so he could duck into his office to grab his coat.

Ella followed him in. "Everything okay?" she asked, keeping her voice down.

"Yeah, we talked. It's all good. I'm going home."

"Oh. You are?"

"Yep. I just got married, and I don't want to be here."

"Okay, then. Have a nice evening."

"You do the same." Wade returned to reception, where Mia was talking to Emma. "Ready?"

"If you are."

Hunter came out of his office, holding papers in his hand. "Hey, Mia, before you go, could I have a word?"

"Sure."

Wade wanted to ask his brother what kind of word he needed to have with his wife. But he didn't ask. Instead, he waited patiently for her to take care of whatever Hunter had to ask her.

She came out a minute later and smiled at him. "Ready?"

"What's up with Hunter?"

"He just needed to confirm my Social Security number. It's all set."

Wade put his arm around her and told Emma he was leaving for the day.

"Have a good one," she said.

He squeezed Mia's shoulder. "Oh, I plan to."

CHAPTER 20

"There is no end of craving. Hence contentment
alone is the best way to happiness."
—Swami Sivananda

Hunter stared at his computer screen, not sure what to do with the info staring back at him. The Social Security number Mia had given him belonged to a woman who'd died in 1972. There was no record of the number having ever belonged to her.

What the hell did he do now?

As a matter of course, he ran background checks on every new employee, beginning by validating their Social Security number. He was almost afraid to continue the process. Rubbing at the stubble on his jaw, wondering if he should quit now or keep going.

Hunter Abbott didn't cut corners when it came to overseeing his family's business interests. He was methodical and thorough. He didn't make exceptions—ever. But this was his brother's wife.

He shut down his computer, stood and grabbed his coat. "Be back in a few," he said to Emma on his way by the reception desk.

"Got it," she said.

She'd been a great addition to their team, but he still missed seeing Mary every day. According to Cameron, her dad and Mary were having the time of their lives traveling together. Mary deserved the grand adventure of her romance with Patrick. She was a great person.

Everyone deserved a chance to be happy, which was what had him so torn about the information he'd uncovered about Mia.

Wade was clearly crazy about her, had been for quite some time, according to Hannah. It didn't surprise Hunter that he'd never caught a hint of Wade's affection for Mia. His brother kept to himself, always had, even when they'd all lived at home.

Hunter remembered when Wade had claimed the oversized closet and turned it into a bedroom, so he wouldn't have to share a room with Colton anymore. That was typical Wade—while the rest of them zigged, Wade zagged. He was self-contained, didn't feel the need to share his every thought with others.

Hunter had never been self-contained. He'd shared almost every thought he'd ever had with his twin, Hannah. Now his thoughts were divided between those he shared with Hannah and those he shared with his wife, Megan.

Crossing Elm Street, he made a beeline for the diner, eager to see his wife and talk it out with her. She'd know what he should do—and he could trust her to keep the matter confidential.

Her eyes lit up with delight at the sight of him. Would he ever get tired of being received that way by her? No, never. For the longest time, he'd nursed a secret crush on her while she'd pined for Will. Those days seemed like a long time ago now that they were married and trying—as hard as they possibly could—to get her pregnant.

He couldn't wait to see her round and glowing. Taking a seat at the counter, he leaned in to accept a kiss from her.

She rested her hand on his face. "What's the matter?"

It didn't surprise him that she could tell he had something on his mind. They were so in tune with each other that he could tell, just by looking at her, when something was troubling her—and he loved that. Looking around to make sure they wouldn't be overheard, he said, "Mia applied for a job with the company."

"That's cool. That means she's sticking around, right?"

"Yeah."

"So, what's the problem?"

"I do background checks on every new employee—no exceptions."

Her face fell with dismay. "Oh no…"

"Her SSN is a fake."

"Oh God, Hunter. What do you do about that?"

"I have no idea. That's why I'm over here. I'm hiding."

"Be right back." She went to refill coffees and rang up two customers before returning to him. "You have to tell Wade."

Groaning, he dropped his head into his hands. "Don't want to."

"You have to."

"I know, but he'll be mad with me."

"It's not your fault that she gave you a fake SSN."

"No, but he'll accuse me of being suspicious for checking it."

"You just said you do that for everyone, no exceptions."

"Yeah, but—"

"No buts. You checked up on her as an employee, not as his wife, and that's what you found. He can't fault you for that."

"I hate this for him. He's so happy with her."

"I know. They were in for lunch, and he never stopped smiling. I can't believe he's the same Wade."

"Maybe there's a good reason for the fake number."

"Maybe."

But what good reason could there possibly be? "I very rarely hate my job, but I do right now."

"Will you tell your dad?"

"No. I'm only going to tell Wade and take my lead from him. I don't want this to blow up into an Abbott-family scandal. Not that my dad would tell people, but you know what I mean."

"I do, and I think that's wise. Will you call him now?"

"No, she's with him. I'll talk to him alone in the morning. That's soon enough to ruin everything for him." He groaned. "And here I thought the sex-toy demonstration would be the low point of my day."

"I'm sorry you have to deal with this." She smoothed her fingers through his hair. "Guess what?"

"What?"

"Look at me."

He raised his head and smiled. "Nothing I'd rather look at."

"I'm late," she whispered.

"For what?"

She raised her brows. "And people say you're *so* smart."

Suddenly, her meaning dawned on him. "Are you saying what I think you're saying?"

"I'm only saying I'm late."

"How soon can we find out?"

"Soon."

"I can't wait that long."

"Yes, you can. I'll keep you very busy so you barely think about it."

"Busy how exactly?" he asked, feeling like a little boy on Christmas. He often felt that way since she came into his life and made every day feel like Christmas.

"Wouldn't you like to know?"

"Yes, I would. I really, really would."

Laughing, Megan said, "Go back to work so you can go home sooner. I'll tell you all about it when you get there."

Reaching for her, he laid a hot kiss on her before bolting out the door to go finish his workday. He had much better things to do these days than linger at work any longer than necessary. As always, talking out his problems with her made him feel better.

It would kill him to break this news to Wade, but he'd do it because that was his job as the CFO and human-resources director. And then he'd help Wade figure out what to do next because that was his job as Wade's big brother.

Wade and Mia arrived home, and the first thing they did was change their clothes and roll out yoga mats for a relaxing, invigorating workout that she insisted on leading him through. He tried to keep his tongue in his mouth while watching her bend and stretch and arch her elegant neck. When she bent over into downward-facing dog, he lost his patience and molded his body to hers.

"Um, excuse me, Mr. Abbott, but it's not appropriate to touch the yoga instructor in such a *familiar* way."

"It's very appropriate when the yoga instructor is your wife."

She giggled and pushed her ass into his abdomen. "We're not finished."

"Do you know how crazy you made me that first day, watching your body move? I swear I was hard from the first second I laid eyes on you." Holding the pose, he slid his hands around her and cupped her breasts, dragging his thumbs over hard nipples.

"Is that right?"

"Uh-huh. It took every ounce of self-control I could find to keep my hands to myself that day and every time I saw you afterward."

"Every woman at that retreat was talking about the hot guy with the long hair."

"Are you mad that I cut my hair? You can tell me the truth."

"God, no. You're even hotter with short hair, if that's possible."

"Stand with me." He guided her into an upright position and took her hands to stretch her arms into a sun salutation. They moved together through a variety of poses, their bodies pressed together. No words were needed as they went from one to the other, each seeming to sense the other's next move. The feeling of harmony between them moved him profoundly.

"Savasana," he whispered, bringing her down on top of him for the corpse pose that was supposed to be relaxing at the end. With her on top of him, it was anything but relaxing.

She moved ever so slightly so his erection was pressed between her ass cheeks.

Wade groaned and ran his hands over the front of her, from hips to breasts. "Best yoga practice ever."

"Mmm, for sure. Can we do that every day?"

204 | MARIE FORCE

He wrapped his arms around her, his breathing and heartbeat in time with hers. "Yeah, baby. We can do that every day."

"You're supposed to be relaxing." She flexed her glutes and drew a deep groan from him.

"I'm never going to relax if you do that."

"Do what?" She flexed again. "This?"

"*Mia*," he said, half laughing and half groaning.

"Yes, dear?"

He slid his hands from her breasts to her abdomen and below, drawing a gasp from her when his fingers pressed against the heat between her legs. "You're supposed to be relaxing."

"Relaxing is overrated."

"I'm glad you agree." He turned them so she was facedown on the mat and drew her yoga pants and panties down to her thighs.

"Wade…"

"Shhh, just like this. Is this okay?"

"*Yes.*"

He grasped his cock and teased her. With her pants holding her legs together, the fit became tighter. Something happened to him when her heat connected with his rock-hard flesh. Whatever it was had never happened before with any other woman. He lost track of time and place and anything that wasn't about her and the feeling he had whenever he was with her this way.

Grasping her hips, he slid all the way into her and held still until he regained control over his body and his emotions. Dropping his head to her back, he took deep breaths.

"Wade," she said, sounding urgent.

"What, honey?"

"Are you going to…"

He tilted his hips, and her internal muscles quivered in response. Holding still inside her was a thousand times better than full-on fucking had ever been with anyone else. "Feels so good."

"God, yes... You feel so good." She gripped the hand he'd propped on the mat next to her.

"Just like this," he said. "Like this." He stayed perfectly still, barely breathing in the effort to control himself and the sensations stampeding through him. Holding still inside her was the most erotically charged thing he'd ever done. Encased in her heat, his cock throbbed and expanded, setting off a new wave of fluttering that tested his resolve to remain still.

"I can't... Wade..."

Reaching beneath her, he pressed a fingertip to her clit, and she exploded, screaming from the strength of her release.

He was right there with her, coming so hard he saw stars.

"Holy... What the... How did you..."

Wade laughed and came down on top of her, finally relaxing. Somewhat anyway. He could never fully relax when he was still inside her. "That was awesome."

"I didn't even know it could happen like that, without moving."

"I've never done that before."

"How'd you know to do it?"

"I didn't. I just went with what felt good, and being still inside you felt better than anything ever has." It occurred to him that he'd once again had unprotected sex with her, but he'd decided to trust her, which meant he trusted her when she said she was taking the pill. He'd seen them on the counter in the bathroom, but he hadn't actually seen her take them. He hoped they would have children someday, but not right away. Not when they were still getting to know each other and getting used to living together.

They had time for babies and every other thing life had in store for them.

"How about a shower?"

"Followed by a nap? Marriage is exhausting."

Wade laughed and withdrew from her, wondering how long it would be before he could have her again. If this was madness, sign him up. He loved every minute of it.

In the shower, they took turns washing each other, and he was fully aroused again by the time they toweled off and slid into bed together, their bodies wrapped around each other.

He stared down at her gorgeous face, drinking in every detail as he kissed her, noting that the bruises were beginning to fade.

Mia wrapped her arms and legs around him, trapping him in her sensual web.

He'd never been so happy to be trapped anywhere. For the longest time, all they did was kiss. They made out like teenagers about to get caught by parents. The frantic urgency of it made him forget that they'd planned to nap, that she was exhausted, that he'd just had her fifteen minutes ago. He needed more. He'd never get enough.

He wouldn't have done anything about the urgent need, but when she curled her hand around his cock and raised her hips, he followed her lead and slid into her again, breaking the kiss to take a badly needed deep breath. "Tell me if it's too much."

"Never too much. I can't get enough."

Groaning, he gorged on her, desperate to touch her and taste her and consume her. "Mia…"

"Tell me. What're you thinking?"

"I'm thinking about how much I love you." He kissed her face, her lips, her neck. "That I've loved you from the first time I ever saw you. That I'll never have enough of you or this or us."

"I love you, too, Wade. I've never yearned for anything the way I did for you when I couldn't see you or be with you."

Those words had never been more powerful or packed a greater punch than they did coming from her. For the first time in years, he felt like he could breathe again, that he wasn't missing the most essential thing in his life by missing her. He gave her everything he had, holding her so close to him that her sweat became his. And then, abruptly, he withdrew from her and began to kiss his way down the front of her.

She squirmed beneath him, but the lower he went, the tenser she got.

He looked up at her. "Tell me why you don't like it."

"You… You don't have to… If you don't want to."

His brows arched toward his hairline. "Don't want to? Why would you think I wouldn't want to?"

"I… Not all guys like to. That's all."

"This one does, especially when it's you."

Her heart beat so hard, he could see it in the wild pulse in her neck. "It's not one of the bad things, is it?"

She shook her head, but he wasn't convinced.

Kissing her belly and making a circle around her navel with his tongue, he said, "Tell me."

"I shouldn't… Not now."

Her thighs quivered against his ribs when he moved down, kissing her hip bones and the crease where her leg joined her torso. "Yes, now."

"He said I didn't, you know…"

"Taste good?"

Her entire body seemed to blush as she looked up at the ceiling and nodded.

Wade wished he could kick the shit out of the asshole who made her doubt herself. What he wouldn't give for five minutes alone with that guy. "Mia."

"What?"

"Look at me."

"No."

"Mia…" He kissed her inner thighs and used the width of his shoulders to ease her legs farther apart.

She gripped the sheets like a lifeline, her knuckles white and her body tense.

That wouldn't do. "Sweetheart, look at me."

"I can't."

He playfully bit her inner thigh, which got her attention. "There is nothing about you that I find unattractive. Not one single thing. Do you hear me?"

"How do you know you'll like *that* when you've never done it?"

"I'll like it because I *love* you."

"If you don't like it, you don't have to—"

Wade buried his tongue in her, and her body went completely stiff. At least he had her attention. He held her legs apart with his hands and went to town on her, licking and sucking and fucking her with his tongue. He never let up for one second until she came, nearly pulling the hair from his head as she did.

"Any other questions?"

She was breathing so hard, she couldn't talk, but she shook her head.

Wade wiped his face on the sheet and moved up, stopping to give attention to each of her nipples before continuing to kiss her lips. "Are we good now?"

"Mmm-hmm. Very good."

"And we agree that *he* was a fool who had no idea how lucky he was to have you?"

"We agree."

"And you believe me when I tell you that every single sweet inch of you is beautiful to me and that nothing, and I do mean *nothing*, could make me not want you?"

"Yes," she said between deep breaths. "I believe you."

"Excellent." He pushed inside her again. "Now, where were we?" When he was fully encased in her heat, he used his hips to pin hers to the bed and pushed himself up on his arms so he could look down on her. He didn't want to miss any of her myriad reactions.

Her back arched and her breasts thrust.

He'd never seen anything sexier. *Ever.* She was it for him. Had been from the start, and he was so, so glad he'd waited for her, even if the waiting had been torture at times. That they got to do *this*, anytime they wanted, for the rest of their lives was the best thing to ever happen to him. He wanted to be the best thing to ever happen to her, too, and as he made love to her, he focused exclusively on her pleasure. Kissing and touching and caressing her into a series of orgasms that made him feel like he was on top of the world because he got to make her feel good.

They'd taken the edge off earlier for him, so he was able to make it last until her legs trembled with exhaustion and his arms threatened to give out.

"Come with me," he said, picking up the pace. "One more time."

Her fingertips dug into the muscles on his back, and her legs tightened around his waist. "I can't."

"Yes, you can." He moved his fingers lightly over her clit.

She was so primed that her body seized in response to his touch.

"Told you," he whispered. He gathered her into his tight embrace and buried his face in her hair as he lost himself in her. Rolling to his side, he brought her with him when he collapsed, completely spent and happier than he'd ever been.

CHAPTER 21

"Happiness, contentment, the health and growth of the soul,
depend, as men have proved over and over again, upon
some simple issue, some single turning of the soul."
—George A. Smith

Mia slept like a dead person and woke to darkness.

Wade was wrapped around her, his body heat keeping her nice and warm.

For the first time in years, she'd found true contentment with him—and his incredible family. She'd never experienced anything like the dynamic between Wade and his siblings and cousins. The family was a bonus. He was the true prize.

She snuggled in closer to him, breathing in the woodsy, outdoorsy scent of his skin, running her fingers through his hair—because she could—and touching him anywhere she could reach.

He loved her.

She loved him.

She'd never had a dream come true until now. And she'd never dared to dream anything like what she had with him. Earlier, when he'd shown her that no part of her was unattractive to him, he'd undone years of damage done by Brody, who'd made her feel less than desirable in every possible way, even as he kept her in his iron grip. Once, she'd asked him why he was so determined to hang on to her if he found her so unattractive.

212 | MARIE FORCE

He'd told her to shut the fuck up and not ask questions she didn't want the answers to. That had been her life.

If only she'd had the strength and courage to leave him long before she did. But if she had, he might've gotten away with his criminal activity—and he might've made good on his frequent threats to kill her if she'd ever had the audacity to leave him.

Perhaps that was why things happened the way they had. Maybe she was meant to be there just long enough to stop him. She'd paid an awful personal price for that sacrifice, but she'd do it again if it meant one less kid would be introduced to heroin because of him.

In the message she'd gotten from Larry earlier, he'd mentioned that they were talking to Brody about his supply chain, hoping they could entice him to flip on his suppliers in exchange for a more lenient deal for himself. She doubted Brody would take the deal, but it gave her hope that perhaps the nightmare could end sooner rather than later.

The most important thing had already happened—she could never be forced to marry a man she'd grown to despise. Again, she relived the horror of him telling her to get ready for their wedding because he was coming home with a justice of the peace and had already gotten a marriage license. He'd never expected her to run. He thought she was so afraid of him that she wouldn't dare defy him. She wished she could've been there to see his smug face when they told him she'd married someone else.

"What're you thinking about?" Wade asked, his hand moving gently over her bruised ribs that felt a thousand times better since they'd applied the smelly cream from the store.

"I wish I could've been there when they told Brody I was permanently off-limits to him. I would've liked to have seen that."

"You don't need to think about him anymore. He's the past. The present is so much better than the past." He cupped her breast and ran his thumb over her nipple.

Her body tingled in response. How was that possible? She'd lost track of how many orgasms she'd had earlier. How could she want more? "The present is absolutely delightful."

"I'm glad you think so. Still want to go out to dinner?"

"Only if you do."

"I do, and not because I need to keep an eye on my buffoon of a brother, but because I've never once taken my wife on a real date, and I need to fix that."

"Your wife would be perfectly content with a night at home with her sexy husband."

"There'll be plenty of those, but tonight, we're going out."

"What should I wear?"

"Jeans are considered dressed up in this town."

"I might be able to do a little better than that."

"You could wear a burlap sack and be sexy."

"You might be a tiny bit biased."

"Mmm." He nuzzled her neck. "I'm extremely biased. I have the sexiest wife who ever lived."

"I have the sexiest, most insatiable husband who ever lived."

"I've never been insatiable until I had you. In fact, you'd better shower alone, or we might never get out of here tonight."

"True." She sat up, letting the covers fall to her waist, and pushed her hair back from her face.

Propped up on one elbow, Wade watched her.

"What?"

"I never want to stop looking now that I can."

She smiled at him. He was so sweet to her and always had been, even when they were just friends. But honestly, had they ever been *just* friends? "I know what you mean. Anytime things got to be too much for me in the last couple of years, I would close my eyes and picture you. It used to make Brody so mad when I'd do that. He had no idea what I was thinking about, but he knew I wasn't thinking about him."

"I thought about you all the time. When I was supposed to be clearing my mind during meditation, there you were. When I was in meetings at work or at dinner with my family, you may as well have been sitting right next to me, because you were always on my mind."

214 | Marie Force

"That should be our song. 'Always on My Mind.'"

"I love that song. An old classic, and yes, it should be ours, because it's the truth." He traced the tattoo on her ribs with his finger, following the path of the vine. "What's the meaning behind this?"

"It represented the possibility of growth to me, of something more in the future. Plus, I thought it was pretty."

"It is pretty—and very sexy, too."

She smiled. "I'm going to shower now. Don't you dare join me."

"Wouldn't think of it."

Mia laughed and got out of bed, feeling his gaze on her as she headed for the bathroom. In the shower, she stood under the warm water and closed her eyes. Being with Wade was the easiest thing she'd ever done. It came naturally to her, like breathing or blinking.

She washed her body and rinsed off the soap, feeling as if she was rinsing away the filth of her past with every day she spent with Wade and his family in the magical town of Butler.

In just a few days, she felt more at home here than she ever had in Rutland, where she'd always felt like an outsider around people who'd known each other all their lives. She was an outsider here, too, but Wade made her feel welcome.

She toweled off and put on Wade's red plaid robe that hung from a hook on the door. Belting it around her, she went to the bedroom to find something to wear to dinner with her husband.

Her *husband*.

The words made her giddy and excited for everything still to come for them. Now that she was here, where she'd wanted to be for so long, there was nowhere else she wanted to be but with him. At some point, she needed to call her mother and tell her she'd gotten married.

Mia couldn't wait for her mom and stepfather to meet Wade. They would love him, and her mother would be relieved to hear that Mia wasn't with Brody anymore.

They'd drifted from each other during the years Mia had spent with Brody, and now she hoped they could bridge that gap. Maybe Wade would be up for a trip to New Mexico at some point. Mia had never seen her mother's new home and would love to.

Through the bedroom door, she could see Wade crouched before the woodstove, stoking the fire. He'd put on jeans, but his torso was bare and gilded from the glow of the fire. He loved her. He really did, and he had for as long as she'd loved him.

Miracles had been few and far between in her life until she found him in the most unlikely of places—a yoga retreat that had attracted all women except for the one man who'd captured her attention from the start. That man had put the rest of them to shame with his incredible flexibility and intense focus, not to mention the killer body honed from years of yoga practice. And now that man was her *husband.*

Mia hadn't known what to expect when she came here looking for his help, but he'd given her everything without hesitation. She would love him and care for him for the rest of her life—if he let her. She wouldn't ever be able to repay him for the enormous chance he'd taken on her, but she would try as hard as she could to make sure he never regretted it.

There weren't many things Lucas Abbott took seriously, but a date with a beautiful woman who was also an expert on sex toys? That was something to be taken very seriously. He showered, scrubbed the grime off his face and shaved the beard he'd been sporting since Christmas. He usually kept it until mud season, but Amanda seemed like the type who would prefer clean-shaven to burly-bearded.

Not that he knew her well enough to judge such things, but he hoped to know her much better after tonight.

He combed his hair, put on a bit of cologne and buttoned the shirt he'd ironed for the occasion and smoothed his shirttails over dark jeans. This was as dressed up as it got for him, and he hoped it was good enough for a classy woman like Amanda. Women liked him—and his twin. They had never suffered from a lack of female attention. But lately...

Things had gotten a little... boring. It was too easy. The thrill was gone. He hated to think he might be growing up—*horrors*—but it had happened to his older brothers. *It* being *maturity*. Lucas usually hated that word and everything that went along with it—responsibility, commitment, adulthood.

Watching his younger brother, Max, dedicate himself to single father-hood had been sobering, and Lucas knew that Landon agreed. They couldn't have *Max* making them look *bad*. That wouldn't do.

Lucas had been thinking for a while that he needed to expand his playground, so to speak, beyond the local women who'd kept him and Landon—and Max, once upon a time—entertained in recent years. They were all nice people. Well, most of them were, but none of them presented much of a challenge.

He could walk into any bar in the Northeast Kingdom, strike up a conversation with a pretty woman, and be warming her bed within an hour, if that was what he wanted. He wasn't necessarily proud of his track record where women were concerned and would never deny that he'd had more than his share of fun with women.

But that was all that it had ever been. Fun. Watching his siblings with their life partners had him wondering if maybe there wasn't something beyond fun that might be worth exploring. That wasn't to say he was ready to settle down with one woman for the rest of his life, but it might be fun to have… a girlfriend.

There. He'd said it. Or rather, he'd allowed himself to think it, which was a huge first step for a guy who'd made a career out of avoiding that word and everything that went with it. Many had tried to get him to take on the title of boyfriend, but none had succeeded. Why commit to one woman when there were so many to choose from?

That had been his philosophy, and Landon's, since they were old enough to understand that women liked them. A lot.

Maybe it was time to try something new. Not that Amanda would be the something new. No, she was in town for only a week or so, and then she'd be moving on to her next assignment. This date would be about "practice." It wasn't about scoring or any of the usual games. It was about taking a nice, attractive woman who interested him to dinner.

He could do that. Just because he hadn't done anything like it since his senior prom didn't mean he was incapable.

As he zipped up his coat and stepped into his boots, he decided he was perfectly capable and he would prove that to himself tonight. He drove into town thinking about Amanda's presentation and the way she'd talked about subjects that would turn other women into silly, giggling fools. She'd been the consummate professional, taking questions and offering answers with practiced ease.

What was all new to them was routine to her. She'd probably done that presentation a few hundred times, so it was no big deal.

Lucas was fascinated by her career choice and had a lot of questions he hoped she would answer for him tonight. He parked at the inn and walked on snow that crunched under his feet to the front door, where he kicked the snow off his boots. At the front desk, Mrs. Hendricks lit up at the sight of him.

"This is a nice surprise," she said. "Landon?"

He shook his head. "Lucas."

"I never guess right with you two."

"No worries. Hardly anyone but our mom gets it right every time."

"It helped when you had the beard."

"I'll grow it back just for you."

She smiled and flushed. "Such a charmer. What can I do for you tonight, hon?"

"I'm here to see a guest. Amanda." Lucas realized he had no idea what her last name was.

Luckily, Mrs. Hendricks knew. "Amanda Pressley. I'll ring her room for you."

Amanda Pressley.

It was a good name, a strong name. Amanda Pressley.

Mrs. Hendricks hung up the phone. "She'll be down in just a minute."

"Thank you. We have reservations for seven in the dining room."

"Your brother Wade and his new missus reserved a table at the same time." Mrs. Hendricks leaned on the counter. "What's she like? His new wife?"

Lucas didn't let on that he was annoyed that Wade and Mia would be spying on him and Amanda. "She seems really nice."

"Is it true that none of you knew her before he married her?"

"Wade knew her. That's what matters, right?" He was saved from contributing further to the Butler gossip machine by Amanda's appearance. She wore a sweater he recognized from the store, along with jeans and black leather boots that showcased a great pair of legs. Her dark hair was shiny and smooth, her smile warm and welcoming.

"Hi there," she said.

"Hey."

"Your beard is gone."

"Good luck figuring out which one is Lucas and which one is Landon without the beard," Mrs. Hendricks said.

"I'll make sure she knows the difference," Lucas said. He offered his arm to Amanda. "Shall we?"

Amanda tucked her hand into the crook of his arm. "Yes, please."

"You two have a nice dinner," Mrs. Hendricks said.

"Oh, we will," Lucas assured her.

CHAPTER 22

*"I am fascinated by what is beautiful, strong, healthy,
what is living. I seek harmony."*
—Leni Riefenstahl

Wade had told Mia to dress for the weather. Everything in Butler was casual, even the dining room at the Admiral Frances Butler Inn, the one place that had rooms for rent in their tiny town.

She came out of the bedroom wearing jeans that hugged her sexy curves and a sparkly top that she'd paired with a soft black sweater. "Is it safe to wear leather boots, or am I better off with the rubber ones?"

Wade was so busy staring at her that he didn't hear the question.

She waved her hand in front of his face. "Earth to Wade."

"Hmm? What did you say?"

"Leather boots or rubber?"

"Rubber. I wouldn't want the leather ones to get ruined in the slush." He slid his arms around her and buried his face in the crook of her neck, breathing her in. "I still can't believe I can do this whenever I want to."

Her hand curled around his neck, her fingers toying with the ends of his hair. "That's the best part of being married, isn't it?"

"There are so many good parts of being married that I'd hate to single one out as the best." Moving his hands down, he cupped her ass and gave it a squeeze. "I wouldn't want the other parts to get their feelings hurt."

Her soft laughter delighted him. After everything she'd been through, hearing her laugh was the sweetest music he'd ever heard.

"Let's get going before I forget that I'm supposed to be taking my wife on our first official date tonight."

"If you don't want to go out, we don't have to."

"I want to go, and we do have to. I wouldn't want you to think I'm only after one thing from my lovely wife—although that one thing is rather spectacular."

"It is rather spectacular, isn't it?" she replied, flashing a saucy grin.

"The most spectacular I've ever had."

"Me, too."

When she looked at him that way, she made him feel like king of the world, or maybe just king of *her* world, which was more than fine with him. He held her coat for her and followed her to the truck. His motion-sensitive lights illuminated the way for them and lit up the yard. Wade took a good look around as he held the door for her and waited for her to get settled.

It would be so easy, he thought, for someone to walk right onto his property, even with cops watching the place, and he'd never know until it was too late. The thought sent chills down his spine that had nothing to do with the cold. He recalled the things people had said about Mia online and how he couldn't be with her around the clock, as much as he might want to be.

Maybe he should show her how to use the pistol he kept under lock and key. Just in case she ever needed it. Although the thought of her needing to defend herself in their home threatened his sanity. He would keep her safe no matter what he had to do.

"What's wrong?" she asked when they were on their way into town.

The state cop positioned at the end of the driveway pulled out behind them. They'd gotten used to being followed and barely noticed the cops anymore, but Wade was damned glad they were there.

"Nothing. Why?"

"You're tense. What happened since we left the house?"

"I was thinking…"

"About?"

"Security at home."

"What about it?"

"We need more of it." He glanced at her. "Do you know how to shoot a gun?"

"God, no. I've never even touched one."

"I want to teach you. Just in case you ever need it."

"You have a gun?"

"I do, but only for protection. Thankfully, I've never needed it."

"I don't think I could do it."

"If it came down to your life or an intruder's life, you bet your ass you could do it."

"It freaks me out to talk about guns and shooting people."

"I'm worried because people who support Brody know where you are now. If they blame you for what happened to him, it's not outside the realm of possibility that they could come looking for you."

"They'd never find me. Your place is so far off the main drag."

"Babe, all they'd have to do is ask around in town. People know where I live." He reached across the center console for her hand. "I'm not saying this to scare you. I only want you to be safe and aware and able to defend yourself if need be."

"It scares the hell out of me to think I might ever have to defend myself with a gun. I hate them."

"I'm not a big fan of them either. I only have one because I live in the middle of nowhere, and I'd rather be safe than sorry. I've never needed it."

"Until I came along and brought criminals into your life."

"Those are your words, not mine." He gave her hand a squeeze. "I'll show you where the gun is and how to use it, and then we'll forget about it, okay?"

"If you really think it's necessary."

"I hope it'll never be necessary, but I'll feel better about leaving you home alone if I know you can take care of yourself if you have to." He pulled into the parking lot and noticed that Lucas's truck was already there. After killing the engine, he turned to Mia, who had her bottom lip between her teeth. "I don't want this to ruin our night." He tapped on her abused lip, and she released it.

"It's not going to ruin our night."

"What're you thinking?"

"I want to be free of all this, you know? Brody and the case and... All of it. I want it to go away and leave us in peace."

"I love the way you say *us*."

"My situation affects you, too, and I hate that most of all. I feel like I was really selfish to come here and involve you, but I didn't know what else to do when he said he was going to force me to marry him. I was afraid he would kill me if I refused again."

"You did exactly what you should've done, and you've made me very happy."

"It wasn't just about escaping Brody. I hope you know that."

"I do. I get it. It was about us getting what we both wanted at the same time."

She nodded. "I did want you. So badly. I was afraid to even think about how badly I wanted you when I was still with him."

"All that matters now is that you're here, we're together, we're married and we're going to make it work. No matter what." He cupped her cheek and ran his thumb over her soft skin. "Now I'm going to take my wife out to dinner for the very first time. No more talk of anything that isn't about us and the future and all the things we have to look forward to, okay?"

"And spying on Lucas."

Wade laughed. "That, too. Especially that. Wait for me. I'll come around for you." When he got out of the truck, frigid air brought tears to his eyes and had him moving fast to collect her and get inside as quickly as possible. Inside the door, they took a second to catch their breath. Wade blew warm air into his hands. "Whose big idea was it to go out tonight?"

"I believe it was mine. Not the best idea I ever had."

Wade put his arm around her and kept her close to him as they walked toward the lobby. "Our first date is long overdue. Despite the cold, I'm glad we're getting that taken care of."

"So we can rejoin the honeymoon already in progress after dinner?"

"I do like the way you think, Mrs. Abbott."

"I do like when you call me that, Mr. Abbott."

He squeezed her shoulder and marveled at how he, who'd craved solitude his entire life, suddenly couldn't imagine not having her by his side, in his bed or firmly entrenched in his heart. Wade's dad had always told them that when the right one came along, they'd know it—and he'd known right away that if he couldn't have her, he wouldn't want anyone else.

Mrs. Hendricks was working the front desk when they came into the lobby. "It's the newlyweds!" She came around the desk to greet them. "I'm *so* glad to meet you." She hugged Mia, who was startled by the gesture. "Welcome to Butler!"

Wade gently extricated his wife from the older woman's embrace.

"And you," she said to Wade. "Keeping such big secrets." Leaning in toward Mia, she added, "It's always the quiet ones you have to watch out for. They're the sneaky ones."

"Are you sneaky, Wade?" Mia asked, clearly amused.

"Um, not really."

"Oh, come now! You pulled off the story of the year in this town, showing up with a new wife no one had ever met. If that's not sneaky, I don't know what is."

"Well, I wasn't intending to be sneaky," he said, trying not to squirm. "I'm just kind of private. That's all."

"What did your mama have to say about you getting married?" Mrs. Hendricks asked, settling in for a full inquisition.

"She was very happy for us," Mia said. "All the Abbotts were, especially when they found out how long Wade and I have known each other." She gave a tug on Wade's hand. "Don't we have a reservation, honey? We ought to get going."

Hearing her call him "honey" did weird things to his overly taxed heart. Just when he thought this day couldn't get any better, she'd called him honey. "We sure do," he said. "Nice to see you, Mrs. Hendricks."

"You, too. And congratulations. Everyone is so happy for you both."

"Thank you." When they had walked away, he said, "This town. Ugh. Sorry about that."

"No need to apologize. It was very entertaining."

"I'm glad you thought so. People around here don't have much to do, especially this time of year, so they tend to get a little too involved in other people's business. Just ask Cameron what it was like when she hit Fred on the way into town. It's all people talked about for weeks, until they caught wind of Hannah dating Nolan."

"Typical small town."

While they waited at the hostess desk, Wade scanned the room and saw Lucas tucked into a corner with Amanda, the two of them engrossed in conversation. When the hostess returned, he gave his name. "We'd like to sit close to them," he said, pointing to his brother.

"No problem," the hostess said. "Right this way."

The look on Lucas's face when he saw them coming was nothing short of priceless. Wade had to fight through the urge to laugh—hard—at his brother's dismay. "Don't mind us," he said.

Lucas scowled at him. "I don't need a babysitter tonight, big brother."

Wade held Mia's chair for her. "Who said anything about babysitting?"

"Go away and sit somewhere else."

"We like it here, close to the fire. Mia is cold."

She shivered dramatically.

Lucas rolled his eyes at them before returning his attention to Amanda.

"Well played, love," Wade said. "You're going to be an awesome sister-in-law."

"You really think so?"

"You already fit in like you've always been here."

"I guess."

"You don't think so?" he asked, surprised to hear that.

"I do... Everyone has been so nice, but I'm sure they're privately reserving final judgment until I prove myself to them."

"You don't have to prove yourself to anyone. The only ones who matter in this equation are you and me."

"That's sweet of you to say, but it's not realistic. We live in Butler, surrounded by your huge, loving family that closes ranks when one of their own is threatened."

"Mia, honey, where is this coming from? I don't feel threatened, and no one in my family thinks I'm being threatened. They can see how happy I am with you."

"They'll be paying very close attention to me and how I treat you, which is totally understandable." She reached across the table and placed her hand on top of his. "They're looking out for you."

"I don't need anyone looking out for me," he said. "Except for you, of course."

"I'll always look out for you, and if I keep doing that, then they'll know my motives are pure and my intentions toward you are honorable." She picked up the menu and opened it. "What's good here?"

"Mia." Wade waited until she put the menu aside to look at him. "You're not on an audition here. I don't want you to think that."

"You're sweet to say so, but I am on an audition with your family. Don't worry, though. I'll win them over. Now, what do you feel like eating?"

Wade let her change the subject, but he remained troubled by what she'd said. He wanted her to feel welcomed and embraced by his family, but he supposed he needed to be realistic and acknowledge that wouldn't happen overnight.

He tried to focus on the menu, but all he could think about was Mia thinking she was on some sort of audition to be part of the Abbott family. She was already an Abbott.

"We should see what's involved with changing your name to Abbott. If you want to, that is."

"I'd like that. I never knew my father, so I have no particular affinity for the name Simpson."

"Hopefully, you'll become very fond of the name Abbott."

"I already am. My *husband* is an Abbott."

Wade smiled. Would it ever get old hearing her refer to him as her husband? "Mia Abbott. I like the sound of that."

"So do I."

The waitress came over with a list of specials that included a vegetarian pasta dish that piqued his interest. "That sounds good to me," he said.

"Make it a double," Mia added.

They ordered white wine that was delivered to their table a few minutes later.

"We're supposed to be spying on Lucas, and all I'm doing is looking at you," he said while they enjoyed their drinks.

"I like when you look at me. I used to stare at you across the table when we'd meet for coffee and wish for everything I have now."

"Did you?"

She nodded. "It was always so hard to leave you and go back to my real life."

"I still wish you'd asked me for help a long time ago."

Running her fingers over the stem of the wineglass, she looked at him. "I used to cry all the way home every time I had to leave you."

"God, Mia…"

Their salads were delivered, and the interruption made Wade realize he hadn't paid an ounce of attention to Lucas or what he was up to. How could he with Mia sitting across from him, sharing her deepest thoughts? What did he care what Lucas was doing?

"I started having panic attacks," she said quietly. "I'd be in line at the bank or getting coffee, and it would come on me out of nowhere. Just sheer panic."

Hearing how she'd suffered made him ache for her and for himself— for all the time they could've been together. "It kills me to hear how hard it was for you."

She forced a smile for his sake. "It was worth it if it was leading me to you."

"You'll never be afraid with me, Mia. Not ever. I promise."

"You're sweet to say so, but that doesn't mean I won't still have the panic attacks."

He understood that she was letting him know that her scars ran deep. "Every day you spend with me will be one day further away from him."

"It might take me a while to stop anticipating disaster."

"I'm not going anywhere. Are you?"

Smiling, she shook her head. "Definitely not."

It was the best first date he'd ever been on, which was no surprise to him. He felt like he'd waited forever for the chance to spend time with Mia, and it didn't matter what they did. If he was with her, he was happy. It really was that simple for him. He loved being able to go home with her afterward, whispering in the dark with her, sleeping with her in his arms and waking up to her face on the pillow next to his.

He'd left her sleeping when he got up to work out and get ready for work. Even his usually solitary morning routine felt less so with her sleeping in the next room.

If he hadn't had the meeting with Amanda, he might've taken the day off, but with her in town only for this week, he needed to take full advantage of her expertise while he could. He experienced a twinge of anxiety leaving Mia alone, but when they'd gotten home last night, he'd shown her where he kept the handgun in a safe on his closet shelf and how to use it.

"I don't think I could do it," she'd said, eyeing the pistol with trepidation.

"If it comes down to your life, you *will* do it. Do it for me. What would I ever do without you?"

"Let's hope it never comes to that."

Wade thought about the conversation on his way into work, unnerved by her reluctance to defend herself. He would talk to her about it again tonight and every night, until she was more comfortable with the idea.

He arrived in the parking lot right after Ella and waited for her to get out of her car.

"How's it going?" she asked.

"Very well. You?"

"I'm fine. Just worried about you."

"Everything's okay, El. We had a great night last night and talked about a lot of things. It's an adjustment for both of us, but we're figuring it out."

"We all have to do that in our own way."

"True."

"I certainly went through it with Gav when we first got together, and we'd known each other for years. We're still figuring it out."

"It helps me to hear that."

"Can I tell you something, and will you promise to keep it between us?"

"Of course."

Her dark eyes shone with joy when she said, "I'm pregnant."

"Oh, El, that's amazing news. I'm so happy for you guys." He hugged her. "I know how much you want to be a mom."

"I'm *so* happy, Wade. I worry all the time that nothing this good can possibly last."

"Sure, it can. Gavin is crazy about you, and he must be thrilled about the baby."

"He is. I can't wait until we can tell people—especially his parents. They'll be so excited."

"Everyone will be. This is such great news."

"We're going to get married in the next few weeks. Just something small for the family."

"Nothing's small with our family."

"That's also true." She placed a hand over her heart. "Sometimes I still can't believe it's real, you know? I wanted him for so long, and now…"

"Now you get forever with him."

Her eyes sparkled with tears. "He's the only thing I've ever really, truly *wanted*."

"I know how you feel. That's how it is for me with Mia."

"How did you end up married before me?" she asked with a playful scowl.

"Damned if I know. All I care about is that it's done and she's mine and no one can ever take her away from me."

"I'm glad you got what you wanted."

"I'm glad you did, too."

She glanced up the stairs that led to the office. "And now we get to go learn about how to orient our lovely sales team to sell sex toys in our country store. This is our life."

Wade laughed. "Let's get it over with. We both have better things to do than worry about work."

"Indeed, we do."

They trudged up the stairs, said good morning to Emma and went to their respective offices.

Amanda was already at work on her laptop in his office. "Morning," she said.

"Morning. You're off to an early start."

"Got a lot to do today."

"How was your dinner?"

"Very nice. Your brother is a sweet guy."

"Hmm. Okay. If you say so."

"He's very charming."

"We're talking about Lucas Abbott, right?"

"Yes," she said, laughing.

"Listen, you seem like a nice person. He's my brother, and I love him. I really do. But he's a world-class player when it comes to women."

"He told me that."

Wade stared at her, shocked. "He did?"

"Uh-huh. He said he's thinking it might be time to change his ways when it comes to women."

"Lucas Abbott said that?"

She laughed. "He sure did."

"Wow. I need a moment to process this."

"Your family should be a reality TV show. You'd be superstars. You're all so funny."

"I'm not being funny. I'm genuinely shocked by this information. Next, you're going to tell me Landon has decided to grow up, too."

"I don't know about that. I only know what Lucas told me about himself."

Hunter came to the door. "Wade, do you have a minute?"

"Sure." To Amanda, he said, "Be right back."

"I'll be here."

Wade grabbed his travel mug of coffee and took it with him to Hunter's office. "What's up?"

"Shut the door, will you?"

A twinge of anxiety hit him in the gut. What now? He shut the door.

"I'm not sure how to tell you this..."

"Whatever it is, Hunter, just say it."

"Mia gave me a fake Social Security number."

At first, the words didn't register. When they did, once again he felt like a trapdoor had opened under him, sending him hurtling through space. What did this mean? "How... How do you know?"

"Because I checked it."

"Why did you do that?"

"I do it for every new employee, regardless of who they are."

Regardless of who they are... "So, you ran Cameron's when she joined the company?"

"Yes."

Wade knew he was focusing on the wrong thing and being unfair to Hunter, but he couldn't seem to wrap his head around the fact that Mia had given them a fake number.

"I asked her to come back in before you left yesterday to confirm the number, and she gave me the same one the second time. It's registered to a woman who died in 1972. It's never been assigned to her."

"I... I have no idea what to do about this."

"I thought you might want to be the one to ask her what's going on."

"Yeah. Okay. Thanks." Wade pushed himself off the door and opened it before turning back to his brother. "Who else knows about this?"

"You and me. And Megan. I told her I didn't know what to do."

Wade nodded and left the room. He went to his office, put the coffee mug on his desk and grabbed his coat.

"Do you want to go over the plan for the meeting today?" Amanda asked him.

"Can't."

"Wade? Are you okay?"

He didn't reply to her or Emma when she asked if he was leaving. He went down the stairs and out the door, the cold air hitting him like a smack to the face. His truck was still warm from the recent ride to town. He directed it toward home, wondering what he was going to hear and how it might change everything.

CHAPTER 23

"When people are living from passion, they tend to be fulfilled, happy, healthy, and love everyone around them."
—Lewis Howes

Mia woke from a deep sleep and stretched muscles that ached in the best possible way. Thinking of Wade and their first official date brought a smile to her face. She didn't normally put out on the first date, but she'd made an exception for her husband. He'd laughed when she told him that.

They laughed a lot together, which was just another thing she loved about being with him. She'd slept better in his arms the last few nights than she had in years and was finally losing the edge of restless exhaustion that had plagued her over the last difficult years.

Hunter had said he'd let her know when they found a job for her within the company, so she had the day free to finish unpacking and getting settled into Wade's cozy home. Last night, he'd told her about a farm he wanted to buy and how it was run-down and needed some TLC to get it back to habitable. The thought of restoring an old farmhouse with him, of filling it with little Abbotts and watching them grow up was better than any fantasy she could've dreamed for her life.

He was better. The reality was better than the dream.

She took a hot shower and washed her hair. Then she put on Wade's robe, which she preferred to her own because it smelled like him, tied it at her waist and went to the kitchen to brew coffee. She was enjoying her first cup when he came in the door, startling her because she hadn't expected him.

"Hey," she said, smiling. "This is a nice surprise. Did you forget something?"

He stood inside the door staring at her, his face devoid of expression.

"Wade? What's wrong?"

"Why did you give Hunter a fake Social Security number?"

Shock ricocheted through her. "*What?* I didn't do that."

"Yes, you did. He ran the number, and it's not assigned to you."

"It's the only one I've ever had."

"It's a fake."

"That's not possible. I've had other jobs with it. How can it be a fake?"

"I was hoping you could tell me that."

Her stomach turned at the cold tone to his voice. She'd never heard that tone from him before, and it frightened her. Right when she felt happy and settled into a new life, the rug was pulled out from under her again. "I'd have to ask my mother where it came from. I've had it all my life."

"Call her."

"It's really early in New Mexico."

He had no reply to that, but it became clear that nothing between them was going to be right again until she could explain how she'd ended up with a fake Social Security number. She picked up the phone and called her mother, waking her well before dawn New Mexico time.

"Mom, it's Mia. Wake up."

"Mmm, I'm awake. What's wrong?"

"I need to ask you something, and I need you to tell me the truth."

"Okay…"

"Why do I have a fake Social Security number?"

Dead silence.

"Mom!"

"Mia…"

"What? Just tell me, will you?"

"I don't know how to tell you this. I've dreaded this day for years…"

Her blood went cold inside her veins. "What are you talking about?"

"Hold on a minute."

Mia's heart raced as she listened to rustling sounds on the other end of the line.

"Okay, I can talk now. Jerry is still asleep." A deep sigh echoed through the line. "I never wanted you to know this. When you were still a baby, your father and I went through a horrible divorce."

"You told me you were never married to him!"

"I know, and I'm so sorry I lied to you. He was going to take you away from me, Mia. His family... They had money and lawyers. I had nothing but you. So I took you, and I ran away."

Mia's legs went liquid under her, and she slid to the floor, leaning back against the cabinets. "You took me from him?" she asked in a whisper.

"I was so afraid, Mia. He was going to win, and I'd never see you again. I didn't know what else to do. I had a friend. He helped me with new identities for both of us. He swore the numbers were legit."

"Oh my God. Mom... You told me you didn't know for sure who my father was, and all this time, I've been living a gigantic *lie*?" She wiped tears that slid down her cheeks. "My whole life, I wondered about him, and you knew exactly where he was."

"Mia, please try to understand."

"No! I don't understand. I'll never understand this!"

Wade came into the kitchen and sat next to her, reaching for her hand.

Mia pulled it back. She couldn't bear to be touched, even by him. "Who is he? Who is my father? And don't you dare lie to me!"

"His name is Cabot Lodge. The last I knew, he lived in Boston."

"I'm from Boston?"

"Yes. You were born there on January twenty-ninth."

Her birth certificate said she was born on February third in Burlington, Vermont. "Is my name really Mia?"

"Yes, that was the one thing I didn't change. But your real name was Mia Elizabeth Lodge. Mia, honey, everything I did was out of love for you."

"No, Mom, this isn't about love."

Her mother's sobs echoed through the phone. "It was about love and fear. I was very young, and his family was prominent and well connected. I'm so sorry you had to find out this way."

"I found out when my new husband's brother checked my Social Security number and discovered it was a fake. Now my new family has yet another reason to wonder about the woman their son and brother has shackled himself to. Thanks for that, Mom."

"You got married? Not to Brody. Please tell me..."

"No, not to Brody." Mia wiped away tears. "To a kind and decent man who has done everything for me, and this is how I thank him. By passing a fake Social Security number to his brother."

"I'm so sorry, honey. All I can do is tell you I did what I thought was best at the time."

"You could've told me this years ago when I turned eighteen. Why didn't you?"

"I was afraid you'd never speak to me again. Tell me that's not going to happen now... Please tell me, Mia."

"I don't know. I don't know anything right now. I have to go."

"Mia, please..."

"I can't, Mom. Not now." Shell-shocked by everything she'd learned, she clicked the button on the phone to end the call.

"What can I do?" Wade asked.

"I'll understand if you want out of this. I would if I were you." She wiped more tears that continued to flow despite her efforts to stop them. "My whole life is a lie. I'm surrounded by criminals. What decent guy needs this crap in his life?"

He reached out to her, but for the first time since she'd known him, she didn't want him to touch her. The information her mother had given her made her feel dirty and unworthy of him.

"I need you in my life," he said.

His sweet words brought more tears to her eyes. "No one needs this insanity. I wouldn't blame you if you said it was too much."

"I want to call Grayson and get him over here to advise you on how to proceed. Would that be okay?"

Since she didn't know what else do, she nodded. Her father was out there. His name was Cabot Lodge. *Cabot Lodge.* Her real name was Mia Lodge. How might her life have turned out differently if she'd known about him? Had he tried to find her? Would he be happy to hear from her?

Wade took the phone from her and called Grayson, asking him to come over right away. "He'll be here in twenty minutes."

"I, um, I should get dressed."

Wade got up and helped her off the floor. "Come here," he said, wrapping his arms around her.

She let him hug her because he seemed to need it, but she didn't return the embrace. How could he love someone who didn't even know who she was? What did Hunter think of her giving him a fake Social Security number, and how had it never been discovered before now? She felt like total shit.

Wade released her, and she went into the bedroom to get dressed, moving through the motions like a robot. Underwear, jeans, sweater. She ran a brush through her hair and made the mistake of looking in the mirror. She looked as bad as she felt.

Standing in the bathroom, she tried to recall every vague answer her mother had ever given her when Mia asked about her father, which she had done frequently until she realized her mother was never going to tell her anything other than she wasn't sure who he was. When she was seventeen and asked her mother how that was possible, she'd said, "Someday, you'll understand."

Well, she didn't understand. She didn't understand any of this.

She heard the house phone ring and Wade talking to someone.

"No," he said. "I won't be back today. Go ahead without me."

He was missing work because of her. How long would it be before he started to hate her for the drama she'd brought into his life?

The phone rang again, and Wade came to the bathroom door. "Your mom is on the phone."

"Tell her I can't talk to her right now."

"She says it's urgent."

Mia took the phone from him. "What?"

"I'm afraid of what will happen if you tell him where I am."

"Because you kidnapped his daughter more than twenty-five years ago?"

"Yes."

"I have to go."

"Mia—"

She pushed the button and handed the portable phone back to Wade. "I think I'm going to be sick."

"Sit," he said, closing the lid on the toilet and bringing the trash can closer in case she needed it. "Take some deep breaths. Find your center."

Mia would've laughed, but he was trying to help her, so she didn't laugh. *Find her center?* She didn't even know who she was. How was she supposed to find her center? Her whole life was a huge lie. She took the breaths and tried to focus on getting air into her lungs rather than thinking about the chaos swirling around her.

"I woke up happy this morning," she said after a long silence.

"Me, too."

"I'm sorry, Wade. I… I didn't know it was fake. I didn't know any of this."

"I know you didn't." He kissed the top of her head. "We'll figure out what to do, okay?"

"It's not your problem. I'd understand if you…"

"What? Left you because of something you didn't know about?"

"It's all so sordid." She shook her head. "It makes me sick. I can't imagine how you must feel."

"I feel sad that you were kept from your father. I feel sad for him that he was kept from you."

"What if… What if he doesn't care about me?"

"He was fighting for custody of you. It's probably safe to assume he cares—and that he'll care greatly about hearing from you."

A knock sounded on the front door.

Wade kissed the top of her head. "That'll be Grayson. Come out whenever you're ready, okay?"

"Okay."

He left her, and she took a few minutes to pull herself together before she joined them in the living room.

"Hey, Mia," Grayson said as he accepted a cup of coffee from Wade. "I was going to call you guys this morning. I talked to the *Herald* reporter, and it turns out that while the reporter wouldn't say who his source was, he confirmed the person was at the yoga retreat where you met. That's how the reporter confirmed you guys have known each other for two years."

"Well, that's one mystery solved," Wade said.

Mia couldn't make herself care that they'd resolved that issue when another one required her full attention. Would it ever end?

"Has there been a development in the case with your ex?" Grayson asked.

She shook her head. "No, something else."

"Do you want me to tell him, hon?"

She didn't know what she wanted. "Sure, thanks."

Wade told Grayson what'd happened that morning, from Hunter alerting him to the fake Social Security number through her call to her mother and what had been uncovered.

"Holy shit," Grayson said on a long exhale. "Your dad is *Cabot Lodge*?"

"That's what she said. Why? Who is he?"

"He's a Boston city councilman. Has been for more than twenty years. His search for the daughter who was abducted by her mother is big news in Boston. He's never stopped talking about you or looking for you. His family is very prominent in the city. His grandfather was the mayor. His mother's family was in the steel business. They're loaded."

Mia absorbed the information like a hungry sponge. The most important thing she heard was that her father had never stopped looking for her. "I... I need to get in touch with him."

"He's going to be elated, Mia. I knew him a little when I lived in Boston. There was always something so sad about him. People said that losing you broke him."

"What will happen to my mother when this gets out?"

"I don't know. I could put out some feelers and find out, if you want me to. We should do that first. We may be able to negotiate leniency for your mother because she told you."

"Only because I forced her to. How is it possible that no one discovered the fake number before now?"

"They probably didn't check it. Most people aren't as thorough as Hunter is."

"That's a fact," Wade said. "He takes anal to a whole new level."

"I might never have known this," Mia said. "I could've gone my whole life thinking my father didn't give a shit about me, when in reality…"

"He's been searching for you all this time."

"I don't want him to wait any longer," Mia said. "He's waited long enough."

"Let me make a few calls," Grayson said. "I have contacts in Boston who can advise me on how best to proceed."

Wade handed him the phone and then put his arm around Mia.

"You have an important meeting at work today."

"Nothing is more important to me than you are."

Grayson paced the length of the living room as he made one call after another, working from the contacts in a cell phone that was otherwise useless to him in Butler. "She's concerned about what'll happen to her mother," he said. "No, I think that needs to be a condition of her coming forward. She'd like to meet him, but she wants to know first what'll happen to her mother." After a pause, he said, "Let me give you the number where I can be reached." He gave them Wade's number and ended the call, promising to wait to hear back from whomever he was talking to.

"That was the agent in charge of the FBI's Boston office," he said.

Oh my God, Mia thought. *The FBI?*

"The case got a lot of attention when the abduction first happened. There's been a warrant for your mother's arrest since the day you disappeared." The date he mentioned would've been when she was just over a year old. For twenty-seven years, her mother had been wanted by the FBI. Dear God. How was that possible?

They waited a very long hour before the phone rang again.

Grayson took the call and did a lot of listening before he said he'd consult with her and get back to them. "He spoke to the US attorney, and it's not as simple as you not wanting her charged."

"I would very much like to meet my father, but the only way that's going to happen is if there are guarantees that my mother won't be charged. That's my final offer." She had no idea where the strength was coming from, but she knew this was her only chance to negotiate leniency for her mother. Whether she thought her mother deserved it was a debate for another time.

"I'll call them back." Grayson made the call and conveyed her wishes to the US attorney. After he hung up, he said, "They're notifying your father now that you've made contact. He has to agree before they can accept your condition."

Mia's hands were sweaty and her stomach felt sick. Needing to move, she got up and went into the kitchen to do the few dishes that were in the sink.

The phone rang, and she jolted.

"This is Grayson Coleman." He was quiet for a long time, so long that Mia's nerves were completely shredded by the time he said, "Got it. Okay. Will do." Grayson stood to face her. "Your father has agreed to allow the charges against your mother to be dropped in exchange for the opportunity to see you. The prosecutor said he cried when they told him you'd been found. The only thing he wanted to know was how soon he could see you."

Overwhelmed.

That was the only word Mia could think of to describe the emotions swirling inside her. Her father had cried when he heard she'd been found.

That news brought new tears to her eyes. He wanted to see her so badly, he was willing to drop the charges against her mother.

"We'll go to Boston today," Wade said. "Right now."

"You have work and things… Amanda is here. The store."

"Fuck that. I'm taking you to Boston to meet your father. Today."

CHAPTER 24

"Marriages... need constant nurturing... the secret of having it all is loving it all."
—Dr. Joyce Brothers

Less than an hour later, they were on Interstate 93 South for the three-hour trip to Boston. Wade had called Hunter to let him know what'd happened and asked him to pass the word to the rest of the family that they were going to Boston and would be back in the next day or two.

"Are you freaking kidding me?" Hunter had said when Wade told him what had come of the fake Social Security number.

"I wish I was."

"How's Mia?"

"Rattled and shocked and... I don't know." She'd kept her distance from him since learning of her mother's deception. He hoped that once she got her head wrapped around it, she would turn toward him rather than away. But for right now, there was only distance as she processed this latest blow.

"Let us know if you guys need anything," Hunter had said. "I assume it's okay to tell the others?"

"Yeah, go ahead. It's not going to be a secret for long." Wade dreaded the publicity that would rain down on Mia once it got out that Cabot Lodge's long-lost daughter had been found. Hell, something that sensational would probably make the national news. He hoped the mess with Brody didn't get brought into it, too.

As they drove out of the mountains, Mia's phone came to life, beeping with texts and voice-mail messages.

"Do you want to check that?" he asked.

"It's probably more stuff about the *other* criminal case."

"It might be your mother trying to call you again."

Mia withdrew the phone from her purse. "I'll text her to tell her I took care of getting the charges dropped and that she should leave me alone for the time being."

"That's probably for the best. You can reach out to her when you're ready to."

"*If* I'm ready to." She looked over at him. "It was bad enough that I brought the Brody crap into your life. If I'd had any idea this was going to happen, too..."

"What? You wouldn't have come?"

"No, I wouldn't have."

"Why do you think this changes anything for me?"

"It should change everything. Your wife isn't who she said she was. She's running around with a fake Social Security number." She shook her head. "It's sordid and disgusting and horrible."

"Sweetheart, just like what happened with Brody, this was done *to* you. You're a victim in both cases."

"I've attracted the wrong kind of people from the day I was born."

"You can't help who you were born to or what happened to you when you were too little to have a say in it. That's no reflection on you."

"How can it not be? She *raised* me. She taught me the difference between right and wrong, and all that time, she was keeping me hidden from my heartbroken father? How do I ever reconcile that?"

"It'll take some time to wrap your head around it, but you have to keep telling yourself you had nothing to do with what went down between your parents, Mia. You were a helpless baby caught in the middle. What your mother did was wrong, but she probably did it out of love for you."

"Or so she says."

"Have you ever doubted for a minute that she loved you?"

"No. She used to say it was the two of us against the world."

"Did you have everything you needed growing up?"

She nodded. "We were never well off, but she worked two jobs to pay the rent and put food on the table. She came to all my stuff at school and was my Girl Scout leader for a couple of years."

"That sounds like a very dedicated mom to me."

"How could she take me from him, though? How could she do that to a man she must've loved at some point? She was *married* to him."

"I don't know, honey. My mom always says no one knows what goes on inside a marriage except for the two people in it."

"I suppose that's true. What if he's a bad guy like Brody?"

"Gray said he's very well respected in Boston."

"Brody was well respected in Rutland."

"He cried when he heard you'd been found. That says a lot to me about what kind of guy he might be."

"Yeah, I guess."

"You have good reason to be wary where men are concerned, Mia. Reserve judgment until you meet him. Nothing says you have to welcome him into your life. You're doing the decent thing by going to meet him. Whatever happens after that is up to you."

"I'm still getting used to having the power to determine my own life."

"You're the boss, baby. Whatever you want is what you should have."

"Is it really that simple?"

"It is for me."

"What if I said my fondest desire is to live in Europe? Would you move with me?"

"Honestly, I don't know. I want to be where you are, but I sure do love living in Vermont and working at the store with my family, as annoying as they can be sometimes. Maybe we could compromise by living somewhere in Europe for a month and visiting other places while we're there?"

"I don't really want to live in Europe. I was just wondering what you'd say to that."

"Oh, phew. That's a relief, because I wasn't sure how I could help you make that happen."

"I do like the idea of a month there sometime. That'd be fun."

"Yes, it would. Where would you like to go?"

"I've never been anywhere, so it wouldn't matter to me where we went. Anything would be an adventure."

"We'll have lots of adventures together." He reached out over the console. "My hand is feeling lonely over here by itself."

Smiling faintly, she took his hand.

"Ahh, that's better," he said, relieved to feel her coming around after the terrible shock she'd sustained earlier.

"When are you going to tell me I'm too much trouble?"

"When you're too much trouble."

"Seriously, Wade."

"I'm dead serious. We're not there. If we get there, you'll be the first to know."

Lincoln Abbott slid into the booth across from his father-in-law, Elmer, who already had a cup of coffee in front of him.

Megan brought over a cup for Linc and filled it at the table.

"Thank you, honey."

"You're here about Mia," she said. "Move over."

Startled, Lincoln slid over to make room for her in the booth.

Elmer smiled at her. "You're definitely an Abbott now, sweetheart."

"Thank you. I learned through years of observation. What do you know?"

"I know that she gave Hunter her SSN when she applied for a job with the company, and when he checked it, it came back registered to some woman who died in 1972."

Elmer's eyes bugged.

"Wait," Megan said to her grandfather-in-law. "You haven't heard anything yet."

"Hunter told Wade, and he went home to ask Mia why she gave Hunter a fake SSN."

"What did she say?" Elmer asked, hanging on his son-in-law's every word.

"She said it's the same one she's always had, and she called her mother to ask where it came from. That's when she found out that her mother *kidnapped* her during a custody dispute when Mia was a baby."

Elmer blinked rapidly, his mouth falling open and snapping shut.

"All this time," Linc added, "her father has been looking for her. He's a bigwig in Boston. Grayson knows him and had heard about the guy's missing daughter. Apparently, he never stopped looking for her."

"This is just unbelievable," Elmer said. "Poor Mia must be reeling."

"She is," Linc said. "Wade called Hunter to tell him what was going on. They're on their way to Boston now so she can meet her dad."

"What I want to know," Elmer said, "is what about her mother? What happens there?"

"From what Wade told Hunter," Megan said, "they got Grayson involved, and he talked to the US attorney, who agreed to drop the charges after he talked to the father. Mia said she'd only meet him if the charges against her mother were dropped."

"You gotta wonder how she feels about her mother after finding out she kept this from her all her life," Linc said. "And the poor father. My heart just breaks for him."

"This young lady our Wade has hitched his wagon to certainly hasn't led a boring life," Elmer said.

"To be fair, none of it was her doing," Linc said.

"But still..." Elmer said. "It's a lot."

"It's a lot for a new couple in a new marriage to deal with," Megan said.

"Right," Elmer agreed. "But he does seem very..."

"Smitten," Lincoln said. "He's gone over the girl. That's obvious to everyone who's seen them together. Even Mrs. Hendricks said something to me about how happy they seem when I saw her at the post office earlier."

"Mia is the most interesting person to land in Butler since Cameron hit Fred," Megan said.

The two men laughed at her blunt assessment.

"That she is," Lincoln said.

"Although we had plenty of interesting people around here before then," Elmer said. "Take yourself, for instance."

"Awww, you're very sweet to say so, Elmer, but I'm nowhere near as interesting as Cameron and Lucy and Mia."

"Why would you say such a thing?" a deep, familiar voice asked from behind her.

Megan spun around to find her husband standing behind her, his brows furrowed. "I just meant that they've been out in the world and I haven't. That's all."

"That doesn't make you less interesting than they are," Hunter said.

"That's right, honey," Elmer said, patting her hand. "Look at what you've done with your little corner of Butler. You've created a spot many people think of as a second home. That doesn't just happen. It's because you make us feel welcome here."

"I… I didn't mean to start something. I was just making conversation." Megan got up from the booth. "I'll let you guys talk." She took off toward the kitchen.

"I'll, um… I'll be right back." Hunter went after his wife.

"Ah, young love," Elmer said, watching Hunter go. "Never does run smooth, does it?"

"Sometimes it does," Lincoln said. "Take me and Molly, for instance."

"We have a deal," Elmer said, scowling. "You are never to talk about my daughter in that context."

"What? I simply said that young love ran smoothly for us."

"I believe you've provided ample evidence of that in the ten hoodlums you produced."

Lincoln smiled broadly. "We did, didn't we?"

Elmer frowned. "That topic in relation to my daughter is *off*-limits."

"Yes, sir," Lincoln said, rubbing a hand over his mouth to keep from laughing.

Hunter caught up with Megan in the office and was horrified to find her in tears. "Megan, honey… What is it?"

"I don't know," she said, wiping tears on her sleeve. "I have no idea what just happened. One minute, I was gossiping with your dad and grandfather, and the next, I was making myself feel inadequate, and now I'm crying because you heard me say that, and I don't want you to ever think of me as anything less than—"

He kissed her until she stopped talking and went slack in his arms. "I don't even know where to begin with this. *Nothing* about you is inadequate to me. In fact, you are very, *very* adequate, as you well know."

"I think I might be pregnant. Why else would I be acting like this?"

"When can we take the test?"

"When I get home?"

"Let's go home."

"I can't go now. I have to clean up and make the schedule and—"

"We'll come back later. I'll help you with all of it."

"I'm scared."

"Of what?"

"What if I'm a bad mother?"

"Megan, oh my God. Where is this coming from? You're going to be an *amazing* mother. Our kids will be so lucky to have you. *I'm* lucky to have you. No more beating up on my wife. I love her so much. I can't bear to hear *anyone* speak poorly of her. You got me?"

Nodding, she wiped away more tears.

"Let's go." He untied her apron and raised it over her head and relieved her of the half-empty coffeepot she still had in her hand. Then he bundled her into her coat and led her out the back door to her car, which was closer than his, parked across the street at the store.

Hunter drove them home, taking occasional glances at her. "Hey," he said.

She looked at him.

"No matter what, it's all good. Okay?"

"Okay."

He pulled into the driveway and had the driver's door open before he shut off the engine. Reaching over, he released her seat belt. "Come on."

They went inside, and Hunter directed her straight upstairs to their room.

"Am I allowed to take my coat off?" she asked, amused by his haste.

"Only if you do it quickly."

She took off the coat and tossed it on the bed.

"Do you need my help?"

"I think I can pee by myself, but thanks for the offer."

Smiling, he kissed her and nudged her toward the bathroom.

They'd been trying for a while and had stocked up on pregnancy tests. They'd done this a few times, so he knew he needed to wait only a few minutes, but this was the first time she'd thought she might actually be pregnant. That few minutes might as well have been hours as far as he was concerned.

He was on the verge of hyperventilating when she said, "Hunter."

"What?"

"Come here."

Hunter went into the bathroom where Megan stood looking down at the counter. He remembered installing the slab of slate with the vessel sink. He'd never imagined that one day that slab of slate would figure into one of the most important moments of his life.

"Do you see?" Megan asked, her voice higher than usual.

"I see." The gigantic plus sign was hard to miss.

"We did it," she said softly.

"We did it and we did it and we did it, and now…" He couldn't seem to stop looking at that plus sign, until she tugged on the sleeve of his shirt.

Then he looked at her, and the punch of love that hit him was so big, it nearly consumed him. He wrapped his arms around her and held on tight. "We did it," he whispered.

"You're gonna be a daddy."

"And you're gonna be a mommy. Best day ever."

She nodded. "Best day ever."

"In case I forgot to mention it on the best day ever, I love you so much."

She smiled up at him. "I love you, too."

CHAPTER 25

"Being deeply loved by someone gives you strength, while loving someone deeply gives you courage."
—Lao Tzu

"I'm scared," Mia confessed as they drove into Boston in rush-hour traffic that moved so slowly, it only added to her hyped-up anxiety.

"Of what?"

"Meeting him. What if he doesn't like me?"

"Mia, honey, he's going to love you, at first because he doesn't have to look for you or miss you anymore. And then when he gets to know you, he will love you for *you*. How could he not?"

"And you're not at all biased."

"I'm super biased. I love you best of all. I'm afraid you'll forget all about me when you meet your dad."

"I won't do that."

"Promise?"

"Yes, Wade. I promise."

"I'll be right there with you. There's nothing to be afraid of. He's going to be thrilled."

"This has been the weirdest day of my life, and my life has had a lot of weird days. When I woke up, I'd planned to finish unpacking and then stop by the store to see if you wanted to have lunch."

"I'll always want to have lunch with you."

"How do you know that?"

"How long will it be before you believe that I'm in this for keeps?"

"I don't know. No one has ever wanted to keep me before—at least not for the right reasons."

"Well, now someone does."

"I'm still getting used to that."

"That's okay. Take all the time you need."

The GPS took them to the address Grayson had given them. He'd told them it was in Beacon Hill, one of the swankier neighborhoods in Boston.

"I've never been here," she said, taking in the sights of the city.

"No?"

She shook her head. "I've hardly been anywhere. We didn't have much money growing up, and since I've been on my own, all I seem to do is work and scrape by."

"We'll go anywhere you want. We'll see it all."

"What about that farm you want to buy?"

"We'll do that, too."

"And how will we afford all these things we're going to do?"

"We'll work hard and save our money and do a lot of the work to the house ourselves. We'll make it happen, babe."

"You make me believe it."

"You can believe it. It's all happening. It's already happening." He leaned forward for a closer look at the numbers on the brick-fronted town houses. "That's it right there. Now to find a parking place."

They circled the block twice before Wade found a spot and parallel parked. He shut off the engine and turned to her. "How're you feeling?"

"I'm a mess."

"No, you're not. You look beautiful, as always."

"Thank you, but I'm a mess on the inside."

"Look at me."

She shifted her gaze toward him.

"It's going to be great. I promise."

"Stay close."

"Nowhere else I'd rather be than close to you."

Wade held her hand while they walked around the block to her father's house. Her father... Oh God, she was actually going to meet her *father*!

As they approached the stone stairs to his house, the door flew open and a man let out a shout that startled her. He charged down the stairs and had her in his arms before she could begin to prepare herself.

"My baby girl," he said between sobs. "You've finally come home."

He smelled the way a dad should, like aftershave and starch. That was the first thought she had.

With his hands on her shoulders, he stepped back and took a long look at her. His eyes were red and his face puffy, as if he'd been crying for hours. He had gray hair and a youthful, handsome face. She thought he looked kind, if that was possible.

"You're so beautiful," he said, still staring at her.

"Thank you. Um, this is my husband, Wade."

"Oh, you're married! My goodness." He shook Wade's hand. "It's nice to meet you."

"You, too, sir."

"Please, call me Cabot."

"I will. Thank you."

"Where're my manners? It's freezing. Come inside. Please." He led the way up the stairs and ushered them into the house.

Only when she entered the warm house did Mia realize she was freezing.

A woman joined them, covering her mouth as tears ran down her face.

"This is my sister, Emily," Cabot said. "Emily, meet your niece, Mia."

She had an aunt. Mia hadn't considered that her father would come with a family. *Her* family.

"I'm sorry, but I have to hug you," Emily said. "I hope that's okay."

"Oh, um, sure," Mia said, accepting the other woman's embrace.

"We're making you uncomfortable," Cabot said, "but you have no idea how hard we've prayed for this day."

"Is she here?" a young woman called as she came from the back of the house, skidding to a stop when she saw them in the foyer.

"This is my daughter, Caroline," Emily said. "Caroline, this is your cousin, Mia."

"Nice to meet you," Caroline said, shaking Mia's hand. She had dark hair and big brown eyes.

A cousin! She had a cousin. "You, too."

"Let me take your coats," Cabot said.

She and Wade took off their coats and handed them to him.

Mia grasped Wade's hand, and he gave her a squeeze that helped to calm her. All her life, her family had been her, her mother and her late grandfather. And now... "Is there more?" she asked. "Family, I mean?"

"I also have two brothers." Cabot led them into the kitchen, located in the back of the long, narrow town house. "Fischer is in Philadelphia, and Morgan is in DC, or they'd be here. Fischer has two kids, and Morgan has three."

"Do you have others?" Mia asked Emily.

"Just this one," she said, putting an arm around her daughter.

"What about you?" Mia asked her dad. "Do you have other kids?"

He shook his head. "Only you."

"You can't know what he's been through," Emily said, giving her brother an empathetic look.

"Don't, Em," he said, his mouth set in a hard expression. "It's not her fault."

"I'm sorry for everything that happened," Mia said. "I had no idea. If I had known, I would've gotten in touch long before now."

"It's not your fault, and you have nothing to be sorry about. I want you to know... I never stopped looking for you. I can't believe you were as close as Vermont all this time." He seemed to try to rally, forcing a smile. "So how long have you been married?"

"Not even a week," Mia said, smiling at Wade.

"Oh my goodness! You're newlyweds. Did you have a big wedding?"

"No, my grandfather is a JP, and he married us. We were in a bit of a rush."

Cabot covered his heart with his hand. "Don't tell me you're already going to make me a grandfather," he said with a teasing smile. "I'm not sure I'm ready for that."

Mia glanced at Wade.

He nodded, encouraging her to share with her father what she'd been through.

"I met Wade almost two years ago, and a lot has happened since then."

Three hours later, they checked into the Westin Copley Place, a gift arranged by her father for the newlyweds.

Mia exclaimed when she saw the suite he had reserved for them. "This is crazy! I've never seen a hotel room this nice except on TV!"

Wade took pleasure in her delight, as he had during the evening they'd spent with her family. Her father had hung on her every word and wanted to hear the details of her life, no matter how insignificant. It had pained him to hear of her ordeal with Brody and that she'd been abused by him.

"He'll never get near her again," Wade had assured Cabot when he'd asked Wade what was being done to keep Brody away from Mia.

Emily had ordered pizza, and Mia had spoken to her two uncles on the phone. She'd heard about her grandparents and her father's life and had gotten to know Caroline, who was a recent college graduate.

It had been quite a day, to say the least. When Hunter had first told him about the phony Social Security number, Wade's imagination had gone in unsettling directions, but he couldn't have imagined the series of events that information had triggered. He couldn't begin to know how Mia must feel.

She stood at the window, gazing out at the view of Boston, the Charles River and Fenway Park. "My dad has been here all this time, searching for me. My mom knew that. She knew he would be devastated to lose me." Mia glanced at Wade. "How could she do that to him or to me?"

"I don't know, honey."

"Losing me broke his heart. Emily said he's hardly been on a date since my mother left him and took me. It's so sad."

He held her from behind, his chin propped on her head. "It really is."

"Can we promise each other that, no matter what happens between us, we'll never do anything like that to each other?"

"I can make that promise."

"Me, too. I could never do that to you."

"I could never do it to you either."

"I'm glad we have that resolved." Her smile was reflected in the window. "Thank you for making this trip with me. I never could've done it without you with me."

"Yes, you could have. You don't give yourself enough credit for how strong you've been for such a long time."

"I like the way I look to you."

He pressed his cock against her ass. "I like the way you look to me, too."

She laughed. "That's not what I meant."

"I know," he said, chuckling. "I'm a newlywed. I can't help it."

She turned to face him. "What a week this has been. I got a husband, more in-laws than I can count, a father, an aunt, two uncles and six cousins."

"Don't forget a niece and a nephew," Wade said, amused by her inventory.

"How could I forget them?"

"Ella told me this morning that she's expecting, too, but they're keeping it secret for a while longer."

"That's great news. I'm so used to being on my own, and suddenly I have a huge family."

"You're definitely not alone anymore."

She kissed his neck. "My new husband is my favorite new family member."

"Is he?"

"Uh-huh. He's been so sweet and supportive and understanding of the insanity I brought into his well-ordered life."

"His well-ordered life was kind of boring before you showed up."

"Was it?"

Nodding, he gazed down at her, drinking in every detail of her sweet face. "Your dad said it's going to be like a spring day tomorrow. What do you say we stick around so you can spend more time with him and we can enjoy some warm weather before we head back to the frozen tundra?"

"That'd be okay with me if you can be gone that long."

"It's fine. Ella will cover for me, and I'll pay her back when she takes off to have the baby. That's how we roll in my family." He checked his watch. "Speaking of my family, I should check in. They're probably going nuts waiting to hear how it all went."

"Use my phone." She handed it to him. "Do you know how?"

"Yes, smartass. I do. Max has one."

She shook her head and laughed. "I can't deal with this cell-phone-free planet you people live on."

"*Us* people? Hate to break it to you, sweetheart, but you're one of us people on that planet, and this thing is no good to you in my world."

"That's gonna take some adjusting."

"No worries." He kissed her. "I'll keep you so busy, you'll never miss it." Wade dialed the number, sat on the bed and waited for one of his parents to pick up.

"Hey, Mom, it's Wade."

"Oh, honey. I'm so glad you called. How did it go?"

"It was great. Mia's dad is very nice and so happy to have found her."

"I'll never understand how her mother could've done that to him—or to Mia."

"I'm trying to keep an open mind about her. Two sides to every story and all that."

"Still…"

"I know."

"How's Mia?"

"She's overwhelmed but good. I think."

She smiled and gave him a thumbs-up.

"It's been quite a week for her—and me. It'll take us a while to process, but it's all good. Her dad wants to have a wedding for us."

"That would be nice."

"I was hoping you'd think so."

"Of course I do, Wade. A blind person could see how happy you are with her."

"I am happy." He held out his hand to Mia, and she came to sit on his lap. Wrapping his arm around her, he anchored her to him. "We're going to stay here for a couple of nights. Give her a chance to get to know her dad before we head home. Will you spread the word and let Dad know I'll be out of work?"

"I will."

"Tell Ella she's in charge. She'll know what needs to be done."

"Will do. Oh wait, Dad is saying something. Apparently, Amanda decided to extend her stay into next week, so don't worry about the employee training. It's been postponed until you get back."

Wade wondered if either of his younger brothers had something to do with Amanda's decision to stay longer. "They should feel free to proceed without me."

Molly laughed. "I'll let Dad know that."

"Please do."

"Enjoy yourselves in Boston."

"Oh, we will."

Mia elbowed him, making him laugh.

"That's my signal to say good night, and I love you."

"Love you, too, Mom." He ended the call and handed the phone to Mia.

"Such a nice boy," she said, smoothing her free hand over his face.

"Because I love my mom?"

"That's one of many reasons."

He fell back on the bed, bringing her with him. "Tell me the others."

From her perch on top of him, she said, "You're kind and thoughtful and funny, and you let me bomb into your house with my drama and my stuff and you never blinked an eye. You were sweet to me from the first time we ever talked, and my first impression of you has never changed. And—"

Wade kissed her because he couldn't wait another minute to taste her lips. He felt like it'd been days since he last kissed her like this, when really, it hadn't even been twelve hours.

"And you're so sexy," she whispered. "The hottest guy I've ever met."

"No way."

"Yes, you are."

He rolled his eyes. "Whatever you say."

"That's right. I'm your wife, and what I say goes."

"Wow, I walked right into that trap, didn't I?"

She giggled with delight.

He ached with love for her. Kissing her again, he said, "I've never been so happy to be trapped."

CHAPTER 26

"Where we love is home—home that our feet may
leave, but not our hearts."
—Oliver Wendell Holmes Sr.

In the morning, Wade introduced Mia to the fine art of room-service breakfast, which he served her in bed. They fed each other oatmeal, toast with strawberry preserves and fruit while drinking coffee from a cup they shared. The hotel had even provided soy milk, which impressed her greatly.

"Best breakfast ever," she said with a sigh. "I love room service. Can we get it at home?"

Wade smiled, delighted by her. "I'll be your room-service waiter whenever you want breakfast in bed."

"Ohhh, don't make promises you can't keep."

"I never would. You want it, you got it."

She gazed at him with love and a hint of wariness that got his attention.

"What're you thinking?"

"Nothing."

"Don't say nothing when I can tell it's something."

She rolled her lip between her teeth. "You're not going to suddenly get different or remote or weird or mean or anything like that, are you?"

"I'm not planning to."

"Do people actually plan to turn into jerks?"

"I think some people are born that way. The rest of us would rather be nice than be jerks. My grandfather says you get much further in life with sugar than you ever will with vinegar."

"He's so cute." She looked at him with those gorgeous navy-blue eyes that had captivated him from the start, her hair like a gold-spun halo around her face. "I used to think the bad boys were sexy. Now I know better. Good guys who are also sexy is where it's at."

He drew her into a kiss. "I still can't believe I get to kiss you every day for the rest of my life."

"Yes, please do." Her focus shifted to his lips. "I love kissing you. I knew I would."

"Did you?"

Nodding, she said, "All the time we were apart, I imagined what it would be like to be with you this way."

"And? Is it living up to the hype?"

"It's so much better. So, so much better. If I'd had a day like yesterday before I had you, I would've been a disaster. Knowing you have my back…"

He wrapped his arms around her. "I always have your back."

She nuzzled his neck and squirmed on top of him. "Get back in bed."

"Yes, dear."

"Will you always be so agreeable?" she asked when he had her snuggled into his embrace.

"If my wife is asking me to come back to bed, then yes, I will always be agreeable."

Her giggle made him smile. That was quickly becoming one of his favorite sounds.

"You know what we have to do while we're here?"

"What?"

He took her left hand and kissed the ring he'd recently put on her finger. "We need to get something sparkly to go along with your wedding ring since we skipped the whole engagement portion of the let's-get-married program."

She withdrew her hand. "We don't need that."

"What if I need it? If we'd had a traditional relationship, we would've dated for a week, maybe two, and then I would've gotten down on one knee and asked you to marry me. And I would've had a ring for you."

She raised a brow. "A week, maybe two?"

"If it took that long for me to beg you to marry me as soon as possible."

"You're being silly."

"No, I'm not. I told myself a long time ago that if I ever got a chance with you, I'd make it permanent as fast as I possibly could. So, as you can see, you showing up needing me to marry you worked out rather well for both of us."

"I don't need a ring."

"I want you to have one."

"You want to buy that farm and go on a honeymoon. We shouldn't spend money on a ring we don't need."

"You know what happens when you live like a monk and work all the time and don't date or go out because the woman you want isn't available?"

"What?" she asked, sounding somewhat breathless.

"You sock away a lot of money. You can have a ring and a honeymoon and the farm. If you like the place when you see it, that is."

"I can't wait to see it."

"So, yes to the ring?"

"If you insist," she said with a sigh.

"I insist."

After spending the rest of the morning in bed, they dragged themselves into the shower.

Wade got dressed, and while Mia dried her hair, he turned on the TV where the lead story on the local news was the resolution of Boston City Councilman Cabot Lodge's decades-long quest to find his missing daughter.

The story included an interview with Cabot, who was tearful while talking about his daughter. "Yesterday was the second-best day of my life," he said, reading from a statement, "second only to the day Mia was born. I'm so thankful to have met my beautiful daughter and her husband and to have her back in my life. I can't say enough about the people who supported me during this long ordeal, particularly my late parents, my siblings, nieces and nephews. I never gave up on finding her, and I never stopped loving her." They showed a photo taken last night of Mia standing between Wade and Cabot that he must've provided.

"Such a great outcome to a heartbreaking story," one of the anchors said.

"I know Cabot," the other anchor said, "and can attest to how difficult this situation has been for him. I think I speak for everyone here when I send him our sincere congratulations that his long search has ended so happily."

"Indeed," the other anchor said. "Let's talk about this weather!"

Wade breathed a sigh of relief that there'd been no mention of Mia's connection to Brody in the report.

The local meteorologist explained the reason for the rare seventy-degree day in January as a convergence of high- and low-pressure systems that would give Boston one day of springlike weather before the cold returned the next day.

"It's going to get up to seventy today," Wade told Mia when she emerged from the bathroom wearing the hotel robe.

"In January?"

"A freak weather event. Your dad was just on. They interviewed him about finally finding you and showed a picture of the three of us together."

"It's so weird to be part of things that make the news. I'm looking forward to returning to my normal, boring life that doesn't include reporters."

"Your new life will never be boring, babe," he said with a rakish grin.

"You know what I mean."

"I do. You're not comfortable in the spotlight."

"Not at all."

"Hopefully, it won't be on you for much longer. But we don't need to think about that today. We have the whole afternoon before we're due to meet your dad for dinner. Let's go check out Boston on this gorgeous day."

"I'd love to."

They went to the top of the Prudential Building, strolled along the Charles, had lunch at Faneuil Hall, walked through the Boston Commons and sat in the grass to soak up the warm sunshine.

"Such a beautiful day," Mia said, reclining on her elbows, her face turned toward the sun.

"It's like a little gift in the middle of winter," Wade said, looking at her rather than the blue sky. She was much more beautiful, wearing a lightweight maroon sweater and jeans. If she was nearby, he'd rather look at her than anything else. "Next stop is the jewelry store. I saw one a couple of blocks over that looked nice."

She reached for him, and he leaned over her, waiting to see what she would do while she fixed his hair and studied his face.

"What?"

"I like to look at you."

"I was just thinking the same thing—about you, of course." He kissed her, wishing there was time to linger. But there'd be time to linger later. "Come on. We've got things to do." He helped her up and laced his fingers through hers for the short walk to the store he'd spotted earlier.

Inside the store, a clerk asked if they needed help.

"I need an engagement ring for my lovely wife," Wade said.

"I think that might be the first time I've had that request."

Smiling, Wade glanced at Mia. "We've done everything out of order, but that's okay. It works for us."

The clerk showed them a stunning array of rings in a wide variety of cuts and settings.

"Which one do you like, hon?" Wade asked.

Mia shook her head. "I could never decide. I'm not even supposed to be here for this."

"That's true," Wade said, eyeing the rings and zeroing in on the one his eye kept coming back to. "I like this one." He picked up the ring for a closer look. The band was made of tiny diamonds, and the diamond in the middle was surrounded by a circle of smaller stones. "What do you think?"

"That's way too much."

"You said it's my decision. This is the one I like for you. Let me see it on you." He took her left hand and slid it on next to her wedding band. "That's really pretty. Don't you think?"

"Wade…" She shook her head.

"You don't like it?"

"Anyone would like that ring, but you don't have to—"

He leaned in to kiss her. "I know I don't have to. I *want* to. Please?"

A sniffling sound diverted his attention from Mia. The clerk dabbed at a tear. "You two are simply adorable."

Mia laughed. "*He* is adorable."

"You both are," the clerk said. "It does my heart good to meet two people who obviously belong together."

Smiling, Wade gazed at Mia. "Say yes to the ring, my love. Jennifer says we belong together. The ring will seal the deal."

Mia looked down at the ring and then back up at him. "I say yes to the ring and to you and to everything."

After having dinner with Mia's father, they drove home to Vermont the next day. Cabot had promised to come to Butler for a visit in the next few weeks, and they'd exchanged phone numbers so they could stay in touch between visits.

"What're you going to do about your mom?" Wade asked as they crossed the Vermont state border.

"I guess I'll call her when we get home. It'll take a while for us to get past this, but I don't want to be estranged from her."

"I'm trying to picture us having a real wedding and both of your parents being there."

"I won't invite her. That wouldn't be fair to Cabot. She got all the other big moments in my life. That one should belong to him. As far as I'm concerned, there's no need for them to ever see each other again."

"That might be for the best."

Outside of Butler, not far from where Ella and Gavin lived, Wade took a detour to show Mia the farm he'd looked at a couple of times. The last time he'd been here, the project had interested him, but not enough to pull the trigger on the purchase. Now that he had a wife, a family of his own, his thoughts had again returned to the farm. While he loved his current home, it was small—too small to add to their family someday.

He parked the truck in front of the ramshackle house and killed the engine. "Try not to see what it looks like now, but instead imagine what's possible."

"I love all the land and the view of the mountains in the distance."

"The view was one of the first things I loved about it, too. Let's go take a look."

"Are we allowed to go in?" Mia asked when they walked toward the sagging front porch.

"I know the owners. They won't care."

"What is it with people in this town not locking their doors?"

"That's Butler for you." He opened the door and gestured for her to go in ahead of him. The interior was dirty and ridden with cobwebs and reeked of neglect. "I was thinking we could remove some walls, open up the kitchen into the living and dining rooms. New floors and windows, rebuild the fireplace. That could be an office in there, and there're three bedrooms and two bathrooms upstairs, one of them in what could be a master suite."

"Can I see it?"

"Sure. Go on up. Just hold on. I don't know if the stairs are solid." He followed her up the stairs and watched her inspect every room. The last door she opened was the spacious master.

"Oh, there's a fireplace up here, too. I love that." In the attached bathroom, she let out a squeal at the sight of the grungy claw-foot bathtub.

"It needs a lot of work, but I think we could really make it into something special."

"Wade… This is just… I can picture us here."

He put his hands on her hips and gazed down at her. "And maybe some little Wades and Mias in the other rooms?"

She rested her hand on her heart, the new ring on her finger catching the light from outside. "It's too much."

"No, baby," he whispered as he kissed her. "It's everything you deserve."

"Can we afford this?"

"If we do most of the work ourselves, we can. My cousin Noah is a contractor who would help with the big things, and my brothers will help, too."

Mia's cell phone rang, and her eyes lit up with delight. "And there's cell service here! Sold!" She took the phone from her pocket, and her smile faded at the sight of Larry's name on her caller ID.

"It's okay," Wade said. "Take the call. No matter what it is, it can't touch us if we don't let it."

Nodding, she pressed the button and put the call on speaker so Wade could hear, too. "Hi, Larry."

"Mia, I'm glad I caught you. I tried the home number you gave me, but when there was no answer, I figured I'd take a chance on your cell. There's been a significant development in the case, and I wanted to let you know right away."

Wade put his arm around her, and she leaned into him.

"What kind of development?"

"The kind in which Brody realizes he's totally screwed if you testify against him. He's indicated his willingness to accept a plea deal that would require him to name names of the much bigger fish who were feeding his organization. We told him the only way we'll cut a deal with him on the drug charges is if he also pleads guilty to assaulting you."

Mia looked up at Wade, her shock apparent.

"This is Wade, Larry. What did he say to pleading guilty to the assault charges?"

"He said he'll do it to get the plea deal."

"How much time will he serve?"

"He's looking at fifteen to twenty on all the charges. Mia? Are you still there?"

"Yes, yes, I'm here. I just... I can't believe it. I never thought he'd admit to any of it."

"When he heard you'd married someone else, I think he knew the jig was up. He was looking at up to twenty years in prison on the drug charges alone. This deal gives him a chance of parole while he's still young enough to enjoy it."

"So, it's over, then? It's really over?"

"We still need to get the judge to certify the plea, but that should be a formality. So as far as you're concerned, yes, it's over. This victory is as much yours as it is ours. Without everything you did, we wouldn't have had enough to get to this deal. You ought to be very proud of yourself, and if you're ever interested in a job in law enforcement—"

"No, thank you," she said, laughing through tears. "I've had enough of law enforcement to last me a lifetime."

"I'll let you know when the deal is approved by the court."

"Thank you so much for everything, Larry. Especially for believing me."

"That's all thanks to you. You built a very believable case. I'll be in touch."

Mia hung up, let out a scream and jumped into Wade's outstretched arms. "It's over! It's really *over!*"

Wade swung her around, caught up in her joy. "I'm so happy for you and proud of you."

"I couldn't have done it without your willingness to marry me. You heard what Larry said. That tipped the whole thing."

"Marrying you was the single best thing I've ever done."

She hugged him tightly. "I can't believe it's over, and I'm finally free of him."

"I love that this news is the first thing to ever happen to us in this house. That's a sign, don't you think?"

"The cell service was the sign."

Wade laughed and put her down, but kept his arms around her. "What do you say, Mrs. Abbott? Should we buy this place and make it our home?"

"We should, Mr. Abbott. We absolutely should."

EPILOGUE

Lincoln slid into the booth across from Elmer, who greeted him with a huge grin.

"What a week, my friend!" Elmer said.

"I know! I can't keep up with everything happening in my family these days. Wade got married, and they're buying a farm. Hunter and Megan are expecting. Ella and Gavin are expecting, although we're not supposed to know that yet—and planning to get married very soon. Lucas and Landon are fighting over a woman, and Hannah adopted a baby moose. Did I forget anything?"

"Nope. That about sums it up."

"Where do we begin with all this?"

"Let's start with Wade. The news about Mia's ex taking the plea deal was the banner headline, if you ask me."

"Agreed. Thank God that's resolved and they can put it behind them."

"I read the coverage in today's paper, and now that Brody has pleaded guilty, the details are being released. Mia was instrumental in bringing down Brody's operation. Without her, the prosecutor said, they might not have gotten him as soon as they did. Not to mention, he handed them three guys the DEA has been after for *years*."

"My new daughter-in-law is an impressive young woman, that's for sure."

"That girl has been through a lot in her life. If anyone deserves happiness with a guy like our Wade, it's her."

"Couldn't agree more. Wade took next week off, and they're heading to Florida for some fun in the sun."

"Good for them. They have a lot to celebrate. Now what's up with Hannah and the moose?"

"Apparently, she conspired with Dude to lure the little one away from Fred. They built a pen for him, and she's feeding him right from the bottle. Dude is guiding her, and Nolan wants the two of them locked up in a loony bin. But you know Hannah when she sets her mind to something."

"Indeed. Someone ought to tell poor Nolan that the ship has already sailed."

"What's going to happen when Fred finds out where his little friend is being kept?"

"That's anyone's guess."

"Speaking of wild animals, what's this about Lucas and Landon fighting over a woman?"

"You heard me right. They're both interested in Amanda, and neither will step aside for the other. I've never seen them so at odds. And poor Amanda doesn't know what to make of all the attention."

"Did I hear she extended her time here in Butler?"

Linc nodded. "Initially, it was because Wade had to go to Boston and the employee training was postponed. But now I think her extended stay in Butler has more to do with the twins than it does with work."

"Very interesting," Elmer said, stroking his chin.

"For the record, if she ends up with either of them, it goes in my column. That product line was my idea. She wouldn't be here otherwise."

Elmer rolled his eyes. "You're grasping at straws, but I'll let you have this one since you're so far behind anyway."

"No matter who gets the win, we need to keep an eye on those two. Neither of them has ever been serious about a woman before, and isn't it just our luck that they set their sights on the same one? Nothing good can come of that."

"Agreed. We'll keep an eye on them—and on her. If the two of them are intent on her, she'll need all the help she can get."

***

Thank you for reading *Here Comes the Sun*! I hope Wade and Mia's story was worth the long wait! I loved writing them and their unconventional romance. When I had the idea for them to get married before they even dated, I couldn't wait to write the rest! If you enjoyed the book, please consider leaving a review at the book retailer of your choice, as well as Goodreads, to help other readers find their story. Please make sure you're on my newsletter mailing list at marieforce.com to keep up with the latest news about my books.

Join the Here Comes the Sun Reader Group to talk about Wade and Mia's story: www.facebook.com/groups/HereComesTheSunReaders/ and make sure you're a member of the Green Mountain Reader Group at www.facebook.com/groups/GreenMountainSeries/ to never miss news of the series or upcoming books.

As always, thank you to my husband, Dan Force, and the incredible team that supports me behind the scenes, including Julie Cupp, Lisa Cafferty, Holly Sullivan, Isabel Sullivan, Anne Woodall, Kara Conrad, Linda Ingmanson and Joyce Lamb. I couldn't do what I do without their help and support.

Profound thanks to the readers who make this amazing career possible. I appreciate each and every one of you!

xoxo

Marie

OTHER TITLES BY MARIE FORCE

The Gansett Island Series

Book 1: Maid for Love *(Mac & Maddie)*

Book 2: Fool for Love *(Joe & Janey)*

Book 3: Ready for Love *(Luke & Sydney)*

Book 4: Falling for Love *(Grant & Stephanie)*

Book 5: Hoping for Love *(Evan & Grace)*

Book 6: Season for Love *(Owen & Laura)*

Book 7: Longing for Love *(Blaine & Tiffany)*

Book 8: Waiting for Love *(Adam & Abby)*

Book 9: Time for Love *(David & Daisy)*

Book 10: Meant for Love *(Jenny & Alex)*

Book 10.5: Chance for Love, *A Gansett Island Novella (Jared & Lizzie)*

Book 11: Gansett After Dark *(Owen & Laura)*

Book 12: Kisses After Dark *(Shane & Katie)*

Book 13: Love After Dark *(Paul & Hope)*

Book 14: Celebration After Dark *(Big Mac & Linda)*

Book 15: Desire After Dark *(Slim & Erin)*

Book 16: Light After Dark *(Mallory & Quinn)*

Book 17: Victoria & Shannon (Episode 1)

Book 18: Kevin & Chelsea (Episode 2)

The Green Mountain Series
Book 1: All You Need Is Love *(Will & Cameron)*
Book 2: I Want to Hold Your Hand *(Nolan & Hannah)*
Book 3: I Saw Her Standing There *(Colton & Lucy)*
Book 4: And I Love Her *(Hunter & Megan)*
Novella: You'll Be Mine *(Will & Cam's Wedding)*
Book 5: It's Only Love *(Gavin & Ella)*
Book 6: Ain't She Sweet *(Tyler & Charlotte)*

The Butler Vermont Series
(Continuation of the Green Mountain Series)
Book 1: Every Little Thing *(Grayson & Emma)*
Book 2: Can't Buy Me Love *(Mary & Patrick)*
Book 3: Here Comes the Sun *(Wade & Mia)*

The Treading Water Series
Book 1: Treading Water *(Jack & Andi)*
Book 2: Marking Time *(Clare & Aidan)*
Book 3: Starting Over *(Brandon & Daphne)*
Book 4: Coming Home *(Reid & Kate)*

Single Titles
Sex Machine
Sex God
Georgia on My Mind
True North
The Fall
Everyone Loves a Hero
Love at First Flight
Line of Scrimmage

The Erotic Quantum Series
Book 1: Virtuous *(Flynn & Natalie)*
Book 2: Valorous *(Flynn & Natalie)*
Book 3: Victorious *(Flynn & Natalie)*
Book 4: Rapturous *(Addie & Hayden)*
Book 5: Ravenous *(Jasper & Ellie)*
Book 6: Delirious *(Kristian & Aileen)*

Romantic Suspense Novels Available from Marie Force:
The Fatal Series
One Night With You, *A Fatal Series Prequel Novella*
Book 1: Fatal Affair
Book 2: Fatal Justice
Book 3: Fatal Consequences
Book 3.5: Fatal Destiny, *the Wedding Novella*
Book 4: Fatal Flaw
Book 5: Fatal Deception
Book 6: Fatal Mistake
Book 7: Fatal Jeopardy
Book 8: Fatal Scandal
Book 9: Fatal Frenzy
Book 10: Fatal Identity
Book 11: Fatal Threat
Book 12: Fatal Chaos

Single Title
The Wreck

About the Author

Marie Force is the *New York Times* bestselling author of contemporary romance, including the indie-published Gansett Island Series and the Fatal Series from Harlequin Books. In addition, she is the author of the Butler, Vermont Series, the Green Mountain Series and the erotic romance Quantum Series. In 2019, her new historical Gilded series from Kensington Books will debut with *Duchess By Deception*.

All together, her books have sold 6.5 million copies worldwide, have been translated into more than a dozen languages and have appeared on the *New York Times* bestseller list many times. She is also a *USA Today* and *Wall Street Journal* bestseller, a Speigel bestseller in Germany, a frequent speaker and publishing workshop presenter as well as a publisher through her Jack's House Publishing romance imprint. She is a two-time nominee for the Romance Writers of America's RITA® award for romance fiction.

Her goals in life are simple—to finish raising two happy, healthy, productive young adults, to keep writing books for as long as she possibly can and to never be on a flight that makes the news.

Join Marie's mailing list for news about new books and upcoming appearances in your area. Follow her on Facebook at https://www.facebook.com/MarieForceAuthor, Twitter @marieforce and on Instagram at https://instagram.com/marieforceauthor/. Join one of Marie's many reader groups. Contact Marie at *marie@marieforce.com*.

CPSIA information can be obtained
at www.ICGtesting.com
Printed in the USA
FFOW03n1837310118
44818987-44984FF